TSUNAMI DOLPHINS

AN "ANIMAL EYES" STORY

JUSTIN MORGAN

Copyright © 2022 Justin Morgan
All rights reserved.

Justin Morgan asserts his moral right to be identified as the author of this work.

Although inspired by real events, this book is a work of fiction. Any resemblance to actual events, places or persons, living or dead, is entirely coincidental.

No part of this publication may be reproduced, distributed, or transmitted in any form or by any means, including photocopying, recording, or other electronic or mechanical methods, without the prior written permission of the publisher.

Cover Photograph by Waschi Washborne @pixabay
Dolphin Illustration by Viktorija Čeliković

ISBN (paperback): 978-1-7399570-2-5
ISBN (digital): 978-1-7399570-3-2

Published by Paws On Publishing

The *Animal Eyes* Series

The Dogs of Chernobyl

Tsunami Dolphins

Apes of the Wildfire

∼

I really hope you enjoy this book.
If you do, kindly consider leaving a review or rating online.
Even one word is a big help!
Sincere thanks,
Justin

In March 2011, Japan faced the triple horror of earthquake, tsunami and nuclear meltdown.

This book is dedicated to the victims of the disaster, and to all who lost their home.

TSUNAMI DOLPHINS

1. A Grave Insult	1
2. The Spawning	11
3. A Very Silly Little Thing	21
4. A Sleeping Vision	31
5. The Ripping of the World	40
6. Beached	51
7. Smoke from the Shore	61
8. Impure Rain	71
9. The Riverside Shrine	82
10. Repaying a Debt	92
11. The Sullied Lagoon	102
12. A House with a Boat on its Roof	114
13. Attack of the Shadow	122
14. Lurkers in the Deep	132
15. A Gift from the Fallen	143
16. The Herding	154
17. Slaughter at Blood Cove	164
18. The Mourning Ocean	175
19. A Chilling Truth	186
20. Hanging in the Balance	197
21. A Sickening Victory	208
22. Parting	219
23. The Ocean of the Future	230
Historical Note	239
About the Author	241
Acknowledgments	243

1

A GRAVE INSULT

Coastal Waters off Tohoku,
Japan

Behaving himself didn't come at all naturally to Mako.

With the sun nearing the shore, his pod was slowing. They'd swum all day, yet still the spawning grounds lay out of reach, and with other pods far ahead of them, it was likely now that the only thing awaiting them there was a blanket of mackerel scales sparkling on the seabed.

It was all the boys' fault, of course. They took the blame for everything these days. A calf got slapped with a tail fluke? The boys did it. A hunt failed because the prey heard giggles? Must have been those boys again. One day, they'd cop it for the changing direction of the currents.

With the adults now resting, Mako peeled away with his friends, Hideki and Karoo. 'They should be thanking us,' he chirped. 'Wandering off like we did probably saved their lives.'

Hideki stretched his neck back and gave a whistle of agreement. 'Imagine if we hadn't! Nio would have led the pod into those orca clans for sure.'

With a broadening smile, Mako threw out a sonar signal. 'And *that* is why we should wander off again.'

Reading the echo that came back to him, Mako gave a disappointed quack. No ships were passing, meaning no fun was to be had surfing in the waves of their wakes. But then, further up the shore, a picture began to emerge of an odd construction standing out from the shallows. With its lines and precise angles, it was evidently something put there by humans.

'Are you getting that, boys?'

Hideki emitted a worried creak. 'I see it. But do you really think it's wise to go off?'

Mako went into a spin and raced off up the coastline. 'You can do what you like. But I'm bored of being good.'

He stopped only when he reached the structure. How curious this thing was! Two wooden posts, lit by the radiance of the setting sun, towered up from out of the water. Sat across their top was a bar, its upturned ends like a fish-eagle's pointed wingtips, and just below this was a second crossbeam.

Mako glided among the posts, then called his friends over, who'd trailed him up the coast. Hideki and Karoo approached with trepidation, studying first the stone blocks bearing the posts, then, as they held themselves above the surface, the full structure.

Observing his friends' confusion, Mako began to chirp. 'Nio is always looking for shrines — like the shipwreck we found that time, and the coral husk in the middle of that reef. We use those shrines to pray to the trout-god, right? Well, my father said humans pray to him using their own shrines. I think this is the gateway to one of them.'

He'd barely finished imparting his theory when a boat came puttering from around the corner. The instant its human riders saw the spyhopping dolphins, their faces lit up with smiles, and Hideki and Karoo excitedly span off to greet them.

Mako, however, stayed where he was. Up on the promenade, something interesting was taking place. Unless he was mistaken, there was an opportunity up there that seemed too good to be true. But before he could investigate more closely, his friends came racing back, chuckling.

'You've got to see this, Mako! Humans *love* us! They go *"Ooooh! Aaaaah!"* and they clap their hands when we leap!'

Mako turned to his friends with mischief in his eye. 'Love us, you say? Well, we'll see about that. Come with me. And watch.'

With care, Mako manoeuvred through the shallows. The wall of the promenade stood barely above the height of the water, and in its centre were three dark plinths, each marked with symbols. Between these plinths were bowls, from which delicate curls of fragrant smoke rose into the air.

Hiding themselves beneath the water which lapped at the wall, the dolphins watched a human busying himself before the plinths, carrying on like Nio did during one of her thanksgiving rituals. They listened as he uttered his odd, monotonous speech, and when this came to a halt, the human walked away, leaving behind, exactly where his feet had just been, a fish.

Wasting no time, Mako sprang up and snatched the fish in his jaws with a celebratory quack.

The startled land creature gave a shout. 'Hey, naughty dolphin! That wasn't for you!'

Hideki and Karoo stared at one another with shocked eyes. 'Have you gone crazy, Mako? If this really is a shrine, then that fish was an offering. You can't take what was given for the god of the sea. It's a form of offence.'

'A delicious form,' giggled Mako. 'Now, are you going to wait here with me until the human brings another fish? Or are you going to swim away crying for your mothers' milk like the babies you are?'

'Wait until Nio hears about this, Mako. You're really in for it this time.'

Mako clapped his jaws beside Karoo and issued a nip to the flesh behind his flipper. 'You're going to tell on me? For taking a fish that was going to waste?'

'It's an offence against nature to take what's meant for Moshiri,' said Hideki. 'Only an impure mind would even consider doing such a thing.'

And with that, Hideki and Karoo sped off.

But Mako, seeing the human making his way back towards the plinths, remained exactly where he was. The man drearily mumbled some words and placed down a second fish, and the moment he stepped aside, Mako popped up and clasped it away in his beak.

This time, the human didn't call out. He simply walked away again, making a noise which to Mako sounded like a chuckle.

As Mako swallowed this second fish down, all he could do was laugh. Free food! To think of the energy he'd wasted all this time hunting for his own meal, when he'd had to do nothing more than show off a little bit!

The human came back again, now with some companions. This time, rather than place the fish at the foot of the plinths, he turned to the ocean and held it aloft in his hands, and Mako sprang up.

Squeezing the muscles in his core to stay above the water, he held himself face-to-face with the human, and simply looked at him. The eyes of the land creature were so strange! Not only were they hooded, they were fronted. How did these odd creatures see *behind* themselves? They had their own kind of sonar perhaps, at frequencies not perceptible to marine life. But the eyes were expressive, too; they were curved up, like little smiles. The creature was, unmistakably, friendly.

With care, Mako took the fish from out of the human's hands. But rather than sink back below the waves, he swallowed it where he was, allowing the creature to watch him while he ate. The other humans he'd brought became suddenly excited and clapped their hands, and the boat which had gone by earlier began making its way back up to the wall.

Mako peered inside the clapping folk, to see hearts beating in their centres. This species certainly wasn't built for fighting! With their long limbs, so easy to grab a hold of, they were vulnerable. And how thin the necks were! They had no blowholes at the top of their heads, and took in air instead through the two small openings at the front of their faces. It was a horribly flawed system: if anything pressed on their necks, or if a fish became lodged in the narrow pipes running through them, humans would surely be starved of air.

By now, the boat had pulled up alongside the promenade, and a length of rope was wrapped around a metal post, keeping it tethered in place. The humans inside the boat were delighted by Mako's presence. They held dark machines to their eyes, which clicked mysteriously at irregular intervals as the riders pointed them at him.

The human on the promenade now held out a fourth fish, and Mako couldn't help but giggle. Nio's accounts of her time with land creatures made them sound like beings of extraordinary intelligence, who understood the ways of Moshiri and built monuments to communicate with him. Yet here they were, clapping their hands, pumping their fists and hollering gleefully, all because a dolphin was eating a fish!

The riders on the boat didn't have such a good view as those on the promenade, so Mako dipped underneath the waves and glided to the far side of their craft. Then, to roars of great pleasure, he leapt out from the water in a full somersault, earning himself some strips of dried squid that one human poured into the ocean for him.

Partly to repay this kindness – though mainly because he'd become oddly greedy for their attention – he rose vertically out from the water and began to move across the surface with a controlled swaying of his tail flukes.

The humans, appreciating his mimicry of the way they themselves lumbered gracelessly upon the solid ground, went wild.

This was all just too much fun! Mako considered all the other tricks he could use to impress his land friends, and was just about to breach the surface again to do a backflip for them, when a bull dolphin appeared beside him.

So distracted had he been, Mako hadn't even seen his father coming.

∼

Predictably enough, Mako's mother was furious.

'You left to play with your friends? Even though *you're* the reason Wakka Totto's pod is going to reach the spawning grounds before us? What were you even doing at the shore?'

Mako kept quiet.

'Go on,' said his father. 'Tell her.'

'I took a fish.'

'Took? From where?'

Mako looked at his father, hopeful that he might spare him having to admit the terrible thing he'd done. But the bull remained silent, leaving Mako no choice but to come out with it. 'From a shrine.'

His mother's eyes flashed with rage. 'You *stole* from the trout-god?'

The bull glared at Mako. 'That's not all, though. Is it, son?'

Sulkily, Mako turned away.

'I caught him performing.'

'Performing? For *humans*?!' His mother was even angrier about this than she was about the theft. She turned to Mako and clapped her jaws fiercely beside his face.

Mako blew a bubble and scanned around at the many individuals of the pod, wishing he were any other dolphin but himself.

'Well?' squawked the cow. 'What do you have to say for yourself?'

But what was there to say? There was no point arguing. He couldn't do *anything* right. Even when he tried to keep out of everybody's way he got into trouble. He turned to face his father, and accidentally let out the briefest of chuckles, making his mother even more furious.

'You think it's funny, do you?'

'No,' said Mako, which was quite obviously a lie.

'Well, let's see if you think it's funny when you're tending to the seniors tonight.'

'What? Mama, no!'

'You're to travel at the back of the pod with the elderly, Mako. Their pace will be your pace. You'll bring them food, stay with them when they spout, do anything they ask of you. And when you've done that, you can go to the maternal pod and help with the podlings. Now,' she said, turning to the bull, 'get him out of my sight, will you? I've had all I can take for one day.'

Mako's father flicked his tail and turned sharply away. 'Come, boy,' he said.

By now, the pod was moving north again through the clear coastal waters. They'd made up for some lost time by cutting short their rest, but still it was doubtful they'd reach the mackerel spawning anytime soon. Mako didn't care about that right now, though; as he trailed his father towards the rear of the pod, he had to suffer the embarrassment of being seen by all his smirking friends.

'You don't get why she's so angry with you, do you, son?'

Mako's beak swayed from side to side. 'Hideki said it's a crime against nature to steal from Moshiri.'

'Then Hideki has paid closer attention to Nio's lessons than you have. But that's not what your mother was so upset about. We've never told you what happened to your mother's father.'

Mako's energy suddenly changed. When his mother was cross with him, she usually pushed and pushed until he too got angry. His father, though, knew better, and used stories or history to take the heat out of his mood. And *this* was especially exciting: neither of his parents ever spoke about his old grandfather. Now no longer of a mind to want to argue and resist, Mako quietened.

'Your grandfather was a long-awaited blessing,' said the bull, as he led Mako though the failing light of day to the slower animals at the pod's rear. 'His mother and father – your mother's grandparents – had all but given up trying to have a calf of their own. So when they finally succeeded in making a child, right at the very limit of the age when such a thing is possible, it was a cause for celebration for the whole pod. Nio used to speak about it all the time during ceremonies. She was certain that her prayer had been heard, that Moshiri himself had blessed them with new life. She never mentions your grandfather's name any more though. Not since before you were born.'

The adolescent let up a bubble. 'Why not?'

'He died young, Mako. Not young in the way you and your friends are, but young for a dolphin. He should have seen forty-five summers. Yet he lived only to his thirtieth. Do you know why his life was so reduced?'

Mako let his mind conjure a multitude of scenarios before he settled on his answer: 'Orca.'

'Humans.'

The shock of what his father said sent a jolt along Mako's spine. 'You mean, a human *hurt* him?'

'Not at all,' said the bull, with a glumness that was

uncharacteristic. 'Humans *saved* him. You see, as a child he got beached, and a human came and carried him back into the water. Your grandfather never forgot the kindness of that individual. In fact, he became enraptured with land creatures after his encounter with one. So much so that, years later, during a migration to the south islands, he, well, you see, he—'

'He what, father?'

'—he *deliberately* beached himself .'

Mako's eyes widened. 'Deliberately? But why would he do such a thing?'

'Because he wished to be with them. And indeed, his wish was granted. He ended up in captivity. For seven summers.'

'What does it mean, father? What is captivity?'

'It means he was not free. The choice of where to roam, when to eat, who to play with – these things were taken from him by humans. But even though he was denied the open ocean for all that time, he was provided with what he needed to survive. He was fed throughout the day, given companions to mill beside. And he learned much about the humans – in fact, some say he knew more about their nature than Nio herself.'

'But, father, if he was in captivity, how was my mother born? How did he sire his own children?'

'Because,' creaked the bull, 'the humans freed him. When his strength began to fail and he could no longer perform the jumps and tricks the humans so loved to watch, they carried your grandfather back to the shore and sent him out into the open water. It took him a whole year to find the pod again. But, you see, Mako, a dolphin in captivity experiences something so unusual that it reduces the length of their lives. So, now you understand why your mother was so angry.'

Mako's beak drooped with remorse. At the pod's back end at last, where Nio and the rest of the elderly animals were swimming, he realised he deserved this punishment.

His father wasted no time saying goodbye, and headed back up to the other bulls, leaving Mako to introduce himself to an old bull and an old cow. And right as he did, a sound like thunder came from below.

Debris began to billow up as the seabed rattled. The seniors didn't seem particularly fazed by it, but all Mako could think about for the rest of the journey was the fish he'd taken from the shrine.

He had, as his friends made clear, insulted Moshiri, the great backbone fish of the world on whose mighty spine the whole ocean rests.

And the trout-god was obviously unhappy about it.

2

THE SPAWNING

IN AN OCEAN that fizzed with the chirruping of dolphins, Fusa emerged from her slumber, and smiled.

Today was one of the good days. A true spectacle of nature, this frenzy of feasting and play gladdened the hearts of every member of her pod, and muscles which had ached from the strain of the migration finally felt soothed.

With a kick of her tail flukes, Fusa threw a scan wide into the bay and glided across to her infant daughter, Misa, who greeted her with a whistle of impatience. 'At last, mama! The mackerel will all be gone soon!'

'That's nothing to worry about,' Fusa chuckled, reading the echoes as they bounced back to her. 'A spawning as big as this could feed the entire ocean. Come on then, Shrimp.'

The pair thrashed into a spin, gliding through the herds together until they reached the fish, where they happily ate their fill. Rare was the day when such delicious food was abundant enough that a dolphin barely had to open her jaws to catch a meal, but the annual mackerel spawning offered just that luxury. *This* was why Wakka Totto insisted the pod kept up its pace for days on end – and why that elderly leader wanted today's thanksgiving ceremony to be extra special.

Today was Fusa's turn to give the calves their lessons. She'd already chosen a bay that promised perfect surfing waves, so, before the skittish infants had the chance to grow tired from the fun of hunting, she sent a whistle through the throng of bodies to summon them.

The podlings gathered at once, and the small group turned towards the coast. But just as Fusa pulled off, she spotted Toshi coming in on her right side. Misa gave a cheerful whoop — 'Dad's coming surfing with us!' — but Fusa knew there was no chance of that. Toshi did whatever he wanted to do. And that seldom included spending time with the calves.

Toshi got straight to the point. 'Have you thought more about what we discussed, Fusa?'

'I have. And as I said before, I think breaking away from the pod is foolish.'

'No, Fusa. Allowing ourselves to be slowed down by all these herds – *that's* foolish. We've become a super-pod. We easily could have been late to this spawning.'

'Yet we were first to arrive, Toshi. By a long way. Even with the biggest maternal pod, we're still the fastest in the ocean.'

Toshi, unsatisfied by this, let out a frustrated creak. But then, as he looked more closely at Fusa, he calmed again. 'What's wrong?'

The question caught Fusa by surprise, and she bucked. 'What do you mean?'

'I know you. And I know when something's troubling you. What is it?'

Fusa shook her beak. 'Nothing's wrong. Today's one of the good days.'

But now that Toshi had mentioned it, Fusa realised he was right. Ever since she'd awoken, a vague feeling of dread had been lingering. Like a puff of ink from a startled squid, this ominous shadow clouded the waters around her – and she had absolutely no idea why.

The day's lessons were twofold.

While she herded the calves together, Fusa introduced the first activity. 'Right,' she said, 'are we all ready for a bit of sonar practice?'

Misa and her friends began to whine. 'Again? But we know how to catch fish already!'

'Maybe so,' Fusa agreed, positioning her body to face west. 'But echolocation is about more than hunting prey. It could save your lives one day.'

A frisson of excitement rippled through the young, so Fusa, knowing very well how easily this could turn to silliness, put a quick stop to it. 'Oki,' she said. 'Come and face me. Send a beam in my direction and tell me what you see.'

Oki emitted a brief click train towards Fusa. 'I see you.'

'What part of me?'

'Your shape.'

'Good. Now do it again, but this time make your click train longer, and scan your head slowly from side to side.'

The others laughed when Oki practiced the movement, but the infant kept her focus well on the task and followed Fusa's instruction perfectly.

'What do you see as well as the shape of me? Be more specific this time.'

'I see things inside you, auntie. Your heart. And the melon in your head.'

'Good,' said Fusa. 'The rest of you, come and do as Oki did. Beam your sonar at me. But make your click trains longer than you normally would.'

The calves swayed as they used the air in their lungs

to send out long signals. Then, when their echoes returned to them, they set about on a mad dance of spins and flips. Fusa smiled: they were seeing *inside* her.

When they'd calmed sufficiently, Fusa made the youngsters face west to echolocate the shoreline. As it was some distance away, it took a while for the signal to bounce back, but soon pictures emerged in their minds of a world above the waves filled with all sorts of strange activities.

'That's called a *port*,' Fusa said. She pulled away from where the calves were milling, and led them around to the shore itself, taking care to stay well clear of where the activity was at its most bustling. 'Now, I want you all to come up and spyhop next to me.'

The youngsters, using their fins to hold themselves out of the water, lingered beside Fusa in the coolness of the morning air while she scanned for living things. On the land were beings that shuffled upon long, straight stalks, like flukes split into two halves. These pointy, hairy creatures possessed not the merest hint of a dolphin's grace. She'd seen them often enough before, yet Fusa was always struck by how alien their world seemed. It was a place where no fun appeared to exist at all.

'Send your beams to the port again,' instructed Fusa. 'Try to read the creatures you see moving around.'

Misa's eyelids sagged with just a hint of worry. 'What are they?'

'Those, we call *humans*. Wakka Totto will tell you all about their strange ways one day.'

Fusa led the infants through the swaying columns of a kelp forest, and onto where the coastal shelf met the land at just the right angle. 'Now, let's move onto our second lesson,' she cheeped, when the stragglers had caught up.

This part of the bay was disturbed by no human activity, with the only features of the land being a wide beach and, beyond that, grassy meadows. Finding such a stretch of coast so near the mackerel spawning grounds was a piece of good fortune; there was nowhere safer for a bit of surfing practice.

Fusa turned to her pupils. 'Surfing solo is not like doing it with your mothers. If you get caught in the tide or lose your sense of direction, you can't expect other dolphins to risk beaching themselves to get you back into the water. Once you commit to a wave, that's it. You're on your own.'

The calves – even the older ones – hushed upon hearing this warning, and a flurry of questions quickly came Fusa's way.

'Auntie! What if the shore is littered with corals?'

'Auntie! How do we know which waves are going to roll off into tubes? Don't most of them just swell into humps?'

'What happens, auntie, if the humans come out on their boats?'

Ignoring this barrage, Fusa went on ahead to where the water grew clear and the pressure began to drop. They were reaching the shallows, and the time was coming to leap into the light to catch the peeling waves. Misa was growing quieter with every swish of her tail – and she wasn't the only one.

From the front, Fusa clicked for the party to halt, and they all milled in the bright light that spilled from the sky into the upper ocean. Ahead, huge coastal waves were forming. Surf like this was rare; when she had the youngsters observe the movement of the waves, it was mostly so she could herself read the water's wild and violent behaviour.

Even for Fusa, the effect of the shifting ocean was hypnotic. First, the surface dipped into a kind of crater. Then, as the tide pulled the water closer to the land, the crater's back side began to rise. The broadening wave was too wide to see with her eyes alone, so Fusa sent a beam of sonar out through her head, and was astonished by what the returning echoes revealed: in her mind now was a picture of an enormous wall of water, which crashed onto the surface with an explosive power forceful enough to shape the very rock of the ocean bed.

Even the most boisterous of the boys went silent, their earlier excitement replaced with awe. But suddenly Fusa wasn't much concerned with the waves anymore — her attention now was concentrated on the murky underside of a boat that was moving across the surface. What was it about the sight of it that made her eyes widen and her flippers draw to a halt?

Misa gave a shy cheep. 'Who's going to go first?'

'Nobody's going first,' clucked Fusa. 'You're still too small to do it solo. We're all going together. Just remember. Let the wall carry you. Don't resist it. When it brings you back into the water, you have to roll away and fight with all your power to push back against the tide. Ready? On three.'

'One!' the infants chorussed.

Fusa kept her eye on the boat as it struggled to break through the surf.

'Two!'

The tide pulled back, readying the surface to form the great barrel of a wave. The boat appeared suddenly closer, and a chill of anxiety coursed down Fusa's spine.

'Thr—'

'No! Wait!'

The infants held back. Misa gave a squawk. 'What is it, mama?'

A memory, faint like a distant headland on a day marked by mists, resonated in Fusa's mind.

She'd had a dream.

That was why she'd woken up so darkened by doubt.

She tried with all her might to force it to the forefront of her mind. But aside from the feeling she'd seen these boats before – and that they represented some kind of threat – there was nothing more of substance to it.

Nevertheless, it was enough to bring a premature end to the lesson.

The last thing she would ever consider was risking the safety of the pod's young.

∽

Toshi, snapping his jaws together crossly, launched into a tirade the moment he saw Fusa returning with the podlings.

'What are you doing back so soon? The other cows are at the ceremony.'

Fusa's face prickled with shame. She herself would have felt aggrieved to find Misa brought back early during another auntie's turn to have her, yet this was the very thing she was doing now to them.

'Just watch them for me, will you? I won't be long.'

Toshi's eyes bulged. 'You want *me* to watch the podlings?'

'You're only filling your beaks with mackerel here anyway. Just keep them with you until I get back.'

'Back from where?'

Fusa considered explaining what was about to happen, but since she couldn't say for sure what that even was, she thought better of getting into it.

Toshi, however, was persistent in his protests. 'Us bulls have our own duties, Fusa. Have I ever asked you to watch out for orca clans?'

'Please, Toshi. She's your daughter, too. Just watch over her and her friends a while.'

'Alright, if it pleases you, I will. That's what we need to do, isn't it — make compromises. So just remember that when we next discuss breaking away from this super-pod.'

Wasting no more time, Fusa hurried off to find the pod's leader. The elder was going to want to know *exactly* what she'd envisioned in this dream of hers, so, as she swam, she forced herself to remember as much of it as possible.

By the time she found Wakka Totto, however, barely any more of it had materialised, and as she approached the elderly cow, Fusa tried to conceal the embarrassment – and fear –she knew must be visible in her eyes. This mysterious old dolphin had always unnerved Fusa, and until now she'd had very little to do with her.

Wakka Totto had already begun the thanksgiving ceremony, which started, as always, with the milking of the pufferfish. The elder was pressing the fish so that it released a murky cloud, which she promptly consumed from out of the water. She'd then begun to tidy together the spiral shells brought by the adolescents.

'Dolphins,' Wakka Totto whistled, her eyes bulging lightly now with the effects of the fish's narcotic emissions. 'We gather once again to thank Moshiri, the maker of the seas and the storms on whose mighty backbone our entire world rests, and to offer to him these beautiful shells.'

Watching from the edge, Fusa took care to avoid the troublesome young males as they scrambled and squabbled for whatever was left of the discarded pufferfish's intoxicating fluid. Was there anything in the ocean more maddening than adolescent boys? Afraid to interrupt the elder as she communed with the trout-god, she waited for the right moment to approach.

But Wakka Totto went on. 'Every year, when the currents shift, the mackerel come together to make their next generation. And that means a feast for the first pods to arrive. Dear Moshiri, we thank you for guiding us along the quickest currents, that we should be those very dolphins. We hope that you will hear our thanks and accept our offerings as the afternoon goes by, and that you will steer us safely onward across the strait to my ancestral home of Squid Hood Bay.'

The boisterous boys, given energy by the leftover

pufferfish they'd pilfered, hung close to the elder. 'Wakka Totto,' one of them said, not in the least bit concerned about interrupting, 'tell us what was here before the ocean.'

Wakka Totto gave a nod and took in another pufferfish's belched fluid. 'In the beginning,' she chirped, speaking more slowly than before, 'there was only swamp – dark water of the most polluted kind. Just one creature dwelt within it, the great trout Moshiri, whose mighty body stretched between its very boundaries, with his head in the west, where the sun falls, and his tail in the east, where it rises. Moshiri brought together the pollution to form the lands, clearing the ocean for us all to live.'

'But why must we thank him?' asked another of the adolescents.

'Our whole world rests on the trout-god's great spine, and his gentle movements help us know the direction of the currents. Since it is through his breaths that the tides ebb and flow, and through his soft swaying that we are able to find our food, we owe him our gratitude.'

On these words, Fusa sped forward with a kick of her flukes. She'd waited long enough.

Wakka Totto turned her bulging eyes towards Fusa, and saw at once something was wrong. 'Tell me, young Fusa. What brings you to me with such worry?'

'I'm sorry to come now that the ceremony has begun. But I recall you telling us once about visions put into your dreams by the mighty trout-god. Is it really true? Does Moshiri show you things which later come to pass?'

'Indeed he does! Though moments of deep sleep are rare for mature dolphins, we do, every once in a while, allow both our eyes to close. And when that happened to me in my younger days, I would glimpse future events.'

Wakka Totto suddenly appeared concerned. She brought her face close against Fusa's own, and held it beside her. 'Why? Have you seen some shadow cast over the pod?'

'I wish I could tell you I had. But the threat was just so faint. All I know is that when I saw fishing boats riding out into the surf earlier, I had a peculiar feeling that some ill would follow.'

Throwing her head back up to the shallows, Wakka Totto let out a long click train. She hung a while in silence, waiting for the echoes of her scans to return – and when they did, she nodded her beak gravely. 'A fleet is heading out through the spawning grounds right now. It is indeed possible that the trout-god has warned you of something that should be feared. You were right to inform me of this, young Fusa. We must act at once.'

'But what if it was only a dream?'

'We won't take that chance,' whistled the elder. 'We leave now. We must move further from the coast and the human trawlers.'

'But Wakka Totto,' came a voice from among the other seniors. 'What about the pufferfish? So many have been gathered already.'

'There are always more to be found. For now we must listen to what Moshiri has told this young one, or bad things are sure to follow.'

And with that a message went out that the entire pod was to abandon the spawning grounds at once – a message that was going to make Fusa the most unpopular dolphin in the ocean.

3

A VERY SILLY LITTLE THING

At the rear of the pod, in the dead of night, Mako was listening to the seniors as he swam alongside them.

What had seemed to him at first to be a punishment was in fact a treat. One by one, the elderly dolphins were recollecting incidents from their lives, and in their age and wisdom Mako found a hopefulness: perhaps he wouldn't *always* be quite such a silly little thing.

Nio, who was especially full of stories, was presently remembering her own childhood, when the pod's encounter with an extraordinary creature brought them a deeper understanding of their world.

'I find it hard to even imagine how we got by before we knew humans. You know, I still recall first seeing land. An island, it was, like that one there. I asked my grandfather: "How can it be so firm that we can't swim through it? Why are there things that dwell above the waves?" And he answered simply: "That's just the way things are."'

The others gave a chuckle. 'Such ignorance!'

'I would call it a lack of curiosity,' stated Nio. 'Some simply don't question what is around them, or how it came to be there.'

At this, Mako grew self-conscious – was she making a

point about *him*? – and he turned his beak away. The adults of the pod spent so much of their time going on about the trout-god, and Nio was constantly on the hunt for shrines. But it was all just stories, wasn't it? There didn't have to be a *reason* why things were the way they were. Did there?

As though Nio had seen inside Mako's mind, she gave him a gentle nudge with her flipper. 'Little Mako is wondering, too, how that island came to be there.'

Turning shyly back to the leader of the pod, Mako let up a bubble. 'You say that Moshiri stirred up all the impurity in the swamp and made it into land. But how do we *know* that?'

'Because,' clicked Nio, 'we were blessed. Blessed with the friendship of a human. Our former leader – you're too small to remember him – bonded very closely with a human female. He spent much time with her in a special dwelling she made that could accommodate both marine and land creatures, and through that friendship he came to know much of what she knew.'

While the seniors continued to chitter away among themselves, Mako pondered how exciting it would be to actually *live* with a human. Nothing to do but play and snack, and bask in their adoration day in and day out. That old dolphin had truly won at life.

Together, the pod advanced further north, taking advantage of a kelp forest's cover to rest awhile. The young busied themselves playing in the seaweed strings, but Mako, obligated to remain with the elders, could do nothing but look on with envy.

Once, during a bow-riding excursion, some unknown dolphins had said something unusual to Mako which continued to puzzle him. 'Some boys I surfed with once,' he chirped softly now to Nio, 'called the leader of their pod a *priestess*. They said she can speak directly with Moshiri.'

Nio gave a nod. 'That would be my old friend, Wakka

Totto. Let's just say we don't see eye to eye on that particular matter. *Every* dolphin can communicate with the great trout-god, provided they do it at a shrine.'

'Wakko Totto. What a funny name!'

'It might be, little Mako, but don't think that old one isn't a serious force in this ocean. By now her pod has probably gulped down every last mackerel. With any luck, the old dear has been distracted with one of her ceremonies. The toxins of pufferfish aren't exactly known for helping much when you're in a rush.'

Just then a large bull — one of Mako's father's closest friends — came hurtling through the herds to reach the rear. For a brief moment, Mako's hope grew that he was about to be released from his duty, but the look of worry on the bull's face indicated something more serious.

'Orca ahead.'

Nio's eye flashed with concern. 'Have they echolocated us?'

'Yes, but we should be alright. The pod is tight today.' The bull looked pointedly in Mako's direction. 'Unlike yesterday.'

Mako felt suddenly shamed, but the large dolphin thankfully made no more of it.

'Then we stay tight,' clucked Nio to the other seniors at the rear of the pod. 'Orca are no threat when we're all together.'

The pod assembled into a dense scrum of bodies, and made its way steadily along the current. Accompanied at its head by many of the adolescent males were the bulls. The maternal pod, containing the podlings and their older brothers and sisters, formed the centre of the journeying entity, with the elderly making up its tail.

Concentrated tightly like this, Mako felt less cut off from his friends, and now, with the light of the skies pocked with twinkling points of light, he was looking for ways that he might squeeze in just a little play without catching his mother's attention. Yet each time he broke away from Nio and her elderly friends, his mother yelled for him to stay tight.

The pod stopped to rest when the night grew darkest. Nio, determining that the orca were now far enough away, permitted the youngsters to swim freely for a while. Mako was allowed, too, provided he attend to his duties, which presently meant ensuring the older animals had something to eat.

Thankfully, the shallower coastal waters meant fish were plentiful, which would spare him some energy. Tuna were passing nearby, and he was about to set off to drive them towards the pod's back end when he was suddenly startled by another loud rumble.

It came out of the rocks below, and was even more intense than the earlier one. A thunderous grinding, it was enough to make even some of the adults recoil.

The infants went darting back to their mothers. This was a great frustration to Mako, who needed these little ones to help with a certain task.

After some time, the quaking ended, and the podlings' confidence returned to them. Mako, able finally to convince them to come away once again, chased them playfully around the shallows of the shore, then, when they were comfortable with him, he set to work persuading them.

'That rumble you heard just now,' he said, as they raked their beaks through the sediment in search of hiding flatfish, 'just goes to show how dangerous the world is. You know, don't you, that there are orca all around these shores? And they'll gobble up podlings, just like you're gobbling up those little fish.'

The infants let out squeals of fright, but Mako was quick to offer comfort, aware that they might rush back again to the safety of their parents. 'But that's not anything for you to worry about. Because Mako is your friend, and he will protect you.'

On hearing this, the podlings went skittish with relief.

'Poor old Mako, though, has been working all night helping with the slower and weaker members of our pod, and *still* he hasn't finished. But here's a good idea! You can assist Mako in taking care of that, and help him keep his energy up, then he can look out for you like the good friend he is. Does that sound fair?'

'Yes!' chirruped the little ones. 'We must help Mako keep his energy up!'

Moving his head from side to side, Mako scanned all around to check who might be listening, but thankfully many of the adults were suspended at the ocean's surface, enjoying some quiet moments of rest. 'Great! Then here's what I want you to do. You're to swim over to those tuna. They're going to spread apart as soon as they see you, so it's important that when you get close enough you fan out nice and wide to encourage the fish to regroup and head in this direction. Got it?'

'Yes, Mako!'

'Tell it to me like I told it to you.'

One small girl, who's click trains were barely yet developed, attempted to reiterate Mako's plan. 'We go… to there,' she said. 'We be quiet for the tuna. Then we all go out, dolphin on this side, dolphin on that side.'

Mako gave a nod. 'Good. And you're not to stop until you see me. When you drive the tuna to me, I'll take over.'

'What will you do with them, Mako?' asked a little boy.

'I'll do the same as you: drive the fish the last little bit of the way to the older dolphins. Once all our energy is restored, we'll be ready to continue our journey to the spawning grounds. Now, let's do it. Head for that shoal, there. And stay together!'

Wasting no time, the podlings accelerated off. Mako threw scans at the tuna; discouragingly, the returning echoes revealed the fish were already alert. The infants, though, did a surprisingly good job of springing apart just at the right moment and, sure enough, the fish came speeding through the tunnel they'd created and into the open water where Mako was waiting.

Before he even knew it, he was surrounded by all the tuna he could eat. And, with his appetite high after such a long journey, he could eat *a lot*.

The podlings chittered irritably. 'They're all gone! Mako ate them all!'

Swallowing down the last fish, Mako giggled with glee. 'Yes, they are all gone. But remember, that one was just a practice.'

'No!' protested the infants. 'Mako cheated! We're not helping Mako again!'

'Mako didn't cheat! I just had to check you could do it! Just think about all the scary things waiting for you out there. But Mako will never let them hurt you. Now come on, let's try once more. I promise I'll do the last bit for sure this time. I'll drive the fish the rest of the way to the seniors.'

He sent out a sonar beam to locate the next shoal of fish. But the element of surprise was gone now, and the aloof tuna had moved a little further back from where the first lot had been. Still, the plan had worked so well; in no time at all, the podlings would be right back here with the food. The seniors really would get their meal, and he could finally play with the boys again.

Turning to the sulking podlings, Mako spoke encouragingly. 'Same as before, then. They're not so close now, but do as you did already and it will work just as well. Go on then! Off you go!'

The podlings darted away. But no sooner were they gone than the bull came speeding noisily back through the waters on the far side of the elderly dolphins. 'Orca have surrounded us!' he was whistling. 'Tighten the pod!'

Mako's eyes widened with fear. He gave a shout after the podlings, but with a chorus of distressed squawks now coming from the mothers – *'Where are the calves?! Where are the calves?!'* – his voice was lost.

With as powerful a thrash of his tail as he could manage, Mako went after the little ones. But the tuna had obviously been suspecting another ambush and had moved even further away, and the podlings, still fanned out, had kept chasing.

'No!' Mako screeched. 'Forget about the fish! Come back!'

The few who were closest obeyed; many, however, were carrying on ever further out into the expanse.

By now, the adults were splitting the water as they raced around with utmost urgency. Mako felt he should continue with his own attempt to retrieve the infants, but the cows and bulls were doing a much better job of widening the search so he stayed where he was, desperately hoping to see each of the podlings safely back at their mothers' sides.

Through the cacophony of clicking and the bubbly wake of tails swishing this way and that, Mako faintly heard his own name being called. It was his father, instructing him to pull tighter back into the pod. Without hesitation, he obeyed.

Throwing scans in every direction, Mako tried as hard as he could to track the unfolding turmoil, and watched with immense relief as, one by one, the terrified infants began to return. He was probably going to spend the rest of his life tending to the elderly dolphins, but he'd gladly do it if only the last few infants came back safely.

One more appeared.

Then another.

They were all here! Weren't they?

One of Mako's mother's oldest friends began twittering with anguish. 'Chizuko! Where is Chizuko? Where is my baby girl?'

Nio came to the pod's edge, her unmatched sense of sonar needed now more than ever. She threw out click trains into the open water to the south. 'There!' she said, prompting two bulls and a cow to speed off. 'That's Chizuko! But something's heading for her – dear Moshiri! It's orca! Hurry! They're coming in too fast! They're already—'

Nio fell silent, and her beak drooped downwards to a seabed littered with bones.

Mako's stomach, fluttery with the tuna he'd just swallowed, felt like it was about to eject them right back into the water.

The cow wailed out. 'What, Nio?! What is it?! Where is Chizuko?'

But Nio said nothing.

The three adults returned to the pod, their eyes sickened with grief and shock. 'I'm sorry,' said the bull. 'We were too late. Chizuko was taken.'

While Mako waited to go in front of Nio and the heads of the pod's families, he did everything he could to block out the cries of the mothers.

Why didn't they yell at him? Tell him he was stupid, careless, selfish? They should be asking what could have possibly gone through his mind to make him endanger the lives of the little ones in such a way, just to save himself the effort of having to help the pod's older and weaker members.

But instead, they said nothing.

Nobody, at all – even his friends – would say a single word to him. Which left him no choice but to listen to the wails and screeches of the cows.

Staying close to the algae-covered folds of the seabed, the sense of grief was like a physical presence rippling in the water. The death of any dolphin was always met with anguish and sorrow, but the loss of a podling went beyond anything he'd encountered in his young life. It was as though the very force that made the cows' hearts beat were fading. At least when they were angry with him they gave him a piece of their mind and moved on. Now though, they were too distraught to even speak.

The bulls were no less saddened than the cows. The threat of nearby orca was still real, though, so they busied themselves at the pod's eastern edge with herding the pod tight together.

Waiting to be summoned by Nio felt like waiting for a death sentence, and as time passed slowly by, Mako found himself dwelling on some of the other troublemakers from the pod's history. One especially notorious individual was called Tenko. He was already gone by the time Mako was born, driven out by the bulls, but his friend's big brother remembered him well, and once told them all about the young rogue.

Tenko was a troublemaker. As it was told to Mako, he carried in his heart a deep dislike of the other bulls. At every opportunity, Tenko slammed against the older dolphins and raked his teeth along their sides to score marks in their skin. They tolerated it for a time, but one day during a strand-fishing activity at a stretch of beach, when Tenko tried to shove himself to the front of the line and take more than his fair share of fish, one bull snapped his large body around and delivered a powerful tail slap right into his face.

Tenko waited to get his revenge. Some time later, the bulls and their sons were helping humans at the port. For driving the shoals closer to their boats, the dolphins were repaid with plentiful fish. Tenko, seeing the bull who'd hit him milling near the boat's whirring blades, thrust upwards into the older dolphin's body, shoving him into them. The poor bull's dorsal fin was severed in half.

For that callous act, Tenko was taken before Nio, who ordered the bulls to chase him away, and the troublemaker was never seen again.

Mako's heart thumped fast as he considered it. Tenko

merely injured the bull that day; despite his disfigurement, he remained an active and healthy dolphin. Yet Mako knew what he himself had done was worse, since poor little Chizuko was dead.

He let out a soft whine. It was doubtful if any dolphin in his pod's history had ever done anything so terrible as what he had done today.

Shuddering at the ongoing clucking of the grief-stricken mothers, Mako was so crushed with shame he felt it might drown him at any moment. How was he supposed to bear it?

He scanned for the bulls: they were still at the eastern edge of the pod, diligently holding the group together.

In his mind, Mako knew the best way to deal with this was to face up to the terrible decision he'd made and accept his punishment. But he just couldn't do it — and that meant all that remained for him was a single option.

So, pushing away from the huddled mass, Mako left his pod forever.

4

A SLEEPING VISION

FUSA WAS RIGHT: the rest of the pod were indeed cross with her.

She understood why, of course. For days, they'd raced along the currents to be first to the spawning grounds, exhausting themselves and pushing the young far too hard. And it had been worth it; tussles with other pods were avoided as the dolphins got to feast freely on a gigantic mass of shimmering mackerel.

Then, after just half a day, for some indistinct threat which may or may not have come, they'd had to leave it all behind.

Herding now on the summit of a seamount, a safe distance from the coast, the pod was awaiting news from the few bulls who'd stayed back at the spawning grounds. Misa, sensing her mother's discomfort, stayed close to Fusa, but every other member of the pod kept well back while their disappointment eased.

Wakka Totto bore no ill feeling towards Fusa, though it was evident in the way she swam to and fro that the pod's leader was unsettled; while thanks had been paid to the trout-god, their briefness did not befit the bounty bestowed upon them. A full day of ceremony had been reduced to its mere opening, and no creature as devout as Wakka Totto would ever feel happy about that.

The tension of the elders was eased, however, around noon, when a rumbling sounded and the seamount began to shake. At once, the infants darted back to their mothers' sides, but jubilation spread among the adults. 'It worked!' they chirruped. 'Wakka Totto's thanks have been accepted!'

Misa held her body close to Fusa. 'I don't like it when the seabed rattles that way.'

'You've nothing to worry about, Shrimp,' said Fusa, as the trembling died down. 'That's just Moshiri. He's giving his tail a little shake to acknowledge our prayers.'

Any grudges the others held against Fusa quickly vanished, and over the course of the afternoon the usual playfulness of the dolphins returned. While the remaining bulls busied themselves with pufferfish, the maternal pod played hide and seek in the kelp fields, and one of the other cows took the infants off to explore a nearby island.

It was almost as though life were back to normal again.

And then the other bulls rejoined the pod.

Toshi was incensed. Managing only a harsh look at Fusa as he passed, he went right to Wakka Totto, and let fly a volley of angry clicks. 'Why did we squander our hard-won advantage for the sake of some silly dream?'

'Calm yourself, young Toshi,' cheeped the pod's leader. 'Tell us what you saw after we left.'

'That fleet of fishing boats the pod fled from? They came right through the mackerel, as we expected. And they carried on right out into the ocean – and that was the last we saw of them.'

'What about other boats? Were there more around the coast?'

'None!' whistled Toshi. 'Whatever threat Fusa thought she saw was nothing but a moment of anxiety during her sleep. But your decision to act upon it has cost the rest of us dear.'

'What are you saying, Toshi?' asked Wakka Totto.

'What do you think I'm saying? The other pods have arrived at the spawning grounds! Whales, too. It's a feeding frenzy over there!'

Toshi peeled away from the glum-faced elders and came straight across to Fusa, whose heart quivered with remorse. She tried to explain how sorry she was for acting so rashly on so frail a threat, but he cut her off the moment she voiced it.

'You had your chance,' said Toshi. 'I told you we were disadvantaged in a pod this large. A bunch of us bulls are breaking away now. Tell Misa I'll see her soon.'

Fusa let out a desperate line of clicks. 'What do you mean? Where are you going? Toshi!'

But the powerful bull had already fled.

~

Hiding from the world within the swaying towers of the kelp forest, lost in regret for all the things that had ever gone wrong in her life, Fusa was startled by the sudden appearance of her cousin, Turem, who came and lay her flipper across her back.

Turem whistled softly. 'Do you remember when we were podlings, and I hid so well nobody could find me?'

Fusa let out a sad chuckle. 'Wakka Totto had to come.'

'I got in so much trouble with mama that day. But do you remember how much we laughed?'

'I peed on Wakka Totto a little bit.'

Turem squawked with glee, then, after a period of silence, spoke with tenderness. 'It's sad that Toshi has taken off, Fusa. But you can't wallow forever. They're bulls. It's what they do. Why don't you come with me? I want to show you a canyon I've found that's just like where I hid that time.'

Fusa glided along her cousin's body, comforted by the touch, then, keeping tight, the pair swam until they reached the shallows of the coast, by which time the light near the surface was glowing with the hues of early dusk.

Below, scarring the bottom, was a deep chasm set within the inclining ocean bed. Fusa fired signals all through it, reading in their returning echoes a world of arches and tunnels that would make Misa spin with excitement. Like the surface of a sponge, its steep valley sides were pocked and pitted, but unlike a sponge they were also rocky and very, very vast.

Pressing fins with her cousin as they journeyed, Fusa bristled to think of her encounter with Wakka Totto. She respected the elder, as they all did, and had been given no reason at all to fear her, but the old dolphin's ways – especially her ability to communicate with the trout-god – were unnerving.

Voicing a question that had troubled her for some time, Fusa turned her beak to her cousin. 'How does Wakka Totto know so much about Moshiri?'

'Same way she knows everything. Humans.'

Fusa cast her mind back to the odd upright creatures she saw at the port yesterday. It was known to all in the pod that Wakka Totto possessed great knowledge about human matters, but the elder tended only to speak about them to dolphins who asked her directly.

'But why her, though? How come it's only her that knows about them?'

Turem blew a bubble. 'The story Wakka Totto tells is that she once had a human companion.'

Fusa tilted her head towards Turem, shocked. 'A *companion*?'

'A long, long time ago, apparently. When she was just a podling herself. She came across one in the water diving for oysters.'

'Humans can swim?'

'Not really, no. But they do come into the water now

and then. The human didn't want the oyster's meat though. She just wanted the shiny ball inside the shell. Wakka Totto went and helped the human by dislodging the oysters from the rock reefs. And the human treated her nicely after that. She brought her fish and rubbed her belly, and everyday Wakka Totto went to play with her in a tidal pool at the edge of Squid Hood Bay. And there she taught her the human tongue.'

'They can talk like us?'

'They can't speak dolphin, no. But some of us can speak like them. The human taught young Wakka Totto their words for numbers and shapes, then their names for things. And the more time she spent in her company, the more she learned about how the world was made.'

Fusa's smile broadened. For the first time in her life, the thought of Wakka Totto didn't make her stomach flutter like it were full of cuttlefish.

Cheered by her cousin's kindness, Fusa began to look forward to hearing all about Misa's day out at the island. Yet as she swam with Turem back to the pod, she realised that she was tired in an almost unnatural way. From the tips of her flukes to the point of her beak, exhaustion resided in every part of her.

Indeed, when she was listening to Misa's account, Fusa felt her eyes burning with the emotion of the day. Soon, she was going to have to explain to her daughter why her father had left the pod, and the prospect overwhelmed her with melancholy. But so tired was she, that one half of her brain quickly shut itself down for sleep.

With her daughter hanging vertically beside her, the awake part of Fusa's brain took her over the surface to breathe. But the creeping fatigue quickly found its way deeper into her mind, and, for the briefest of instants, everything in Fusa's mind grew quiet.

And that was when the images appeared.

There were long lengths of fabric, swaying between

towering cliffs. And boats, crashing and careening in a way unsuited to their buoyant form. Everything was dragging as though it were in a net, and the dolphins surrounding her were powerless to resist it. The hot and needling water was like blood in its opaqueness, and each of her senses was corrupted, and every hope was lost among the protruding bones of whalefalls down on the seabed.

Fusa lurched awake, her heart pounding. She reached out for Misa, who was still at rest beside her, then, for no reason other than to ease her loneliness, she threw out click trains in every direction.

The horde of bodies comprising the pod blipped in her sonar field. Everything was as it should be. But then some echoes returned from the open water to the north, revealing a most unusual picture.

Travelling side by side were two individuals, who appeared to be wearing box-like objects on their heads. Who were *they*? Fusa thought she knew everybody in this pod, but these two weren't familiar at all.

Monitoring her sonar field, she watched as the two dolphins suddenly separated: one turned for the coast, while the other sped through the ocean on a southern trajectory.

'Misa.'

'Mama?'

'Sorry to wake you, Shrimp. Send a click train out, will you. Tell me what you see.'

Misa let fly a long chirrup, and waited. 'He's funny,' she said.

'Who?'

'That speedy boy over there with the box on his head. Mama, you were making noises. Did you dream again?'

Fusa pushed up with her tail fin, and held herself in a spyhop. She beamed her sonar all around, letting the wind chill her sleek skin as she waited for the echo to return. When she was sure no boats were approaching on the waves, she submerged again, and held her face beside Misa's.

'Come on, Shrimp. Let's swim.'

'But it's late, mama.'

'I know,' said Fusa, thrashing away from where they'd hung.

They glided quietly through the pod until they reached Turem, who was resting beside her own children.

Turem's closed eye sprang open upon sighting her cousin. 'What is it, Fusa? What's going on?'

'Watch Misa for me.'

'Why?'

'Please?'

'Of course, cousin. But remember what I said. If Toshi's made up his mind, there's nothing—'

'This isn't about Toshi.'

Holding her beak against Misa's, Fusa gave a big smile. 'Be good for your auntie, Shrimp. I'll be back soon.'

∽

'Something's coming.'

Wakka Totto nodded at Fusa's words, but remained silent. Appearing sluggish, it was as though the very pufferfish that had made the elderly leader so excitable before were now the very thing that made her grouchy and glum.

'The trout-god showed me more this time,' Fusa said to the elder. 'Not just boats now, but nets, too. And a dreadful, deafening clattering. The boats – they move in a way that's not right. Like they're rolling. And all the dolphins have this same feeling of being… lost.'

Wakka Totto's swollen eyes opened wider. 'Lost?'

'It's like they have no control over their sense of direction. Up and down and left and right – none of that means anything. It's all just… dragging. And the water, it's impure somehow. It's like what you were telling the adolescents, about the whole world being nothing but swamp. It's like the world *before* the world. Wakka Totto, I'm frightened.'

'All creatures fear what they don't understand, young Fusa. Even the humans. But we can't be ruled by fear. After the pod has rested, we're going to head back to the spawning grounds. I think you'll see that we're quite safe.'

'I think it's a mistake.'

'The mistake was leaving before our ceremony was complete. We've been extremely lucky that the trout-god heard our prayers – but we can't push our luck.'

'But Wakka Totto, if it's as you say and my dream really is a vision from Moshiri, then doesn't that mean he's trying to communicate a warning to us? Won't it upset him even more if we fail to heed it?'

The elder swayed, and let up a bubble. 'Perhaps. Or perhaps, sometimes, these things are nothing more than dreams. Let's keep things in perspective, young Fusa. We're far from human boats here, and they can't hurt us if they aren't above us. But since you're obviously so fretful, I'll send some of our remaining bulls out as scouts. If any boats are seen near the mackerel, we'll hold off longer. The whole pod.'

A swirl of protests eddied around Fusa's mind. What good were the bulls, after a day spent swallowing the intoxicating burps of pufferfish? In this state, they'd forget what they were even supposed to be scouting for.

No. That wouldn't do.

'Leave the bulls to rest, Wakka Totto. I'll patrol the shore myself. It's me who's seen the threat, so it's me who should keep a watch for it. If no fleets appear by daybreak, we're clear to return to the spawning grounds.'

Wakka Totto went over the surface to spout, and came back with a more agreeable look in her eye. 'Very well. In honesty, I'm not keen on losing the few bulls we have left

– the mackerel are attracting orca clans, after all. Go now then, Fusa. I'll find a way to break it to the pod if you come back with bad news.'

Fusa nodded, and swam away on powerful thrusts. Following the ridge of the seamount west, she scanned tirelessly for everything that moved. Whales were around at a distance, and orca, and another dolphin pod would soon be arriving at the bay. But human activity on the waves was quiet; save for the occasional lone vessel, the land creatures retained no real presence at all, put off, perhaps, by the gusty weather that made the ocean's surface swell with choppy peaks.

The first hint of dawn began to illuminate the east as Fusa arrived at the coastal waters. With Turem's canyon laying directly beneath her, she reflected once again just how much Misa would love to play hide and seek within its gullies and crevices.

Throwing a scan at the shoreline, a trio of blips registered in Fusa's sonar field. Boats were near. But they were small, and set on a different course to the bay hosting the spawning mackerel. This was no threat at all.

She took a deep breath of air into her lungs at the surface. There was simply no way keeping the pod away from their feast could be justified. Provided every dolphin stayed alert, it could do no harm to head back to the spawning grounds.

Turning back for the seamount, Fusa thrashed her tail flukes and accelerated away. But the moment she did, a deep groan emerged from the seabed, and the rocky shelf began to shake.

The god of the sea and the storms was rattling his scales again.

But unlike the last time, now Moshiri did so with a force that was anything but gentle.

And with that force, the vision that tormented her dream — of a world gone to purest chaos — was coming suddenly to life.

5

THE RIPPING OF THE WORLD

Fukushima Shoreline,
March 11, 2011

The East was beginning to blush with the first light of dawn, yet the promise of a new day was more bitter to Mako than the flesh of any rotten octopus.

For the first time in his life, where he was going mattered not a bit to him. Thrashing his tail flukes with all his strength, the young dolphin pushed on with a single desire: to be as far from his pod as he could possibly be.

Below him sat the picked bones of whalefalls – his only company in this empty patch of ocean. He'd never known solitude like this, yet still he advanced, hopeful that soon he'd come to the edge of the world itself and fall right off. And only then, when he was rolling like a piece of driftwood in an eternal surf to forever lament the awful tragedy he'd caused, could he ever be far enough away.

But echoes rebounding from a great distance – scans

he'd thrown so long ago he'd forgotten all about them – revealed something disturbing in Mako's sonar vision.

He actually wasn't alone.

Orca were out there.

Mapping the course of these hunting clans, an unsettling picture emerged. The orca were journeying south, against the current: they were heading straight for his pod.

Terror washed along his spine. The dolphins he'd run away from had been through so much already this morning because of him. Made vulnerable by their grief, their defences were sure to be weakened.

He drew to a halt, his eyes widening as his inner voice pondered something unfathomable. The orca would rip him apart, of course. Burst him into a cloud of blood. But that didn't matter, not when he had before him the chance to do right by the very dolphins who'd put up with his misdeeds for so long.

He *had* to do it. He had to entice the orca away from his pod.

Swimming now towards the distant blips captured in his sonar field, Mako beat his tail with a frantic urgency. It wouldn't undo the damage he'd caused, but perhaps this deed might serve as the single pure act of his silly little life.

His scans rebounded with increasing speed; what started as mere shadows were now condensing in his mind into sharper images of killer animals.

He was nearing the clan.

With his focus trained on the echoes, Mako read the movements of the orca. Two of them were peeling away from the wider group: they were coming for him. He tucked his beak tight into his underside, and flapped his fins to turn himself over.

Now darting through the water in the opposite direction, he lead the hunters west, away from the pod, throwing out a train of clicks.

Ten seconds passed before the scan returned.

Scan.

Nine seconds.

They were gaining.

He pumped his tail hard, but the fatigue of a night's journeying – and his shameful retreat from the earlier tragedy – was costing him some acceleration. If only he'd known he'd be leading hungry orca on a chase this morning, he could have kept something back in reserve!

Scan.

Seven seconds.

But wait! Only two were coming! He let out an anxious squeal. If the rest of the clan was still on course to clash with his pod, he was sacrificing himself for nothing.

Thrashing harder, he banished the thought. He was doing all he could; his father and the rest of the bulls would do the same. The young and the weak of the pod were safe from orca as long as *they* were around.

With this newfound hope, Mako hastened. Beaming out another scan, however, only six seconds passed until it bounced back.

In his mental map, the coast was appearing, its shoreline wavy with bays and furrowed with inlets which, if he was lucky, would funnel him to safety.

Scan.

Four seconds.

His tail was becoming more tired with every beat, but the ocean's edge was nearing, and something was materialising in his sonar field which looked like a narrow channel inland. This was his only chance.

He banked a few degrees to the south before scanning again.

Two seconds.

The pursuing orca were now close enough that he could see the points of their teeth.

Below him, the water's depth was becoming

shallower where the shelf of rock rose to meet the shore. Within the seabed lay widening trenches; dipping into one was tempting, but it wasn't safe: he could easily end up trapping himself.

Scan.

One second.

The clicks of the orcas' crude language were sounding right behind him.

'Dolphin... snack. Dolphin... bye bye.'

But then the orcas' voices fell silent. They'd stopped chasing and, to Mako's complete surprise, were turning and speeding away.

What was going on? Had they decided to spare him his li—

A ferocious noise, like the world was exploding, sounded below.

And then the ocean actually *moved*.

The maker of the sea and the storms, whom Mako so rudely offended, had found him.

Moshiri had shaken his scales twice already since last night – and now he was making his displeasure properly known.

The seabed was suddenly trembling with a force so strong whole sections of the canyons below cascaded into themselves, all while a juddering, grinding groan roared from inside the fabric of the ocean's vast floor.

'Forgive me!' Mako called out. 'Great Moshiri, forgive me!'

He numbed with fear. With the entire ocean sat upon the trout-god's gargantuan spine, no plan Mako could possibly come up with was worth the energy of devising it.

With that thought, his panic ceased. Fighting against this show of strength was as pointless as trying to reverse the direction of time's current. Nature was pleasing itself now. And its children, of which Mako was merely one, had no choice but to let it.

Mapping the environment was pointless, too, since it was changing so rapidly all around him. He didn't even bother to time the terrible quaking, although it went on long enough that he began to question whether this tremulous vibrating might now be the world's permanent state.

Eventually, however, its intensity began to dim, and the bed below stopped rattling. Mako's thundering heart calmed by a degree. Was that it? Had Moshiri delivered his lesson? If so, Mako had most definitely learned it. To behave impurely was to be impure, and the trout-god wished only for cleanliness in the oceans he bore upon his back. Never again would Mako insult the backbone fish the way he did last evening.

Going up to spyhop at the surface, however, Mako realised that the lesson had only just begun:

A wave the size of the ocean itself was heading his way.

The trout-god, at last, was about to have his vengeance.

~

"All creatures fear what they don't understand, young Fusa."

Wakka Totto's words had made sense when she spoke them in the darkness of night. But amid an event as shocking as the one now taking place, Fusa was starting to see just how right the elderly leader had been.

No scene had ever struck such terror into her heart – and none had ever been so absolutely impossible to comprehend.

From out of the seabed, a groan was emerging, a droning din that gave the impression the very rock were crying out in pain. Rumbles and rattles were frequent occurrences in the ocean – Wakka Totto told them as calves not to fret at it – but what was happening now was on a scale that defied belief.

Positioned at the top of the southern cliff of Turem's canyon, Fusa's body was paralysed with fear against the husk of some long-gone coral. She listened as the noise steadily took on a grinding quality — as though two separate slabs of matter, each of unfathomable vastness, were scraping against one another in a kind of contest to see which could push the other away.

Sediment was billowing in low clouds, pockets of it swirling here and there where eddies whisked it into fleeting columns, and the fact that Fusa could see the carpet of starfish moving along the rocky ledge suggested those inert critters were reacting with utmost urgency.

The teeth-rattling friction then halted. Fusa, however, sensed that the battle raging in the depths was readying to conclude with one final, devastating blow, and sure enough, with barely a second gone by, a victor emerged – one slab thrust the other upwards.

The ocean bed had just ripped itself apart.

The coral's husk now stood away from Fusa by a dolphin's length: the force of the released tension had shunted the seabed closer to the coast.

As the world convulsed with a sickening violence, the vast canyon began to disintegrate below her. Just last night, when she and Turem had explored its many crevices, Fusa had thought how very ancient this structure seemed. And now, as though it were made of nothing more than wet sand, it split, then collapsed into the space that had stood between its steep walls.

On and on the quaking went, minute after minute, with the roar of a million explosions. Deafened and dizzied, Fusa had no idea which direction she was even facing, her senses becoming ever more confused as the ocean around her darkened and fragmented, until eventually the intensity gave way to shorter, but only slightly less tremorous, jolts.

And now, as if she hadn't already had her fill of traumatising chaos, some other force was arriving to terrorise her, something so strange and hypnotic that she felt like she were experiencing it from outside of herself.

Surveying the solid shelf below, Fusa noticed that the anemones stuck on its surface had all gone flat; as though reaching for some prize, their tentacles stretched out to the open ocean. The rocks, too, had done something peculiar: they'd headed halfway up to the surface, where they now simply hung in the water.

But rocks weren't living things. Were they? With her senses still dazed from the seabed's convulsions, Fusa wasn't sure of anything right now. She didn't even know her own location relative to other things, a feeling of disorientation made worse by the fact the canyon had vanished into itself.

She threw out sonar scans in every direction, but the echoes came back abnormally, seemingly unable to find her, and at this point she suddenly realised why: she was being moved against her will.

Some unknown current was pulling her to the east. The anemones weren't grasping for something: they were being flattened by the same force that was dragging her.

Dragging!

Her chilled heart shattered into shards of ice. This was it: the vision in her dream, put there by Moshiri himself, made real at last.

With her oxygen levels low, Fusa ached to spout, to feel cool air in her lungs. Yet the combined strength of all the dolphins in her pod wouldn't be enough to break free of this current's astonishing clutch.

The possibility of drowning served to intensify her panic; with her blood racing around her body this way, it wouldn't be long until life left her and she sank like a boulder to the bottom, a banquet for the worms.

A sense of peace overcame her; the present quiet was all the more serene after the cacophony of the world splitting apart. She allowed her eyes to close. All the anguish she'd carried around inside her – Toshi abandoning the pod, Misa's inevitable upset at finding out – didn't much matter at all in this moment. Right now she craved just one thing: a long and dreamless sleep.

But just when Fusa's thoughts began to dim and the light of life started to fade, she became aware that the pull was weakening. She kicked out her tail – and moved forward!

Impulsively, Fusa darted higher through the shallow coastal waters, her lungs burning as her nostrils fought off the urge to drink in the ocean. Although no thoughts troubled her in this mad scramble to the surface, she was mindful enough to feel thankful: had she been any deeper when this pandemonium broke out, she would have drowned for sure.

Finally, with a heave of her body, she broke through the waves to release a huge spout of mist up into the sky.

Remaining in a spyhop position above the surface, a blaring sound came drifting across from the land, its frequency rising and falling in a constant pattern. Fusa turned to see boats, but rather than trailing nets like in her dream, these empty vessels weren't a threat of any sort. Beyond the boats, on the shore, a few land creatures were scrambling to get inside their wheeled machines.

For the first time since the awful quaking started, Fusa felt something approaching ordinariness. Soon, she'd get her breath back and return to her daughter. Misa was going to be so cross that she'd been left with Turem, but when she heard the incredible tale of her mama's morning, she'd have nothing to offer but love and affection.

Still, Fusa wasn't completely calm. Some sense that all was not well was troubling her, and this was made worse when echoes returned from the open water to the east.

She twisted her body around. If her sonar was to be

trusted – difficult, given her recent disorientation – there was something wide heading her way along the surface of the ocean. Wide seemed inadequate a measurement, though; whatever this was, it stretched on in both directions out beyond the range of her scans. What was more, it was moving at a speed so unbelievable that Fusa concluded something had indeed gone wrong with her senses.

A human on the shore behind her was moving with increasing urgency, screaming a word over and over again: 'Tsunami!' Fusa wasn't overly familiar with the behaviour of the long-limbed land creatures, but she was easily able to perceive that it was in a state of panic.

She watched the open ocean and listened to the echoes of her clicks, which began to build a disturbing picture of the water. It was doing something very odd. She supposed it could be called a swell – yet a swell was found where there was a trough and, discounting this mysterious line of water protruding from the surface, the ocean was reasonably calm.

It was a wake then, was it? That was possible. But what kind of boat could have left a wake as wide and as fast as this one, and why hadn't she seen that vessel pass?

The wall of water was beginning to slow as it came closer to the shallower depths of the shoreline, but that was no reason to feel cheerful, since what it had lost in speed, it had made up for in height:

This thing was *growing*.

She dived beneath the surface, where the sound of tumbling water was simply incredible. The wave – or wake, or whatever it was – was drawing closer, filling her with an overwhelming urge to head to the shore. But what was she supposed to do once she reached the water's edge?

She sent out a scan; her sonar returned nothing interpretable as an escape route, so she went above the waves again.

And as she spyhopped there, she saw that the surge of water coming her way could not be escaped.

The end – for what else could this be if the very ocean had just torn itself apart? – was the only thing left to experience. The world was being returned to its original swamp state.

A gentle wave bobbed her up and down – a foretaste of what was about to follow – and it occurred to Fusa that the coming devastation may in itself be a mere ripple. Did something lay beyond it, ready to destroy whatever was left of the oceans and the land that sat upon them?

She began to weep at the thought of Misa and the rest of the pod out in the ocean, whom this wall of destruction must surely have flattened by now.

Desperately, she sent out sonar signals, but the returning echoes weren't quite readable: they revealed odd shapes, which tumbled and rolled along the face of the coming wall of water.

A shudder passed through Fusa as she identified them as boats. In her dream, humans were the cause of her horror; here in the waking world, they were merely another of its victims.

Plunging back into the ocean, she swam as hard as she could to the south. The surge was going to push her onto the land, so it was better it did so where the terrain was open and flat.

She powered her flukes to get as far from the port as possible, and began to feel debris in the water prickling the skin of her left flank – her first sense of the wave's awesome power. This was it: she was now being shunted towards the shoreline, and whatever lay upon it.

Throwing clicks every which way, Fusa perceived all manner of objects being pushed with her. Alongside the boats were long poles of metal, wooden boards, plastic barrels, tin cans, glass bottles and giant spiky stones like very odd starfish, each one heavy enough to crush a whale.

After one last leap to take as deep a breath as possible, she returned below the surface to a noise now so loud it made her head ring with pain, but that didn't seem to matter very much because suddenly she was tumbling, barreling, flailing – her propulsion no longer anything to do with her own effort and everything to do with the force of the surge of water.

Scanning frantically, no echoes returned. Or perhaps they all did; caught in the explosive face of the wave, it no longer mattered what the chaos of objects around her looked like.

She felt a large force smash into her belly, followed just a moment later by something very heavy hitting her on the head. Momentarily, a flash of bright light shone in her eyes, and Fusa gulped down a breath before the water span her over once again. She became aware that she was passing now over land — her back was scraping against a hard surface – and then a great pain raged in the centre of her body where she was slammed into something tall and narrow.

And with that, she was suddenly in a calm place.

No longer a young mother separated from her daughter, she was just a little podling again, somewhere far away, and lovely.

6

BEACHED

BY THE TIME the great wave was finished with him, Mako couldn't even remember why he'd fled his pod.

The surge had shoved him toward the coast with an incomprehensible force, as though the entire ocean had been set on an incline and was somehow tipping from a higher place to a lower one, with him caught upon its very edge.

He'd wondered if he might die – at one point he suspected he *was* dead – which was why, when he eventually came awake again and surveyed his surroundings, he thought his spirit was now in some new world.

Water encircled him, but he wasn't at sea.

This was *inland*.

A hard material dug into the skin of his belly. Weakly, he tried to turn himself with a push of his flipper, but the filthy water in which he lay, polluted as it was with all manner of inorganic material, was too shallow.

He was beached.

Against his left side was a wall, which had evidently stopped the wave carrying him even further into the land. By some quirk of fate he felt he didn't deserve, no heavy object had come in after him to crush him against it. Even luckier was that his blowhole had remained above the surface of the water where he now lay. How easily he could have been trapped in the swampy quagmire! Pinned beneath one of the many heavy pieces of debris surrounding him, he would have drowned for certain.

Still, it wasn't much of a consolation. Amid this desolate, ruined scenery, a place that was neither ocean nor land but some corrupted state in between, he was beginning to regret that the wave hadn't just killed him.

With the dry air on his skin, Mako scooped water over himself with his fins and waited for something – anything – to happen.

Although the water was close by and deep enough to swim in, he simply didn't possess the strength to get himself off his belly and into it, so he lay still, taking in his surroundings. This must have been a pleasant environment before the wave had struck it. Open fields of grasses – a kind of foodstuff consisting of thousands of tiny grains – spread out far and wide, with only occasional trees or low walls breaking up the uniform layout of the land.

If his overwhelmed senses were to be believed, the harbour north of here had fared significantly worse. The devastating surge had been channeled in through the harbour's walls, and now the buildings that had run along it were gone, as were the many boats that had so recently bobbed there. Any further north, and he would have ended up there himself, but since his section of the wave had met a wall it couldn't breach, he'd been shoved instead to the south, eventually finding the shore on the other side of a curved bay.

It was impossible to imagine a time where the worst hit portions of the coast would ever return to normal. The dark waters here in this sheltered stretch of land were already beginning to pull back, and as the tide receded all manner of shapes on the fields were materialising in his sonar. Mostly, this was the kind of debris common to human habitations – the land creatures tended to shove the stuff they didn't require anymore straight into the ocean – but as more and more objects became exposed to the clear morning skies, Mako realised that in many cases the shapes were humans themselves.

As the water level continued to pull back, living humans began to appear. They moved on awkward strides, struggling to advance through the waterlogged fields, but they were persistent, and soon were hauling the lifeless members of their kind away on the apparatus they'd brought to carry them.

Watching it all unfold, Mako worked tirelessly to keep his back wet. But the blubber encasing him, so vital in the cool waters where he lived, was acting against him now, and he was rapidly overheating. Even worse than that, though, was the pressure on his underside. Pressed beneath his weight, his organs were being crushed against the hard structure on which he was marooned. He tried to rock himself this way and that, and might have succeeded in flipping himself over, but the risk of ending up like some capsized turtle, unable even to splash water on his exposed underside, was too great, so he remained as he was.

If only his hunger would let up, though. He didn't wish to dwell on the last time he ate, when the podlings had brought him tuna, but the emptiness of his belly was almost painful. He wondered if there might be some trick he could perform for the humans. Something that might persuade them to throw him a snack as they had last evening when they watched him at the shrine. But he knew that in this helpless state, even a basic act of showing off was impossible to accomplish.

As more time passed, greater numbers of humans began to sweep across the saturated fields. They eventually got close enough that Mako felt they should have seen him. Sure, he was concealed from their eyes behind the wall, but why didn't their sonar pick him up? He was right here!

On heavy, plodding steps, the upright creatures continued to walk straight past until eventually, with hunger screaming in his sore belly, he gave voice to his impatience. 'Hey!' he whooped. 'Are you going to just let me dry out completely over here?'

The two human individuals on the other side of the wall went still, then blurted out some words. 'Was that a—?'

Suddenly, two heads peered over the wall. Human eyes were looking right into him.

'Dolphin!' gasped one, whose face drooped in such a way that Mako wondered if he was in distress. 'Imagine, Ryu-san! All the marine life the tsunami has destroyed!'

The other stepped closer to Mako and scooped water across his back. 'Should we lift him, Haroumi-san?'

'I think we must.'

Mako let out a groan. 'Have you got any fish or what? I'm starving.'

The human pair positioned themselves on either side of Mako and wedged their limbs underneath his belly. 'Ready? One. Two. Three!'

The weight on his organs was relieved immediately as the humans hauled Mako up from the hard surface and cradled him in their arms. With a coordination that he had imagined these awkward land beasts to be incapable of, the pair then walked him carefully towards the coast, ensuring their strides were perfectly synchronised.

'Anyway, about those fish?' whistled Mako as he journeyed through the sky ever closer to his ocean home. But his rescuers took no notice as they steadily continued.

Soon, the water was up to the middle of the humans, and they lowered him beneath the surface. Although the ocean was still filthy, becoming fully submerged again brought instant relief to his back and dorsal fin. While he assumed control of his body, the human pair stayed where they were, then, when he was confident the risk of being stranded was now behind him, he brought his head up into the air to converse with them one more time.

'So, no fish then?'

The faces of the humans were less anguished now, though they carried with them an obvious weariness. The shaking of the land, and the great wave that followed it, must have been as terrifying to them as it had been to him. With weak smiles, the two creatures reached out their hands and patted him on his head, then turned back for the shore and waded away.

Mako darted out of the bay, but hesitated before rounding it. Faint echoes of something in his sonar stood out among the appalling volume of detritus strewn within and upon the water.

It was shaped like a dolphin.

He span around. The route to that section of the waterlogged fields was obstructed by boulders and jagged metal objects, but one of his kind was in trouble, and would be feeling as helpless and hot as he had himself not moments ago.

With careful, exact movement, Mako manoeuvred inland.

And then he saw her.

~

What a pleasant, serene place it was.

In Fusa's unconscious mind, she was back with the pod in Squid Hood Bay, swimming side by side with her mother and father after crossing the strait for the first time.

Her tiny body ached from the tip of her beak to the flukes of her tail, but she was filled with pride at what she'd accomplished, and many of the pod's adults came over to the little ones to tell them how very brave they'd been in completing the crossing back to Wakka Totto's ancestral home.

At barely a year old, she'd only known open water until then, so to be at the scalloped edge of the shoreline was a real thrill, and in spite of her tiredness she longed to play in the bright, shallow waters that sparkled in the light of the warm sun.

Her parents were exhausted too. Worry had troubled their faces throughout the entire crossing, and although they'd taken care never to mention their fear to Fusa, she understood well enough how vulnerable they were to an attack by orca or shark. But now they were here, they were relaxed, and it brought Fusa peace.

The rest of the pod were napping, but Fusa was far too excited to sleep. The coast was teeming with life: not just fish, though these were plentiful, but creatures she'd not yet encountered, and on the other side of the cove her undeveloped sonar was returning images of an animal swimming with incredible exuberance.

Ignoring the whirring, juddering racket sounding from the rear of a boat coming out from the surf, she proceeded along the cove until she came face to face with an excitable little creature with large round eyes at the front of its face, and whiskers fanning out from its snout-like nose.

Little Fusa brought her beak close to the animal to investigate, and it held its head gently beside her own as it, too, attempted to figure her out.

'What are you?' she said, but the animal just stared dumbly back.

'I'm Fusa. I'm one. I'm a dolphin. What's your name?'

Still the animal stayed silent. But then, as though he wanted the calf to know how clever he was, he arched his sleek body and performed a tight backflip before sending a flurry of bubbles up to the surface.

Fusa giggled. 'You're a very good swimmer,' she said, and mimicked the flip. Although it wasn't quite as graceful as the one performed by her new friend, he blew more bubbles to encourage her to do it again.

The pair spent a while flipping together until they achieved perfect synchronisation. Fusa was about to ask the creature to come with her to show their trick to her parents, but her attention was hoisted away by the boat, which by now had come overhead. 'Why is it so noisy?' Fusa asked. 'I don't like it.'

The creature blew bubbles and made a heavy swipe of his tail. Little Fusa watched as he then broke through the surface and held himself at the boat's side where, to her amazement, a chunk of fish flesh came flying overboard and landed in the water. The creature took hold of the fish and brought it down to Fusa, dropping it in front of her beak for her to take.

'Thank you,' she called out, and he made his way back up to gobble down the next piece that had plopped in.

She wanted to join him at the surface, but the way the blades at the rear of the boat were chopping into the water put her off. He was clearly having so much fun up there, though: he clapped his fins together, earning himself ever more pieces of fish.

Eventually, Fusa decided to be brave, but as she was making her way towards the rear of the boat to accompany her friend, she heard her father's voice call out behind her:

'Fusa! No!'

Before she even knew what was happening, she'd been shoved away, and the clear water was suddenly cloudy with blood, and when she looked at her father he was thrashing around in pain, his dorsal fin sliced in half through the middle.

Her mother was there a moment later in a state of panic, promptly ordering her daughter to go find the other calves. And as Fusa swam away, her beak drooped as she began to understand what had happened.

'I caused this,' she said sadly to her friends.

The calves rested their flippers upon her own. 'He'll be alright. He'll be alright.'

But Fusa simply stared away. 'I caused this,' she said again.

Presently, light was streaming in through her opening eyes. She was emerging from out of her unconsciousness, and the past was becoming the present.

'I caused this,' she mumbled, groggily. 'I caused this.'

Something hard was beneath her, and half of her body was in the open air. But she was too befuddled by the force of the wave to get any sense of where she was.

Then she heard a dolphin's voice calling out – 'auntie!' – but she couldn't figure out whom it belonged to, nor where it was coming from.

'Auntie!' it said again. 'Who are you?'

Fusa tilted her head around to speak but, disorientated, only a single word came out, and she had no idea why. 'Coral.'

She beamed her sonar, but nothing came back. In her eyes, she saw shapes lumbering nearby; she couldn't be sure, but they looked like humans.

The dolphin called out again. 'Can you move, Coral?'

Fusa craned around the other way. Where the water was slightly deeper beside her, a young male was moving towards her through the filthy water.

Again, she attempted to echolocate. And again, nothing came back. A vague feeling of dread stirred inside her at a thought she battled to suppress.

'You're hurt,' said the adolescent.

Fusa fell back.

'It's alright, auntie,' he called. 'I'll help you.'

'Why are humans here?' she whistled softly.

'They're helping.'

Growing suddenly confused, Fusa began to panic. 'But who are you?'

And even though the helper gave his name, she was far too dazed to take it in, and everything went dark.

～

Mako waited until the young cow's eyes finally came open again, then asked: 'Can you move at all?'

'A bit,' she creaked. 'But my vision is funny.'

'The wave beached you. You need to get into the water or you'll overheat.'

'I feel hot.'

'Shall I push you in?'

'I feel so hot.'

'Coral, listen to me. I'm going to push you into the water. Tell me if I hurt you.'

Supporting his weight with his fins, Mako leaned onto the hard platform on which the female was stranded. With her hooked fin and milky lower body, it was apparent she was a different kind of dolphin to him.

Taking care to be gentle as he pushed his beak beneath her, he gave the cow as firm a shove as he could manage, and successfully pivoted her body to the side, but still the distance to the water was too great. 'I can't do it,' he quacked. 'We'll have to find another way.'

Mako dipped at once back below the surface, and, taking care not to strand himself, retraced his path back to where the humans had brought him out. He then went up into a spyhop and looked around. The human pair were still moving across the flooded fields: at least, it might have been them; it was hard to say, when their kind all looked so similar.

With his loudest voice, Mako chirped across to where the nearest one stood. 'Hey! We need some help over here!'

The humans turned to face him.

'Yes! Here! Please come. A dolphin is in trouble!'

The upright creatures looked at one another, then

waded through the opaque water to where he was floating on the surface.

Mako backed away as they approached; the humans followed.

'That's it! This way!' He turned to face the structure on which the injured cow lay. 'Over there,' he squealed, pointing with his beak.

The humans swivelled their heads around and, to Mako's relief, looked right at her.

Wasting no time, the pair came trudging through the water and approached the wounded dolphin, while Mako glided behind them in the shallow depths. Then, as they had done with him, the humans positioned themselves either side of the young cow and lifted her gently, before carrying her to where the water was deep enough to allow her to propel away.

Mako surfaced again. 'Thank you,' he said, and the humans, as before, allowed a flash of happiness to show on their otherwise wearied faces.

'Come with me, Coral,' said Mako, while the female slowly flicked her tail as though checking it still worked. 'We need to get to deeper water.'

'Why are you calling me Coral?'

'You said it was your name.'

'My name is Fusa. Who are you?'

'I'm Mako.'

Right then the young cow started clucking with distress, drawing Mako closer. 'What's the matter, auntie? Are you in pain?'

'It's my scans!' cheeped the injured dolphin. 'I can't read them! I've gone sonar-blind!'

7
SMOKE FROM THE SHORE

THE LIGHT of the wintry evening grew ever more pale. Then, when the sky became as flat and featureless as a slab of stone, flecks of ice began to drift down.

Fusa was bobbing alone at the surface, dizzy with the pain that now pulsed within her head. Whatever it was she'd slammed into on the wave's relentless face was hard and unyielding, and it had disabled the part of her she relied upon most for understanding the physical space that surrounded her.

At least she had her eyes, though. In the drab light of day, she could discern the faint outlines of humans ambling on the shore and, at some distance across from them, a spit of land. Curving away from north to south, this narrow peninsula shielded the wide, shallow lagoon she now swam in, which explained why the coast here had been only moderately affected by the deluge of surging water.

The wave had stirred up the sediment on the lagoon's bed, however, and in water this foul her eyes were useless. No matter the strength of her determination or the length of her click trains, the echoes that came back sailed straight through her: somewhere between her throat, where the sound waves entered, and her brain, which built the images, the pathway was interrupted.

In addition to her headache, Fusa's stomach hurt, though whether this was nausea or hunger she couldn't say. She threw more scans into the bed of the lagoon, but again, the echoes returned with no information. These waters might be teeming with cuttlefish or octopus, but since she had no means to locate them, she resorted to nudging around with her beak in the sediment, which yielded nothing but a plastic disc and a frayed section of rope.

She came up above the surface in time to hear a loud boom rumble in the distance, and held herself in a spyhop, letting the brittle speckles of ice settle upon her head. Unable to detect the source of the sound, she instead watched the humans in the fields, who'd begun running with a sudden frenziedness. Beyond them, objects she guessed were trees stood in a row, but everything on the other side of those vague, jagged posts was swallowed up by a blurry horizon.

A bolt of fear ran through Fusa's body. This was it: her entire visual range, limited to little more than a single human field.

Remorse throbbed in her heart. She'd left Misa and the others believing she had the experience and strength of a mature bull, which simply wasn't the case. But all she'd wanted was to know the pod was going to be safe. Moshiri had planted a message in her sleeping mind: for Fusa, it felt like a responsibility she couldn't ignore. A threat *was* coming, and since nobody else there was capable enough to watch out for it, she *had* to do it herself.

At the thought of Misa and her pod, angst overwhelmed her. She'd known worry – what creature didn't? – but never like this. The disabling of her sonar capabilities was just about the most devastating loss a dolphin could suffer, yet she'd gladly surrender the rest of her senses to know her daughter was alright.

She tried to imagine the pod as they might be right now, feasting on what was left of the mackerel. The calves would be rushing off in search of waves to surf, the adolescents riding into the shallows on a boat's bow-waves. She could almost hear their chuckles as they played with the mackerel, chasing each other this way and that while they gorged their bottomless bellies.

Imagining the pod continuing onwards to the cool waters of Squid Hood Bay brought Fusa some comfort, yet her unease quickly swelled as she indulged the fantasy. The reality was likely to be much different.

Nothing could have resisted the force of that gargantuan wave.

In her mind, she saw a nightmarish picture of a coast strewn with all manner of creatures, from the mightiest whales to barely visible shrimp. A stranding of unimaginable magnitude, all who dwelt in the oceans – including those she held most dear – must surely now be languishing upon land never meant for them.

It was more than she could bear.

She swished her tail to face the opposite direction. On the other side of the lagoon, watching the business unfolding up on the land, was the boy who'd saved her. It didn't matter what he thought; from out of the pit of her sickened stomach, Fusa let fly screams of inconsolable grief.

∽

Further up the coast, an incident was developing which had captured Mako's full attention. The humans seemed to have noticed it, too; now no longer wading in the surf, they kept their eyes fixed upon the peculiar-looking structure to the north.

Actually, the structure wasn't a single thing, but a

cluster of separate buildings. Mako's click trains came back to him to reveal an assortment of different shapes and sizes. There were towers and tubes; blocks, both short and tall; shiny balls, like pearls.

Where four huge boxes sat in a row, the top suddenly blew off the one in the middle. Then, just as a boom came skipping through the dull air of the evening, a cloud appeared.

Watching it billow, Mako was perplexed. The cloud wasn't fluffy, like ones over the ocean, and it was darker than a raincloud – almost as dark as ink. He wondered if it was a kind of sediment, but since this thing kept pouring upwards it couldn't be; sediment was nothing but particles of dust and debris, which always drifted down.

He remembered Nio telling them once about a substance called fire. Humans, she said, knew how to conjure an element which gave both light and heat, and where that element burned, dark clouds followed. *Smoke*, she called it. That's what this stuff was. Smoke.

One of the humans on the beach began to call out. 'The tsunami's flooded the nuclear station!'

Up until now the land creatures had been moving ponderously, but at the sight of the smoke clouds they grew suddenly animated and ran to the far side of the field, where wheeled machines awaited them. Within these, the humans hurried away.

Mako turned back to the cluster of buildings, but by now a patch of fog had fallen, obscuring his view. With the alarmed voices of the humans no longer disturbing the peace of the lagoon, Mako then became aware of another kind of call. It was the young cow, who was having what could only be described as a tantrum.

'I want my pod! I want my pod! I want to be with my pod!'

A flutter of anxiety stirred in Mako's stomach.

This was a problem.

Sonar blindness was a serious business. Something similar once happened to Karoo the first time they ever tried bow riding. Gliding in and out of the path of a huge ship as it pushed through the deep open waters to the east, Karoo let his excitement get the better of him. Rather than simply leap into the bow waves and flop himself back into the water as the others were doing, he decided he'd like to try a spin as he left the surface. The first couple of times worked fine – Mako was tempted to try it himself – but as Karoo became more and more enthralled by the experience, he took ever greater risks, until the inevitable happened and he slammed head-first into the solid metal of the bow itself before sinking into the ocean.

For one heart-stopping moment, Mako and the other boys thought Karoo was dead. But when Hideki gave him a light slap across the face with his tail fluke, Karoo awoke with a start. In his dazed state, he then complained he wasn't able to tell which direction they were travelling in, or where other dolphins were relative to him, so Mako and Hideki decided to have him wait a while before they journeyed back to their families and, soon enough, he regained his faculties.

The same might be true for the cow. It was possible the shock of the day would soon wear off and she'd be as she was before.

Then again, this wasn't just some bump against a boat.

The flutter inside him grew stronger. It wasn't much of a stretch to think his new companion had been permanently injured today. In the event she was indeed sonar-blind, the life she'd known was over – as it would be for the dolphin tasked with caring for her. If she stood any hope of survival, she would be completely dependent on others.

He swam across and gently quacked hello.

'I want my pod!'

'Did you find anything, auntie?'

The young cow looked up. 'What?'

'In the sediment. You were looking for food. Did you find any?'

'I gave up,' cheeped Fusa. 'It hurt my beak to scrape around among it.'

Mako fired sonar beams until he located what he was looking for, then rushed to retrieve it.

Fusa tipped her head to the side. 'Why are you holding that sponge?'

'If you put a bit over your beak when you probe in the bed, it will stop you from injuring yourself.'

The cow's eyes turned worried. 'I knew that. Of course I knew that. But if you hadn't just said it, I think I wouldn't have.'

Looking down at his own scratched and dented underside, Mako smiled. If only he could have been wrapped in sponge when the surging wave shunted him across the firm land!

To his relief, the cow had calmed, and she bobbed beside him in silence for some moments, the sponge set over the tip of her beak. Then her fins drooped sadly. 'Thanks for the gift,' she wheezed. 'But there isn't any food down there. I think the wave must have shoved everything inland.'

A shudder ran through Mako to hear it mentioned. A more terrible force of nature surely couldn't exist. Such a ferocious swell of water wasn't unique in history – Nio spoke of them often – yet not a single member of his pod possessed a living memory of one.

The young cow noticed his brooding. 'It was terrifying, wasn't it?'

Mako gave a nod of his beak.

'When I first saw it,' she whistled, 'after the ocean floor stopped rattling, I thought it was a fret rolling in from the open ocean.'

'Me too,' said Mako. 'It looked like a giant bank of fog. It was so wide.'

'And fast! When I noticed the speed of it, I knew it was water, not vapour. And that was when I realised I wouldn't be able to escape from it.'

The sensation of tumbling in the wave's face replayed in Mako's memory. But he couldn't bear it, so he voiced the first question that came to mind. 'Where's your pod?'

Fusa looked at him blankly.

'Your pod,' he repeated. 'How is it that you were washed inland, but not your pod?'

The cow's face seemed to suddenly flush with shame, and Mako at once regretted bringing it up. 'Sorry, auntie,' he said.

'It's fine. I wasn't with them when it all started.'

'Why not?'

'I was frightened.'

'What of?'

'I don't know. I thought something bad was about to happen.'

'You were right about that, then,' chirruped Mako.

The cow was too melancholy to notice his playfulness. 'Not really. I was expecting another thing. And when I asked Wakka Totto, she said she'd—'

'*Wakka Totto?*'

'Yes. She's the leader of our pod.'

A flurry of bubbles rose up as Mako gave a giggle. 'Your pod was on its way to the mackerel spawning! We were chasing you on the same current. Did you make it?'

'We did. Actually, we were the first to arrive. But we had to leave again because... well, because of me. So Wakka Totto had to abort the thanksgiving ceremony. We were going to go back, but I wanted to be sure the threat had passed. So I left the pod to go scout.'

'To scout for something that was frightening?'

'For humans in their boats, yes. I thought they were coming to hurt us, so I swam off to keep watch for them.'

Mako's eyes widened. 'You thought the humans

would *hurt* you? Why would you think that? Humans are kind. They saved both our lives earlier.'

'I don't know why. I had a strange dream. I got mixed up I guess.'

Just then a small shoal of passing sardines showed up in Mako's scans, and without hesitation he sped away towards the narrow sandbar that separated the lagoon from the open ocean. The fish, responding quickly, turned towards the mouth of the inlet, and would have escaped out into the expanse, but Mako arrived in time to split the shoal, trapping one half of them in the sheltered waters this side of the spit.

He shared the catch equally with the young cow, whose face showed the slightest trace of a smile as she gulped her sardines. But swallowing down his own portion brought Mako no joy at all.

Merely approaching the sandbar's tip had made his heartbeat quicken with fear — and for good reason. Moshiri, whom Mako had so wronged, had certainly come close to getting him. But while Mako still swam, the great backbone fish of the world had unfinished business.

Right at that moment, the muddied lagoon bed lurched upwards and began to rattle. The cow gave a squeal and held herself close to Mako, who hung at the surface in terrified silence while the convulsing went on. Thankfully, however, this quaking was neither as long nor as intense as the earlier instance.

The cow shook her head from side to side. 'What is *wrong* with Moshiri? Have you ever known him to be so restless?'

At her words, Mako's mouth fell open. It almost felt like an assault upon him, and in his fins he felt a sudden twitch of aggression. 'What do you mean, auntie? Why do you say that?'

'The quaking. That's the trout-god's doing. Whenever he moves, his huge scales rub together, making the ocean bed shake.'

Mako, paralysed with anxiety, remained silent.

'Don't the elders of your pod teach you anything? When Moshiri sucks the water in, he causes the tide to ebb. And when he spits it out again, the tide flows. What happened today was the result of the great backbone fish spitting out so much water that the sea couldn't hold it, and it surged over onto the land. Something must be really troubling him to lash out that fiercely.'

Nausea throbbed in Mako's belly. Should he tell her? Of course he should! What he'd done in stealing from the shrine must truly have been the most despicable act any dolphin had committed in many generations; why else would Moshiri respond so devastatingly?

It was his duty to inform all things of his dreadful crime against nature, since all things would suffer while the trout-god sought vengeance for it. Yet Mako was holding onto so much shame already that he simply couldn't take the weight of it any more. The injured young cow beside him, so scared and lost, needed somebody to look up to while he figured out what needed to be done. He *couldn't* tell her that her dire suffering was because of him. Not just now, anyway.

Voices began to call out again from the shore. Mako and Fusa lifted their heads out to see across the waters of the lagoon. By now, the fog had dissolved into a light haze, making visible on the coast a line of smoke which poured out from the damaged structures. The few humans who'd returned to the beach were fixated on the smoke, and were once again acting with a sense of urgency.

The young cow gave an impatient squeal. 'What's going on up there?'

Mako shook his beak. 'I don't know.'

'Well, can you describe it to me at least?'

'It's quite far, so my sonar's only dim. But humans are lining up outside those buildings. There's a lot of them. Some are heading away in their machines. And some of them seem like they might not be able to move properly, like they might be hurt.'

The cow flicked her beak dismissively. 'That doesn't sound like anything *we* need to worry about.'

Mako gave a nod of agreement. Nothing in the human world could ever be of much consequence to a couple of dolphins.

8

IMPURE RAIN

A LOUD RUMBLE stirred Fusa from her rest, and she opened her eyes to the sight of the seabed quaking.

Moshiri, the great backbone fish of the world, was stirring again.

As before, the sediment, which had barely settled since last evening's convulsion, billowed up into the waters of the lagoon, clouding her vision to everything in the lower half of the basin. Thankfully, though, the sunlit upper region remained clear, and she saw that the boy was hanging at the surface a short swim away.

'Anything happening on the shore this morning?' she asked him.

He remained silent, apparently lost in a world of his own. The quaking, it seemed, was affecting him more than he wished to let on.

'Mako? Mako!'

Startled out of his reverie, the boy turned to face her. On his face was an expression Fusa recognised at once. It was guilt.

Her mother had worn that same expression, once, around the time Fusa's father left the pod. By then, enough time had passed since her father had gone into the boat's blades that the adults stopped worrying whether the bull would be alright. But that didn't mean little Fusa did.

It was true that his wound had healed well. While his dorsal fin had been severed across the middle, he'd been left with enough to stop him from rolling in the water, and though he couldn't turn quite as deftly as he'd been able to before, he still swam with swiftness and grace. But not a single night went by when Fusa didn't worry she would find him the next morning suddenly unable to stabilise himself in the currents, and she gasped with relief each time her click trains located his lively movements.

The day he left, Fusa had been playing in a seagrass meadow that fringed a small island, whose undulating slopes made for great hiding spots. She'd worked out how to make a sea cucumber twirl by flicking it off the end of her beak. It didn't seem all that exciting, looking back on it now, but at the time it seemed incredibly important and she was desperate to find her father to show him. Yet at each location around the island, he was nowhere to be seen.

Eventually, she'd gone to her mother.

'Where's daddy?' she asked.

Her mother twisted her head away. 'He's helping Wakka Totto with something.'

'Are we having a ceremony?'

'We are. Wakka Totto is going to ask Moshiri to divert the orca clans away from our stream.'

Little Fusa had thought no more of it. But then, when she still couldn't find her father later on, she went back to her mother again.

'Where's daddy?'

'He's gone to help chase in some pufferfish.'

But Fusa could hear something unusual in her mother's voice, and she detected a strange kind of wariness in her eyes, almost like… *shame.*

'You're hiding something from me,' Fusa had cheeped, bluntly.

'I'm not,' said her mother. 'Now go find a pretty shell to offer to Moshiri later.'

'What's happening? Where's daddy gone?'

And with that, her mother had confessed that her father didn't want to travel with their pod anymore, and that he'd ventured off into open water by himself.

'You're hiding something from me,' Fusa said to Mako as he held himself in a spyhop.

An embarrassed smile curled up Mako's beak. 'What? Hiding? No, auntie. You're mistaken.'

Fusa held his gaze until his eyes darted away and he said: 'I expect you're hungry.' She knew he was changing the subject, but there was no denying the emptiness of her belly.

'I am,' she replied. 'I can't see here, though. Are you getting anything in your scans?'

Mako let fly click trains in every direction, and a pained expression suddenly clouded him.

'What's wrong?'

'All the fish are out past the sandbar, in the open water.'

'And?'

The boy pretended he didn't hear.

'Mako!'

'What?'

'We need food. Go and drive the shoal into the lagoon so we can trap them.'

'I can't.'

'Can't? Why ever not? Are you sonar-blind, too?'

A few moments passed before a connection was made in Fusa's mind. 'I know why you won't go back into open water. It's the quaking. You're scared.'

Mako suddenly looked like an infant. He was certainly a handsome young dolphin, and there was no doubt when he matured he'd be among the best-looking members of his pod, yet right now, he seemed as vulnerable as a podling, and Fusa felt sorry for him.

'You're worried about another surge, aren't you? You really don't need to, you know. That last tremor was just a tiny movement for Moshiri. Now, I really think you should go get us something to eat, Mako.'

Just then, humans appeared on the beach from across the fields, and the boy turned away from Fusa in order to watch them as they lumbered by.

But Fusa wasn't going to let this drop.

'I'm hungry,' she said.

'I am too. But there's nothing here, auntie. We'll just have to wait.'

Fusa whined. 'Until when? I feel so weak. Why don't we just swim out past the sandbar together?'

'Because,' said the boy, 'it's not safe.'

'Why isn't it? What's the danger?'

Mako suddenly softened. He placed a fin on top of her own, and shyly looked away. 'There's something you should know, auntie. The seabed ripping apart. The fearsome wave that came after it – it was me. I caused it all.'

Fusa let out a nervous giggle. What was this child possibly going on about?

'I did something really bad. I found a shrine with offerings for Moshiri. And I took them.'

Fusa's eyes widened.

'You understand what I'm saying, don't you, auntie? I stole fish from the god of the sea and the storms. And now he's punishing me for insulting him so terribly. He's not going to stop. Not while my heart still beats.'

~

After Mako's confession, the young cow wouldn't say another word to him, and spent the afternoon by herself on the lagoon's west side, where a river flowed into it from the land.

As he'd expected, she was furious. And why shouldn't she be? He'd feel the same way too, if he learned *she* was responsible for it all: the damage to the seabed, his separation from his pod, the loss of his sonar. It was as catastrophic an outcome to a dolphin as any he could conceive.

He'd wanted to keep it to himself, of course. But what he'd done was no secret; by now, his entire pod would know all about it – both the tragedy of little Chizuko, caused by the silliness of his trick, and the terrible offence he'd caused the great backbone fish of the world. Assuming they'd made it to the spawning grounds already, a great many other pods would be learning of his awful behaviour, too. He was destined to be as notorious a creature of the ocean as any before or after him.

While he lamented his fate, Mako spyhopped near the humans, who'd kept themselves busy throughout the afternoon tidying up the detritus that covered their fields in the wake of the wave. Laboriously hurling all manner of clutter into crates, their eyes filled with the same anguish that had troubled them yesterday.

With the light of day now dimming, the humans were presently engaged in a task that was of particular interest to Mako: into one of their boxes, they were piling fish.

His stomach gave a grumble. In spite of the cow's injury, she was astute: he *was* reluctant to go out hunting beyond the sandbar. Perhaps now, though, he'd found a way to get them food without having to leave the lagoon at all.

Mako glided in closer to the shore and spouted. 'Hey!' he noisily quacked to the humans, 'watch this!'

He kept on harassing them until he'd drawn most away from their task. Then, when he was sure they were looking his way – and that he was in no danger of beaching himself – he circled back to create enough space for a launch, before bursting out from the surface with a forward roll.

The faces of the humans beamed with pleasure. While they clapped their hands together excitedly, the rest stopped what they were doing and came down from their fields to the narrow beach. One member of their party then waded into the shallow surf.

Mako went closer to meet him. 'Hello,' he said. 'I'm Mako. I'm sorry for making Moshiri bash up your home. Got any fish?'

The human held out his hand and ran it along the contour of Mako's head. How strange it was to find comfort in the touch of another species.

Odd sounds began to spill from the human's mouth. 'You've had a shock, haven't you?'

As best as he could, Mako mimicked the strange patter. '*Oo-a-a-ock, a-a-ou.*'

'Wow!' said the human.

'*Wow,*' echoed Mako.

The individual turned to face the others while Mako, emboldened for having an audience, manoeuvred for another flip. This he executed perfectly, barely even splashing the individual with whom he'd been talking.

More applause followed, and Mako giggled. If they liked that, they were going to love *this*.

Stretching his body up, he held himself out of the water as tall as he could and, as he'd done for the occupants of the boat beside the shrine, he began to simulate their movement.

'I'm a human!' he laughed. 'Look at me! I'm walking!'

A couple of the watchers began to pass their funny-sounding language back and forth.

'That's one of the two washed in yesterday, isn't it? Handsome chap.'

'He is. Shame they were so close to the shore when the tsunami struck. I wonder why they were separated from their pod?'

'*Pods*. They're different species. This one is a bottlenose. The one over at the tributary is a white-sided Pacific dolphin. We used to hunt them down south.'

'Barbaric business, that.'

'Says a man who loves his dolphin sushi! If you want to eat it, it has to be caught. Anyway, it's part of our history. This modern world is making everything the same. It's good to keep some of our old traditions alive.'

One human, whose arms were wrapped around a basket, pulled a fish out from it and hurled it high into the air. Mako swallowed this whole, then asked for more – and more, and more – and as the basket emptied and his stomach filled, he began to feel an easing of the dread that had lingered inside him all day. Perhaps he'd never have to go out into the expanse ever again.

Just then, a rumble, low and long, sounded. But, unlike the others, this one didn't come out of the seabed, but rather from out of the skies. The darkening clouds, which had been gathering throughout the evening, were bursting, and the first drops of a shower were beginning to fall.

Some of the humans were panicking now. As the rain fell on them, it seemed somehow to hurt them; with a sense of urgency, they pulled their fabric coverings over their heads and began to retreat back across the fields.

∼

Fusa decided that this shielded body of water should be called Snow Crab Lagoon, since its tapered oval shape was so like the carapace of the crustacean.

The boy, who'd been showing off for the humans, had just arrived from the northern rim of Snow Crab Lagoon with a mouthful of fish, which he spat out for her.

Fusa, however, wasn't interested. 'Are they dead?'

'Of course they're dead,' chuckled Mako. 'They'd be swimming away otherwise.'

Fusa clicked crossly. 'Not the fish. Our pods. Our families. Are they dead?'

The boy's face drooped downwards and he turned away from Fusa's intense gaze. Then, after some time passed awkwardly, Mako let up a bubble. 'I wish I knew.'

'They must be. How could anything survive something with so much speed and power?'

'I don't know, auntie. But maybe they were actually safer out in the ocean. You've been surfing, right?'

Fusa, now swallowing down the fish, knew what Mako was getting at. Swells on the surface became waves only when they met the shallows – she'd taught the calves this very fact just days ago. It was conceivable, then, that any marine life further from the coast may not have even *known* about the surge, let alone have been shunted along by it. But then again, that terrible force was so much more than some surf wave.

Although Mako was visibly distressed, Fusa saw no reason to let up. 'They expelled you, I suppose? For taking what was meant for Moshiri.'

The boy rocked his head this way and that, as though merely talking about it were making him writhe with shame and embarrassment. 'I ran away.'

'Like a coward?'

'Yes. But not only cowardice. After I took the fish, I made another very bad decision, and one of our podlings got taken by orca. The adults had enough to deal with, so I left them to it.'

Fusa thought of Toshi, and her stomach fluttered. It didn't matter how strongly the cows felt about them, the bulls always left their pods, in the end.

Mako continued to explain himself, and was growing more distressed with his unfolding account. 'When I was swimming away I saw more orca. They were straying into my pod. So I led a couple away to the coast. That was when the shaking began.'

'There's a few still out there,' nodded Fusa. 'Orca. I heard them.'

Mako gave a squawk. 'Are you sure that's not the whales? I've been hearing whalesong ever since we washed in.'

'I have, too. But if orca are journeying up from the south, we need to leave now.'

'Leave?' creaked Mako. 'We'll be fine if we stay here.'

'We're not staying here, Mako. What you've done is truly terrible. And now you must put it right. If there's *any* chance my pod really did survive the great wave, you must get me back to them.'

Fusa watched as the adolescent wrestled with some inner turmoil. With his jaws parting, he looked to be on the verge of aggression. But after a moment of silence he simply said: 'I can't.'

'If I try and get back to Squid Hood Bay by myself,' said Fusa, 'I'll get lost. You've got to take me back to my pod.'

'If it was that easy, auntie, I would,' said Mako, pulling away from the tip of the sheltering sandbar. 'But you've seen it for yourself. Moshiri is trying to get me. While I'm here, there's nothing he can do. But as soon as I go out into open water, he'll make another surge. Think about the poor humans.'

Fusa followed the stubborn dolphin. 'So you're just going to wait here forever?'

The boy's eyes narrowed as he worked through their options. 'That tributary where you spent the afternoon feeds into the lagoon. Maybe if I swim up it I can avoid his wrath.'

Fusa thrashed her tail fins with annoyance and let out a loud and agitated cheeping. 'You can't avoid the wrath of Moshiri! There's only one way to get the trout-god off your tail. You've got to let him know you're sorry. If you take me back, we can go to Wakka Totto. She's our priestess. So long as she wasn't smashed by the wave, she'll communicate your remorse to him.'

To Fusa's surprise, the boy's head tilted and he gazed into her eyes. She'd expected him to make an immediate protest, yet he simply appeared confused. 'Your Wakka Totto will do *what*?'

'Communicate with Moshiri.'

Mako made a noise halfway between a laugh and a dismissive grunt. 'Communicate… *with Moshiri*?'

'Yes. Exactly as your elder does.'

'Nio does no such thing! Our elder communicates with the trout-god the same way we all do. Through shrines. No single dolphin can access Moshiri directly. It's an insult to say otherwise.'

'And you'd know all about insults, wouldn't you? Mako, there's no choice here. We *need* to find my pod.'

Mako threw lengthy click trains beyond the spit, an expanse that, for Fusa, darkened into total blindness just a short distance away. A feeling of dread crept along her spine. Looking out there, it was obvious she couldn't survive by herself.

When the echoes of Mako's click trains started to bounce back, he began a commentary. 'I think you're right. That might be orca.'

Fusa's heart fluttered with terror. What a cruel quirk of fate this was. Surrounded by her pod, she'd be completely safe from a hunting orca clan. But to get back to them, she'd have to put herself in the path of great danger.

'Wait,' said the boy. 'There's something else out there. A pair of dolphins.'

'From your pod?'

'Strangers.' With extreme reluctance, Mako pulled away from the head of the sandbar into open ocean to get a better read of them in his sonar scans. 'What *is* that?'

'What, Mako? Tell me what you see.'

'They've got something attached—'

'To their heads!' Fusa's brow wrinkled as she strained to remember. There *had* been a couple of dolphins like that out there. She'd seen them herself, and Misa had, too. Not quite mature, they'd had curious boxes fastened to them.

'They're moving south,' said Mako, gliding quickly back into the protected basin on the shore side of the spit. 'No concern of ours.' He then lifted himself into a spyhop, making it clear that he had nothing else to say right now.

Fusa wasn't going to let him off so easily, though. 'You've got to take me,' she squealed, breaking through the surface. 'Get me back to Wakka Totto. If she survived the ocean ripping apart, she'll help you in return. The trout-god *must* hear how sorry you are.'

But conversation was suddenly the last thing on Fusa's mind: beside her, Mako had begun jolting, and then she felt a painful tingling on her skin, like she'd brushed against the tentacles of a man-o-war jellyfish. Yet it was coming out of the sky, not through the water.

It was as though something hot — and somehow *unnatural* — were being carried down with the rain.

9

THE RIVERSIDE SHRINE

THE RAIN CONTINUED to fall into the night, and by the time morning came even the upper waters of the lagoon were charged with a peculiar, prickling impurity.

With the breaking of dawn came chaos in the skies, and Mako wondered just what could be so amiss in the human world. In their metal machines they flew, like impossible birds, endlessly circling the cube-shaped structures from which smoke still came pouring. Sometimes they dipped closer to it, while other times they retreated as though the thing they'd wished to see were in fact far uglier or more terrifying than they'd ever expected.

Fusa had already gone off to poke around in the sediment of Snow Crab Lagoon. He hadn't the heart to tell her there were no snacks down there, though; besides, it was good to have some space from her. The young cow simply wouldn't let it drop.

Throughout one period in the night, every time he breached the surface to take a breath she sent across a whistle – 'we *need* to find my pod!' – until he couldn't stand it anymore and was forced to glide off further away. But wherever he went, she followed, repeating her assertion time and time again. Eventually, it began to work its way deeper and deeper into his mind; even in moments of sleep, he heard those words. Which, of course, was exactly what she wanted all along.

Yet he knew there was a truth to it. In spite of his hope that her echolocation would come back, Fusa remained sonar-blind. It was clear in her sunken eyes, too, that hunger was now beginning to seriously weaken her, increasing the possibility she might not make it. Certainly, she wouldn't without his help.

If she could only get back to her pod, they'd take care of her as all pods did their injured and their elderly. But what was he supposed to do? The moment Moshiri caught him in open water, the great trout-god would lash out. And in the indiscriminate nature of his awful force, the cow was every bit as likely to be clobbered again as he was himself.

Still, she had to feed. Was there *anything* he could safely do? A hint of a smile rose on his mouth as some echoes bounced back from the east. There just might be.

Mako gave a whistle to call Fusa over. Dejected by her failure to find food on the bed, she looked up at him with eyes both expectant and cross.

'We both know you can't go off on your own, auntie,' he said, tenderly. 'Not quite yet anyway. But I've just located a shoal of amberjack. They're about to pass by the head of the sandbar. Why don't you go out and get them?'

'Why don't *you*?'

'You know why,' quacked Mako.

'Moshiri.'

'Not only Moshiri. If your sonar really is gone now, auntie, you need to get some independence. As soon as you go around that spit, your eyes will find the fish. Go and eat, then come back.'

The desperation that lingered constantly on Fusa's face abated, just a little. 'What about you, though?'

'I'll wait at the lagoon's edge. I'll be watching the whole time.'

'I mean, what about food, Mako? You need to eat.'

'You can bring me something if there's any left. But eat your fill. You need to get your strength up.'

'How frustrating you are, Mako!' chirruped Fusa. 'You *are* worried about me, just not quite enough to get me home.'

'Come on,' Mako said. 'Those amberjack won't hang around.'

They swam together to the lagoon's mouth. With frequent glances back, Fusa then proceeded around the spit. Mako, keeping his distance, trained his clicks on her as she thrashed her tail flukes and accelerated after the shoal, then as she gulped down a few of the plump fish.

A sight then appeared in his sonar field that took him by surprise. A lone dolphin – one of the pair with the odd boxes fastened to their heads – was down in the seabed below the open waves. Even more confusing than his unnatural adornment was the suddenness of the individual's appearance. How had he concealed himself so absolutely from Mako's scans one second, only to be there the next?

With incredible speed, the lone dolphin suddenly burst into motion. Heading straight for Fusa, the sight of it prompted Mako to issue an urgent squeal. 'Back, auntie! Now!'

The young cow obeyed at once, and the pair retreated back to the sheltered waters, where Mako kept news of the mysterious dolphin to himself; she'd made a success of the little mission, and he didn't want to cast a cloud on her happy mood.

'Here,' she said, ejecting one of the fish from her jaws.

Mako's stomach groaned at the sight of the food, but this whole incident was too like the tragedy of the podlings, and his appetite was dampened. With any luck, more humans would come down to the shores again later, from whom he could earn himself a few treats, perhaps. But they'd have to be a more cheerful sort than the ones currently shuffling along the fields, whose faces were scored with lines of the deepest worry.

∼

The fish in her belly had given her a boost, but another day beneath the prickly rains that fell upon Snow Crab Lagoon made Fusa begin to feel her energy growing ever fainter.

She'd been sick only a few times in her life. As a newborn, there'd been some difficulty nursing. Her mother had plenty of milk to offer, but for some reason Fusa hadn't been able to quite figure out how to get at it. That problem righted itself after a time, but not before her friends rapidly grew bigger. Consequently, she appeared as a younger dolphin than she actually was, ensuring the eye her mother kept on her was always an overprotective one.

Then there'd been a stomach sickness, and soon after that an infected tooth. During both of these occasions a sense existed that she was unwell, but since her life went on much the same as it always had, the fatigue, the fevers and the nausea caused her no real hardship.

Now, though, she had no real life at all. Confined to a lagoon whose waters were sickening her with their growing impurity, she had only a stranger for company who – not entirely unreasonably – wouldn't risk escorting her back to Squid Hood Bay where her daughter was almost certainly waiting. As such, the ailment Fusa found herself suffering was one of the spirit – a type her mother had kept her from ever knowing existed. She hadn't imagined it was possible for dolphins to have thoughts like the ones troubling her mind now.

Feeling suddenly alone, Fusa spyhopped for signs of Mako and was, once again, disappointed. He'd gone off to investigate the tidal tributary that fed into the western edge of Snow Crab Lagoon, hopeful that food would be easier to come by upriver. But most of the afternoon had passed since he'd swum up it, and a feeling of dread was beginning to creep in. Perhaps the boy was gone for good?

Just as the anxiety was taking over her mind, however, Fusa saw, at the very edge of what her eyes were able to discern, Mako's dorsal fin. With some relieved spins, she rushed off to greet him at the river, reaching him at the very moment an enormous eruption of sound shook the sky to the north.

Together, Fusa and Mako came up. A trio of humans, who were still clearing the mess caused by the wave, were crouching low at the near edge of their field, staring off the same way as Mako. Their cries drifted over the beach and rolled across the surface of the lagoon. 'It's the reactor! It's exploded!'

'It's the human structures again, isn't it?' inquired Fusa, frustrated that the unfolding mayhem was just beyond her eyes' reach. But as she looked on this time, she did actually register something: a streak on the horizon to the north had turned perceptibly dark.

Mako confirmed it with a nervous quack. 'The smoke has changed. It just got bigger.' But since it was of no consequence to him, he turned to Fusa with a smile. 'Go on, auntie. Ask me.'

'You found fish?'

'Loads.'

'And you ate some?'

'Loads.'

'And now you're feeling pleased with yourself, I suppose?'

Mako giggled. 'Is every dolphin in your pod so sharp-tongued, auntie, or is it just you? Listen to me. I think I may have found something important. Want to come with me upriver?'

Fusa, aware that the air was once again beginning to tingle, let herself blithely drop back below the surface.

'Well?' said Mako, sinking beside her.

'Well what?'

'Do you feel up to a swim?'

'I don't know,' she said, pretending to be indifferent. 'Is it far?'

Mako gave her a playful nudge with his beak. 'Who are you trying to fool? I know you're desperate to get out of here. Now follow me. And, no. It's not far at all.'

~

'Will you just tell me?' asked Fusa, as the pair swam cautiously along a waterway that led deeper and deeper into the world of the humans.

'You white-sides are as impatient as you are cheeky, huh?' clicked Mako.

Fusa was secretly glad that Mako had refused to indulge her curiosity. She actually liked to be surprised. As calves, Turem would nag on and on to be told of some secret place Fusa had found, until most of the fun of it was spoiled. Still, her cousin wasn't as bad as some of the others, who grew so irritable by such mysteries that tailslaps were commonplace.

Really, Fusa knew her incessant questions were more a symptom of nervousness than anything else. In rivers like this, the only thing to fear was the tidal shift, but since its level was on the rise, there was slim chance of ending up stranded. Nevertheless, this was the first time she'd been anywhere since the accident, and in her new state of sonar blindness even waters like these, largely devoid of any creature bigger than a fish, gave her a feeling of dread.

Above the brackish water, the skies had grown increasingly busy. Most of the machines that passed over remained out of Fusa's field of vision, but one – a great, dark thing with whirring blades like those which injured her father – came across so low that she stayed above the surface to watch it on its way to the smoking buildings. Things were passing on the land, too: loud things, flashing with lights, whose human occupants wore expressions of apprehension.

Mako slowed when they rounded a wide bend, gliding over to where the muddy banks rose into a wall. He drew to a halt there, and lifted himself above the surface. 'Look,' he whistled.

Set back from the wall, running all the way along the river, was a dense row of trees, broken only where Fusa and Mako were now spyhopping. Within this gap were a few stone structures, amid which a smattering of humans were congregating.

Fusa gave a quiet whistle. 'What am I supposed to be looking at?'

'Oh, come on! Are you blind?'

'Well, I kind of am, yes. Because Moshiri spat the ocean out, and I smashed my head. Remember that?'

Mako's beak sagged and he looked away, and at once Fusa regretted it. The boy was in better spirits than he'd been, and there would be a reason for it, even if she couldn't work out what he was trying to show her. 'Sorry, Mako. It's just, I only see with my eyes now. You've got a better picture of what's going on up there than I have.'

'You don't need sonar, auntie. Your eyes are enough. Just look.'

Up on the wall, the humans stood in a line at a bowl and took turns to catch water beneath a running stream. They then tipped the water out of a small wooden container over their hands. When this was completed to their satisfaction, the humans proceeded, one by one, to a second – bigger – bowl, above which, suspended between two wooden posts, was a length of rope. Angular shapes hung down from the rope; to Fusa's mind, they resembled lightning strikes, or sea snakes thrashing on their way up to the surface. From out of the bowl, fragrant smoke was pouring up into the dusky sky, and something within that wide stone basin seemed to be compelling the humans to clap their hands and repeatedly nod their heads – not just their heads, the entire upper part of their torsos. Perhaps most oddly of all, the lips of the humans moved as though they were speaking, yet in most cases no words sounded.

How did Mako understand any of this? Was it that, as a different type of dolphin, he possessed some ability her own kind lacked? She suddenly felt embarrassed. *This* was Mako's big surprise, and it meant nothing to her.

With a discreet squawk, Mako turned to Fusa. 'See how worried they look?'

That, she *could* see. 'Are they always like this?'

'Humans? Not the ones I've encountered, auntie. They're usually so bright and cheerful. Did you know, they *love* dolphins?'

Fusa remembered watching him yesterday, performing for the individuals, joyfully snatching out of the sky the fish they threw from the beach. They were, indeed, a kindly sort of creature, which made their obvious anguish all the more startling.

But what did any of this have to do with her? She cast a sideways glance at Mako and spouted some air, thinking of a way to ask the question without making him feel bad again. 'Do you think they can help us?' she said at last.

Mako, however, was preoccupied with the water level; with his head pivoting back and forth from the river's surface to the wall, Fusa observed that he was making a calculation.

'We don't need their help,' he replied, eventually. 'All we need is their kindness.'

Fusa blew out a flurry of bubbles. 'Enough of this,' she creaked, her patience now exhausted. 'It's time you started explaining just what—'

'On the other side of the trees,' said Mako, 'there's a gate. I was lucky to spot it earlier. It's a very small one.'

'I don't know what a *gate* is, Mako. Describe it to me.'

'Picture an eagle with its wings spread out. Then imagine its legs are long poles, like those up there holding that rope. That's a gate. They're entrances to human shrines.'

Fusa looked back up to where the people were worriedly bowing at the bowl. 'This is a shrine? So, they're offering prayers to Moshiri?'

'Maybe. Or, if not to the sea god, then to the god of the land. There's something else up there that I've been able to map in my sonar field. Just along the wall there to the left are three stone plinths.' He paused for effect, but Fusa remained blank. 'Three plinths, auntie. Like the ones I stole the fish from.'

Fusa's eyes widened. This was now beginning to mean something.

'I insulted Moshiri. And now he's furious with me. If he catches me in the expanse, he'll send another great surge to get me. That means that even if I wanted to take you back to your pod – and I do want to, auntie – it's likely that we'd both be killed anyway.'

'And you think that by—'

'You say the only way to communicate with Moshiri is through your Wakka Totto, but that's not what my elder says. In my pod, we believe *any* dolphin can give prayers to the trout-god — so long as it's done through a shrine. When morning comes, the river will be high enough for me to get up there and put the fish back. I'll show Moshiri how sorry I am for my terrible insult, and he'll accept my apology. I just know he will. And when he's no longer on my tail, I can get you back to your daughter. This is it, auntie. This is our chance.'

Fusa let herself drop below the surface into the murky gloom of the river. How could her heart contain two such contrasting emotions at the very same moment? She was gladdened by Mako's gesture. Here was a typically boisterous dolphin in his adolescent years, who couldn't help but make bad choices. His remorse, though, was undeniable: he truly regretted that she'd come to harm on account of his behaviour, and was driven to want to put things right, and for that, she was genuinely grateful.

But so too was Fusa saddened by the gesture, and there was one simple reason for it: whether Mako accepted it or not, the great backbone fish of the world, the trout-god Moshiri, could *only* be reached through a priestess like Wakka Totto. Even in the unlikely event that Mako succeeded in getting to the plinths he felt were so important, his plan was certain to fail.

Still, if this was what he needed to do in order to finally take her out into the ocean, then it would be foolish not to support him. She gave him a feeble smile, and asked: 'How will you do it?'

'Easy,' Mako replied. 'I'm going to strand myself.'

10

REPAYING A DEBT

WHILE THE WEARIED young cow rested through the dark hours, Mako worked through a plan which even to him seemed reckless.

The timing was going to have to be perfect. The moment he'd found the shrine, he knew that successfully stranding himself upon its walkway would depend entirely on the ebbing and flowing of the river's tide. So, as the night went on, he paid close attention to the water, carefully observing its changing depth.

First, the river swelled. Then it drained. When it rose again at dawn, he was tempted to chance a leap up onto the land. But since humans loved him so much, it was likely they'd put him right back in the water the instant they saw him out of it.

What they wouldn't do, however, was nudge him off the walkway when the riverbed was exposed: with the waters that low, the drop would be enough to kill him. So long as they didn't wish to harm him — and humans would *never* wish to harm a dolphin — they'd be left with only one option. To put him safely back in the water, they'd have to carry him through the shrine, right past the three stone plinths, to the other side of the site where, even at low tide, the river lapped just below the height of the walls.

Key to his plan was the boat ramp. This slope was cut in its middle, falling away vertically down to the riverbed. Provided he didn't go too high up it, the humans wouldn't spot him — not until he was ready for them to do so, at least.

And that was where Fusa would come in.

With the tide now in retreat, every minute that ticked by made the ramp more visible, so Mako headed off to find her. The time to execute their plan had come.

'Couldn't you find anything plumper, auntie?' he squealed, when he located her eating anchovies.

'There were amberjack here just now,' said Fusa, letting up a bubble. 'But they took off too quickly around the corner. There was no point chasing them.'

Mako threw a scan upriver after them. 'Just get ready,' he said. 'Remember: the humans *must* see you. If they're not taking enough notice, you're going to have to make them. Somersaults. Twists. Backflips. The trick they love best is when you pretend to walk like them along the surface, but that may be a bit much for an old dolphin like you.'

Fusa gave an annoyed chirrup. 'Old? I'm eight, Mako! I've only had four more winters than you.'

'Then you'll have no problem walking for them, will you? Just hold their attention any way you can, for as long as you can. When the tide's all the way out – right down to where I showed you in the night – come find me on the ramp around the bend.'

With that, Mako beat his tail flukes and swam around the sharp meander after the amberjack, locating them by their echoes in a thicket of algae. The fattest of the fish managed to evade him, but he was able to swallow down four middling ones with ease before turning back for the shrine site.

By now, the river had lowered enough to expose the

sheer face of the boat ramp. Mako gulped a deep breath of air and submerged for a few moments to enjoy the feel of water on his skin while he still could. He threw out a click train to check if humans were above already, but the walls on either side of the slope obstructed his signal's path, blinding him to whatever was up on the walkway. It was riskier than he'd have liked. But it had to be now.

With a gentle push, Mako turned into the retreating river to get a good run-up. Then, with a mighty thrash of his tail, he leapt up.

The hard surface scraped against his belly, but he pushed on, bouncing himself up the slope until his flukes were out of the water. He worked the muscles of his stomach, taking advantage of his momentum, and advanced towards the ramp's top until he could power himself no higher.

His beak and flukes and fins flopped onto the stony surface.

He'd done it.

He'd beached himself.

As he settled in to wait, he tried to remain cheerful. His debt to Moshiri was about to be paid, and his life was soon to be his own again. He could travel where he pleased, free from the fear of a force that could devastate the world itself.

The tide continued to pull away, exposing ever more of the ramp's vertical drop. Then, just a short time later, the algae-strewn bank of the upper riverbed was sparkling in the light of the sun.

Already Mako's skin was drying, but he needed to wait a little longer. The whole exercise was for nothing if the humans put him back in here when they found him.

Panic tried to seize him – *what if they didn't find him?* – but he fought it off. Humans *would* come. They came when the terrible surge carried him onto their fields. And they came for his mother's father, too, when he was beached.

At the recollection of his grandfather, Mako felt his spirit darken. The fate of that old dolphin was truly a cause for sorrow. Just thirty summers, he'd lived, his life shortened for his years spent in captivity.

Yet this alone couldn't explain Mako's sudden glumness. Simply remembering his father tell the story made him realise how much he missed his parents. His friends, too – even Nio and the seniors. The feeling of shame pressed upon him with even greater pressure than this uncomfortable slope of rock. How lucky they were not to see him as he was now, stranded – by choice – at the very edge of the human world. His mother's heart would stop beating at the merest glimpse of him.

His despondency, however, was then brought to an abrupt end. A commotion was coming from around the meander. Fusa was on her way — and she was clucking and whistling with the raucousness of an entire herd.

Within moments, humans stood gawping at Mako. Their faces were scored with the exact kind of consternation as the morning they found him washed in. Two individuals stepped down to him without delay, who slid their hands beneath his belly and scooped water across his back. The weight pressing upon his organs was immediately lightened as they hoisted him gracelessly into the air.

Fusa had got the timing just right. The tide was at its lowest; his rescuers would have sent him crashing onto the exposed riverbed if they shunted him in now, so, exactly as he'd anticipated, they carried him up into the site of the shrine.

And as they did, Mako understood why his mood had turned so very gloomy.

It wasn't because of the tragic story of his grandfather's untimely death, nor that it had reminded him of his own long-suffering parents.

It was the possibility that he himself was destined to share the same fate as that poor old dolphin.

By now, Mako would be stranded on the boat ramp, so Fusa brought her head above the surface. The morning skies were darkening with every inch the retreating tide pulled back, but the threat of a downpour was of no concern to the humans, who stood in quiet contemplation while they washed their hands and nodded their bodies at the bowl.

Helping Mako carry out his plan was exciting, yet angst soured Fusa's heart to think how very disappointed he was going to be today.

His pod's belief that *any* dolphin could simply appeal to the great backbone fish was attractive, no matter how silly it was. Certainly, things would be a lot easier for them if Moshiri would just hear Mako's pleas and be done with his wrathful pursuit. There could surely be no joy that would match the joy of this all being over today.

But, sadly, that wasn't how it worked.

On her left side, perched on the wall, a child was dangling a line into the receding water. Fusa observed the little creature with fondness, and glided in closer to look at its bright eyes.

'Hello,' she cheeped.

The child stood, a smile widening across its bizarre, flat face.

'Mama! Come see!' it called.

A pair of adults approached the wall. Their faces also brightened at the sight of Fusa, but unlike the child, their eyes remained too heavy with worry for their smiles to curve very far, and they began to chat fretfully among themselves.

'They're saying the uranium fuel has melted down. You know what that means, Ayumi-san? The Fukushima plant could be the next—'

'No! Don't even mention it! It won't happen.'

'I hope you're right. But we must spare a thought for

the poor mayor of Tokyo. The potential evacuation of fifty million people – imagine it! I bet that man hasn't slept a wink since last Friday.'

'Then he's not the only one.'

A cluster of humans were now peering down from the riverside wall at Fusa. She dipped into the water, diving to its lowest point. Then she rushed upwards, breaching the surface with a powerful thrust, and executed a perfect front roll in the air.

The gloominess of the humans turned instantly to ecstasy. Watching Fusa's aerial acrobatics had brought them to life. Some pointed little machines at her – dark boxes, like the kind she'd observed upon the heads of the two travelling dolphins – while others waved their hands and clapped with glee, seemingly unable to believe their luck that they'd happened upon a dolphin at this time. Mako had been right: human fondness for them was undeniable, and strangely alluring.

She carried on showing off until the shrinking volume of water made it dangerous. With the tide now at its lowest ebb, the moment had come to lure the onlookers away.

'Come with me!' she clicked as she sped around the river's bend. 'I've got even better tricks to show you! Follow me this way! You won't believe it!'

Then, exactly as planned, they spotted Mako.

She watched, breathless, as the land dwellers rushed to him. A pair of them began to hoist his stranded body up off the ramp. Fusa's heart beat hard.

They were taking Mako *into* the shrine.

∽

The onlooking humans parted to open a passage for the two carrying him.

Mako, partially to ease the terror of being in the arms of another species, threw out scans all around. At first, this calmed him, but as the humans hauled him deeper and deeper into the site, his nerves got the better of him and he began to cry.

Just then, the gate appeared in his sonar field. He was getting close! But the humans were too numerous here; a forest of legs made identifying the plinths difficult. Awkwardly, he craned his head around to look with his eyes. Sticking up from a stone block on the ground were three miniature towers marked with human scribblings.

It was the plinths!

At once, Mako violently lurched out of the humans' arms. He hit the ground with a dull *smack*, then rotated himself on his belly to face the monument, while the onlookers gasped with fright.

In a series of thrusts, Mako jerked purposely forwards, quacking loudly. 'Forgive me, Moshiri! Forgive me for my insults!' He squeezed his muscles to wretch up the contents of his belly, ejecting several fish upon the foot of the plinths.

Pandemonium ensued. The pair who'd rescued him began folding themselves at the belly repeatedly, as though making some gesture of apology to the crowd. But the spectating humans were laughing and clapping their hands, jostling to get a look at the dolphin who'd just made an offering to the trout-god.

After another human arrived to pour water over Mako's parched skin, the rescuers lifted him, this time entwining their arms together to ensure they couldn't drop him again. They proceeded with haste until they came to the curved walkway of the river's bend, and, exactly as Mako had planned it, they put him on the wall.

'That's it!' he chirruped. 'Down there!'

But rather than fling him into the river, the humans began a worrisome exchange.

'What if the river is too shallow!'
'We could injure him!'

They turned to the onlookers. 'Please! Fetch us one of the decorator's dust sheets!'

A third human scrambled across to a collection of tools scattered in a corner. Hastily tidying these to the side, he fetched a large square of fabric.

'Quick!' yelled one of the rescuers. 'Get it beneath him! We'll take an end each!'

Mako felt his torso shunted this way and that while the pair struggled to work the fabric into the space between his underside and the top of the wall. Now blinded by the cloth, he gave a squeal of fear. Being trapped this way was not part of the plan, and every impulse was to get himself out of it.

Thankfully, however, water was soon washing across his body as the humans lowered him safely back into the river.

Cheering sounded from the site of the shrine, and when Mako darted around in a wide circle and somersaulted in front of the applauding humans, they pumped their arms into the air with rapture.

'Did you see me?' he whistled to Fusa. 'I did it – I put the fish back, right at the shrine! I knew I could do it. That's it, auntie, we've nothing to fear now. He's forgiven me. The god of the seas and the storms has forgiven me!'

His joy was absolute.

Yet it was also short-lived.

With a flash lighting up the forbidding clouds, an explosion of sound split the sky and rain began to pour. And at that very same moment, the bed of the river — and the walls alongside it — began to rattle.

'Another aftershock!' exclaimed the humans, who ran to the open and lowered their bodies to the ground.

∼

Fusa had to swim as hard as she could to catch up with Mako; the moment the earth ceased quaking, he'd taken off in distress back towards Snow Crab Lagoon, leaving her spyhopping alone in the river's choppy surface.

She found him a short distance downriver. One glance was all it took to see the extent of his dejection. His flippers were slumped weakly at his sides, and where his beak and tail flukes drooped he looked like the very opposite of a smile: a sad crescent, with a crushed spirit.

'Go on,' he said.

Fusa went close and held her face beside him. 'Go on what?'

'Say it. "Your offering failed. Moshiri didn't hear you. You replaced the fish and all he did was shake up another storm".'

'I'm not sure that matters now.'

'You were right, auntie. And now we'll be stuck here forever.' Mako gave a thrash of his tail and drifted down the narrow river.

'We can't be,' cheeped Fusa, pulling abreast of him. 'We're just going to have to brave it.'

With alarming suddenness, Mako stopped. His eyes brightened. 'Unless—'

A smile rose on Fusa's mouth. 'What?'

'It's obvious! It's obvious why my offering didn't work!'

Fusa's mirth faded as quickly as it had come. 'It didn't work,' she peevishly cheeped, 'because ordinary dolphins can't communicate with the backbone fish. Only a priestess can.'

'No,' said Mako. 'It's because that wasn't the shrine I took the fish from, was it? Why would Moshiri hear my apology *there*?'

'Mako! You wanted to do it your way, and now it's done. Let that be the end of it.'

'But it isn't the end of it, auntie! Because the fish were returned to the *wrong place*. I've got to get back to the original shrine. Then Moshiri will forgive me.' He began to chuckle. 'It's so obvious!'

At this, Fusa snapped her jaws beside Mako and whipped her tail flukes, rocking him in their wake. 'What more can I say?!' she yelled. 'I told you it wouldn't work today, yet you did it anyway! What if those humans left you on the ramp? Or took you away to some other place? You risked your life for nothing at all. Now you're talking about travelling back where you came from to repeat this stupid, dangerous plan all over again – and it won't work! Do you hear me? It. Will. Not. Work. And what are you going to say then – *"Of course! It's obvious! They weren't the original fish I stole!"* – even though you already digested those fish? There's *always* going to be some reason in your mind why it didn't work. Every reason except the one that matters.'

Mako turned sulkily away. 'Are you finished?'

'Is Moshiri finished?'

'Leave me alone!' cried Mako. 'I didn't mean for any of this to happen. I took the fish without thinking, then a human brought me more. I shouldn't have taken it, and I'm sorry. Do you hear me, great Moshiri? I'm sorry! And for Chizuko, too! I would never have sent her into harm's way deliberately! Now, please! Leave me alone!'

Mako sped onwards towards the coast, Fusa in tow. Rain drummed against the surface above, and thunder rumbled through the dark skies.

On they went, around the meandering curves – Fusa never quite able to catch up – until a short while later they emerged out of the tributary into the sheltered waters, which appeared much changed from when they'd left it yesterday evening:

From one end to another, Snow Crab Lagoon was now teeming with dolphins.

And a great many of them were quite noticeably unwell.

11

THE SULLIED LAGOON

The new arrivals eyed Fusa and Mako with suspicion.

Occupying every corner of Snow Crab Lagoon was a vast pod which had come in seemingly to shelter from the open ocean. Yet this wasn't a pod; gathered together was an assortment of almost every type of dolphin: striped, spotted, white-sided, rough-toothed, long-beaks and short-beaks.

Keeping close to a pouty Mako as they navigated through the throng of bodies, Fusa was dumbfounded. They'd only been upriver a short time. What had happened to bring so many of their kind into this otherwise-empty basin of water?

With the question swirling in her mind, she was steeling her nerves to interrogate one of the arrivals when she became aware of a strange sensation in the water. 'Do you feel that?' she chirped, quietly. 'It's warm.'

'Not just warm,' replied Mako. 'Impure. It's getting worse.'

Woe consumed Fusa. It was as though the whole body of sheltered water were now a dense web of tentacles trailing some vast jellyfish. Like the earlier rains, it was making her skin prickle and her eyes burn. Journeying up to the riverside shrine had helped her nausea subside, but it heaved now inside her once again. And to top it all, there lingered a sense she had experienced something like this before, somewhere in the dark fog of a very unusual kind of dream.

Following Mako as he pushed a path through the bodies, Fusa winced when they came to the tip of the sandbar. The polluted waters of the lagoon were starting to sully the open ocean, too. She gave a worried whistle. 'It's spreading. Why is this happening?'

The stare Mako fixed upon her was so very intense that Fusa's heart thumped. This boy knew something. But he simply glided away, cutting a route through the horde until he reached the shallows where the humans had tossed him fish.

'They're not here today,' said Fusa. 'You're going to have to hunt for your own meal if you're hungry.'

'I didn't come here just to—'

Stopping suddenly, Mako turned. 'What do *you* want?'

Fusa spun around to see whom Mako was addressing. A female, not quite mature, was milling in the nearby water, passively watching them converse.

'You're friendly,' clicked the stranger.

Fusa moved closer to the girl. 'Don't mind Mako. He's just grumpy because his big idea didn't work out.'

'Idea? What were you planning, pretty boy?'

Fusa shifted awkwardly where she floated. 'He did something bad. And he's trying to make it right again.'

A creaking sounded through the waters behind them – *'Kikuko! Where are you?'* – and the adolescent huffed and craned her neck around.

'That's my parents. They fuss.'

'That's what we do,' said Fusa. 'My daughter's forever telling me off for it. Well, she used to, anyway.'

The ailing eyes of the new girl grew sorrowful. 'Did something happen to her?'

'A giant swell of water slammed across the shore here

a few days ago. It washed Mako and me onto land, but my daughter was out in the ocean with my pod somewhere nearby and now I can't get back to her. I'm terrified she might have got smashed by it, too.'

The older girl's sympathetic eyes softened. 'She'll be fine.'

Mako, who'd remained sulking at a distance, now approached. 'How would *you* know?'

'Because, pretty boy, what your friend is talking about is the quake and the surge that followed it.'

'Kikuko!'

'Alright! I'm coming! We felt that, too, out in the open water. But away from the coast, it's barely more than a brief current. A slight pull, but nothing worse.'

Hope warmed Fusa's innards for the first time since her ordeal began. If what this girl was saying was true, it meant her pod would have made it to Squid Hood Bay intact. The fear that Misa was being baked as she lay stranded deep into the land was an unfounded one.

Mako watched gloweringly as the girl then darted off into the mass of bodies. 'Finally,' he quacked.

Fusa tipped her beak back. 'There was no need to be rude.'

'Just listen, will you, auntie? I figured out what's going on. But I don't want any old dolphin hearing about it. Not just yet, anyway.'

Fusa's heart began to thump hard again. She let up a bubble, and waited patiently while his brain worked through what he wanted to say.

'This impurity,' he whistled at last. 'It's meant for me. Moshiri can't get me while I'm hiding away in this lagoon, so now he's trying to force me back out into the ocean.'

A stunned Fusa tilted away. It was every bit as awful a revelation as she feared it would be. So obsessed was the trout-god with vengeance, so ferocious his wrath, that he was devising ever more cunning – and indiscriminate – ways to enforce it.

Wakko Totto had never spoken of Moshiri deliberately polluting the ocean, though. As the elderly leader saw it, nothing mattered to the great backbone fish of the world beyond the purity of the waters he bore upon his spine. If Mako was right, it meant the trout-god was really only harming himself. But why would he do that?

Fusa's brow creased upon her beak. What difference did it make, why? The lagoon *was* growing contaminated with horrid, acrid disease. Even as she floated here in the shallows, the water needled in her eyes and fouled her mouth with its bitter taste.

A tension crept along her to consider the quarrel that was coming. She'd obliged Mako with his failed shrine plan, and he must now oblige her.

But he wasn't going to like it.

Fusa breached the surface for air, making out the faint shapes of the humans who'd gathered to marvel at the sudden assembly of so many marine creatures. Then, when she was back under, she steadied her nerves and came out with it. 'Moshiri can only give you his forgiveness when he's heard your apology.'

Mako made no attempt to respond, or even show that he'd heard what she said.

'Only a priestess can speak directly to the backbone fish,' she continued, undaunted.

Blankness.

'Moshiri hurt you in his anger.'

Nothing.

'And he hurt me worse.'

A *hint* of a furrowed brow.

'And all the dolphins here now are hurting, too.'

The boy's gaze fell downward.

'But there's a way to make this right.'

Silence.

'Get us to Squid Hood Bay.'

One bubble went up.

'Or every creature in the sea will die. And it will all be because of *you*.'

With that, Mako burst. 'Alright! Alright! I'll take you to your Wakka Totto! Even though Moshiri will smash you and me and every one of these dolphins into flatfish the moment we pass the sandbar! That's what you want, is it, auntie? Then let's do it! Right now! Come on!'

Thrashing through the horde of bodies, Mako cast a piercing glance back as he neared the narrow passageway into the expanse. 'What's the matter? Are you scared?'

'Of course I am, Mako!'

'And so you should be!'

Fusa swam hard past the spit to keep up with him, becoming overwhelmed at once by the darkness of the expanse. Beyond Mako's bubbly wake, she could see nothing at all; so distracted was she by her terror, that when Mako came to a sudden halt, she slammed into his backside.

'What's going on?' she groaned. 'Why've you stopped already? Moshiri hasn't even rattled his scales yet.'

'I'm sorry, auntie. But we've got more immediate problems than the backbone fish.'

Fusa spat out a mouthful of the foul-tasting impurity, longing for clean water to soothe her burning eyes. 'What is it then? The pollution? It's not worse here than in the lagoon.'

'It's not that either.'

'Then what? Why've you stopped?'

'Remember those orca we heard? Well, there's a few more of them now,' whistled Mako, turning around and heading back behind the spit.

'What? Wait, Mako! Where are you going?'

'I want to be with humans.'

'*Humans?* Why?'

'I don't know. I just do. You should come back into the lagoon now.'

'But what about getting back to my—'

'There's hundreds, auntie!' snapped Mako, hurrying off in the direction of the riverside shrine. 'A wall of orca, completely blocking the north. Just waiting for a snack like us.'

∽

As before, the folk at the riverside shrine were gladdened by the sight of Mako. It was as though they'd been waiting for him to come back.

He performed for them enthusiastically, whipping up their whoops and hollers, and by the time he got to the climax of his show, he'd forgotten about the awful mess waiting at the lagoon – and of his duty to confess to its ailing visitors that its impure water was all his doing.

Preparing for his best trick, Mako was just about to come up through the surface again to do the walking display they liked so much, when a very loud noise came chittering out from the shrine.

To Mako's ears, the voice had a different quality than was usual: it was more like a machine than an organic creature. Its effect upon the humans matched his own; upon hearing it, the onlookers grew visibly alarmed.

'*Dear worshippers,*' went the machine/voice, '*please remain calm. Due to the escalating situation at the Fukushima Daiichi Nuclear Plant, the municipal government has declared this region a high alert zone. To ensure our safety from radioactive contaminants, all residents have been instructed to evacuate immediately. The shrine will now be closing. Please make your way to the road.*'

Then, just like that, all the humans simply turned and shuffled away, leaving him on his own.

His good cheer soured. Very quickly, the sense of loneliness became unbearable. He scanned for any sign of life on the land, but everybody had gone, so he took off spiritlessly back downriver.

At Snow Crab Lagoon, he fired sonar scans, but with the multitude of dolphins merging into one another, all that came back on the echoes was a mess of lines, so he swam until he found Fusa in the shallows, holding flippers with Kikuko.

She appeared even more downcast than when he'd left her. Lingering close by were Kikuko's parents, who offered the occasional comforting nudges with their beaks.

Mako forgot about his own heartache at the sight of Fusa. 'What is it?' he clicked. 'Has something happened?'

'No, no,' clicked Kikuko. 'There's just a wall of orca stopping her from reaching her daughter. Why should a young mother be sad about that?'

Mako tipped away with mild embarrassment. 'Nothing else though, right?'

'Well,' said Kikuko, 'the ocean all around here is boiling with poison. And we're all pretty sick. But apart from that, everything is just excellent. How's things going with you, pretty boy?'

The girl's mother flicked a terse look towards her. 'Don't pay any attention to her. She thinks being rude makes her smarter than the rest of us. Now, young fellow. Fusa tells us you've had a tough time.'

Mako's beak drooped.

'You've looked after her well,' said the bull. 'She would have died for sure without your quick thinking.'

'It was the humans, really,' replied Mako.

Kikuko swayed her beak with confusion.

'Humans, dear,' said the cow. 'Those things we showed you once on the land. Terrible creatures.'

The bull nudged closer to Mako and Fusa. 'You seem as though you might be from the northern pods.'

Mako nodded and looked behind himself at the mass

of sickened dolphins, then turned back to the bull. 'We are. What about you? Is this your pod?'

'No. Us southerners prefer to travel in smaller units where we're able.'

The cow smiled broadly, but Mako saw in it little kindness. 'I'm afraid we're rather different to you, with your pufferfish ceremonies and your shrines and your trout-god.'

Kikuko giggled. 'Trout-god?'

'Moshiri,' cheeped Fusa. 'The giant trout, on whose back the whole world sits.'

The older girl gave a bemused glance to her father.

'The northern pods have had dealings with humans over the years, dear,' he wheezed.

The cow nodded in agreement. 'It's always the same when a human bonds with a dolphin. They touch them with their silly ideas and it spreads through their entire pod.'

Mako observed Fusa's eyes widen with the shock of those careless words, and felt his own do just the same.

'The most dangerous creatures you'll ever encounter, humans,' said the bull to Kikuko. 'To be avoided at all costs. We've heard of incidents that would make a little calf's blood run cold. But some dolphins simply can't help themselves. For some reason they become enraptured with them.'

The girl's father went on like this, but Mako didn't want to hear any more of it and pulled away. 'Excuse me,' he said. 'I'm hungry.'

Fusa came hurrying behind him, her face beset with a scowl. 'I cannot *believe* he just called the great Moshiri a "silly idea"! I'm glad you left. Actually, I'm starving.'

But it had merely been a ruse to get away. Mako knew there was no point even sending click trains out. In an area filled with this many bellies, very little to eat would be found.

In awkward silence, he bobbed in the shallows by

Fusa's side, hosting a remorse which reached every part of him. 'I'm very sorry,' he said.

Fusa smiled. '*I* know that.'

Her tone revealed what she really meant. 'But Moshiri doesn't, right?' He thought she was about to begin hounding him again, but when Fusa turned there was a softness to her.

'What do they always tell us about the trout-god?' she asked.

'That he's powerful.'

'Yes…?'

'And he carries the whole ocean upon his spine.'

'What else, Mako?'

'And that he's so big he stretches from horizon to horizon.'

Fusa gave a nod. 'The tip of his tail is far to the east,' she cheeped, 'where the sun rises. And his face can be found where the sun goes down.'

'In the west, you mean?'

Fusa's smile broadened. 'Yes, Mako. But this whole coastline *is* the west!'

Mako looked shyly at the mucky sand below them. 'Is it? I'm afraid I'm not so sharp with where things are. I always just sort of… followed.'

'It must be,' asserted Fusa. 'Out on the other side of the sandbar is ocean that stretches on so far that no echoes bounce back. It goes almost forever, all the way to Moshiri's tail.'

'So, you're saying…'

'I'm saying his head must be along this coast somewhere.'

Mako's stomach fluttered. She couldn't seriously be suggesting…

'You know what we've got to do, Mako.'

'I don't, auntie.'

'We must go before Moshiri himself.'

Mako's mouth dropped open.

'There's no other option,' asserted Fusa. 'He'll listen to us. Then, when he knows you're sorry, he'll settle, and I can go back safely to Squid Hood Bay. Until he's heard your apology, none of us is safe.'

'There's just one problem.'

Mako and Fusa both spun around, startled by the sound of this third voice. Behind them, Kikuko was hanging near the surface.

'How long have you—'

'We're not in the west,' clicked Kikuko.

'Of course we are!' protested Fusa. 'If I'm facing north, and the land is on my left side, and a vast open ocean is on my right, then how could this *not* be west?'

'This whole stretch of shore may look like the edge of the world,' said Kikuko, swaying her beak, 'but it's really just the coastline of one big island.'

Mako and Fusa looked at one another aghast. 'Then where is west?'

Kikuko's parents came gliding in from out of the throng of bodies. 'There's a sea on the other side of the island,' said the bull. 'Four days of swimming across it brings you to the farthest edge of the ocean. *That* is west.'

The cow gave an anxious frown. 'Dangerous waters. Humans cause trouble wherever they roam, but strange things have been happening to dolphins over there for a long time.'

'Then we'll just have to be very careful, won't we Mako?'

Every dolphin turned to look at Fusa, whose face was marked with a kind of determination Mako had not before seen.

'You can tag along with us,' said Kikuko's mother. 'We'll be heading south ourselves to meet my relatives after we're finished with the squid spawning in Lobster Claw Harbour. You can launch your crossing from Oyster Cove.'

'Thank you,' said Fusa. 'But we have to go at once.'

The cow scoffed. 'Just the two of you? But you've barely ten summers between you.'

'Let them do as they wish, dear,' said the bull. 'You'll want to use the strait, though. It's a shortcut. Cuts right through the island further down south. Look for a bridge high up above the water.'

Mako held a deep gaze upon Fusa.

He ought to feel more than he did in this moment, but instead he felt curiously numb.

She was right.

They had to find Moshiri.

He swished a fin and turned about face. Then, without so much as a glance back at this place that had served as their home, he led Fusa towards the sandbar.

Side by side, they vacated Snow Crab Lagoon at last. They banked sharply to the right, keeping close to the shore, out of range of the orcas' scans, swimming, at Fusa's insistence, close together. Mako pretended not to be comforted by Fusa's proximity – but it was obvious she knew he was really.

Just as Mako was settling into his rhythm, a pair of blips appeared fleetingly in his sonar field. Fearing orca, he was relieved to see only the unusual pair of box-wearing dolphins, who were travelling discreetly beneath them in the folds of the bed.

Fusa knew at once he'd seen something. 'What is it, Mako? What are you looking at?'

'Nothing,' he lied. 'Just distracted by all the whalesong out there, that's all. Can't you hear it?'

'Oh yes!' chuckled Fusa, and Mako's tension loosened a little to know that, at least for now, he'd shielded her from the certainty of their being pursued.

'What did the bull say about a shortcut, Mako? Something about a bridge?'

Mako let up a bubble. 'He said it was high up from the water. I'm just going to have to keep scanning for it.'

'Or,' came a third voice from behind them, 'you could let me show you the way, pretty boy.'

Fusa chirped excitedly. 'Kikuko? What are you doing? Where's your mother and father?'

'They'll be fine, auntie. Like I told them, I'm not a little calf anymore. Now, let's go find your trout-god.'

12

A HOUSE WITH A BOAT ON ITS ROOF

The water's foulness had faded just a short distance from Snow Crab Lagoon, easing Fusa's nausea almost right away. But with the trio deep into an arduous day's swim, her mind was still fraught with worry, and she knew precisely why:

She was going to *meet* Moshiri.

Had any dolphin in the history of the oceans ever attempted anything so foolish? His was a power great enough to move the seabed, and she was seeking to bargain with him. She'd be lucky if he even looked her in the eye before he sucked her in and spat her over to the far edge of the world.

Mako and Kikuko, that bit younger than her, had needed to stop for rest. They'd gone straight to sleep the moment they halted near the surface, their flukes swaying by themselves, keeping them afloat. Fusa, however, remained in a spyhop, overcome with worry for Misa and her pod – for everything that dwelt in her beautiful ocean home – until the coming of night took away her ability to see, and she dropped below the surface to close an eye.

But her fatigue felt impossibly heavy all of a sudden,

and her other eye closed too, and before she knew it, it was happening again:

The trout-god was beaming scenes into her sleeping mind.

The vision, as before, was so fuzzy it was hard to determine much of it. Physical things – even emotions – flitted like the skin of a hunted octopus as it desperately mimicked its surroundings. Anger was flashing into denial, which in turn blazed into sorrow of the most abysmal depth. There was panic in one instant, then bargaining in the next – then hatred, hope, disgust, love.

Yet the host of these emotions wasn't her. She wasn't among the vessels that were closing in around the frantic dolphins, and it wasn't through her own eyes that she could see the pair of sheer cliffs either side of the narrow harbour. It was as though she were observing as a patch of the water that was violently gurgling, or as one of the long strips of fabric that flapped overhead.

An overwhelming commotion of pain was sounding: agonised chirps which rose, then rose more, then fell away into silence.

The sound of language – curious, stilted words – was exploding into the sky, along with a din of hammering and the rumble of machinery which made the tightly-packed dolphins even more terrified.

Terrified of...

Land dwellers.

Humans were there, peering over the sides of their boats, their eyes dark with greed and the souls behind them as impure as the very waters the dolphins were caught in.

A calf was there, too, shining with the brightness of the moon. And a handsome young dolphin, flailing at the centre of the writhing mass. This adolescent's eyes were familiar, but water was sullying the face with hot, cloudy blood.

Still, she was able to recognise him.

It was Mako.

With a squeal, Fusa came awake.

Her companions were staring at her with concern. Their presence ought to have calmed her, but the effect of seeing Mako in the flesh right after staring into his spectral form only served to worsen the shock. She continued to squeal, and leapt above the surface to expel her stale air, then raced off blindly towards the rocks.

Mako followed close behind. 'Relax, auntie,' he softly whistled. 'It was just a dream.'

Kikuko, on Fusa's other side, performed a full spin where she bobbed. 'That was a dream?! In my dreams I'm surfing. Eating cuttlefish. Things that, you know, aren't horrifying.'

By now adjusted to her waking surroundings, Fusa felt a flush of embarrassment.

There was just no way to make sense of any of this!

Yet something deep down was telling her that making sense of Moshiri's messages was of the utmost importance to them all.

∽

Beneath a sunless sky twinkling with lights, Mako was in the folds of the coastal bed, chasing rockfish.

He was trying to remember what fun felt like. How long it seemed since he'd glided in the pressure wave of a boat's bow – of twisting in an exhilarating spin, of moving with such speed and effortlessness that it seemed impossible to him now.

Of course, half the fun had been knowing he was doing something he shouldn't. But these days, *shouldn't* didn't really mean anything. Whether he courted danger or did not, the consequences were his, and his alone. It was a thought which, he supposed, ought to have come with a sense of freedom. Yet all it made him feel was oddly hollow.

He snatched away an immature dogfish, then went to the coast to find Fusa and Kikuko, who were ready to set off for a night voyage. For a moment, he wondered if he should mention the dolphin-shaped blips he'd briefly seen again below him. But given the lateness of the hour, Fusa was jittery enough, and he thought better of it.

Kikuko, however, wasn't quite so thoughtful. No sooner had they moved into the taxing currents than the girl made an announcement. 'There's a couple of young bulls down there with boxes on their heads. They're very hard to read. They're almost like shadows.'

Fusa let out a bemused snort. 'I saw that pair. The day before Wakka Totto's thanksgiving ceremony, I think it was.'

'I've seen them quite a bit,' said Mako, concealing his knowledge of their pursuit of the trio. 'Big boys, they are. And fast.'

Kikuko went into a twist. 'How do you know they're the same ones, though?'

'Why would there be more than one pair?' asked Fusa.

'Why wouldn't there be? My father saw something like this before. I've never forgotten what he told me. It gave me nightmares of my own, in fact.'

'Come on then, Kikuko,' said Mako, feeling Fusa squish closer into him. 'Out with it.'

Kikuko began her father's account. 'On the west of the island, where you're going, my dad was travelling in open sea when he came across an injured dolphin. I mean, badly, mortally wounded – his eyes were blind and his fins were cut. Dad went and got him some fish, and as he ate he explained that he'd spent most of his life in captivity.'

Mako recoiled at that word.

'What's the matter, pretty boy? Too scary for you?'

'No!' quacked Mako. 'Go on.'

'This dolphin was captured by humans as a calf and

raised in a pen on a lake. He wasn't allowed to mix with others, and was only let out for short periods every day, and only ever to perform some task the humans set for him.'

'Tasks? What sort of tasks?'

'Mostly retrieving items left somewhere in the lake. But sometimes he was made to deliberately hurt himself by slamming his body into things. Then, one day, there was a loud explosion and the lake's edge blew apart, and the dolphin was able to get through it and into open water. But by then, he was already so damaged he stood no chance of surviving. The truly odd thing, though, was that attached to his flippers were boxes, and when dad asked him what they were for, all the dolphin said was "human eyes".'

Mako chuckled. 'And *that* gave you nightmares? You're even softer than Fusa!'

Kikuko gave a sad smile. 'If you aren't frightened by that, pretty boy, then you either don't have a very good imagination, or you haven't heard what I'm saying. That dolphin was plucked out of the ocean, by humans. He was put to work on tasks he didn't understand – tasks which caused him harm. And it was only luck that stopped him having to live his whole life that way.'

Fusa gave a whimper. But Mako merely let up a dismissive bubble. 'Imagine being scared of humans!' he snorted. 'You may as well be scared of your own shadows!'

~

The eastern horizon was beginning to blush with light.

To Fusa's relief, Moshiri, the god of the seas and of the storms, had neither rattled his scales nor spat out the ocean. Evidence of his earlier strike, however, was becoming gradually visible: town after town, all down the coast, the human lands had been so completely demolished that Fusa wondered whether the trout-god even knew just how destructive his thrashing truly was. Well, if he didn't now, he would after they'd told him.

From their spyhop, the trio watched the scenery grow ever more horrifying as the sun's light crept up the banks of the bay. On a road which coiled around a foothill, wheeled machines were juddering by one after the other, like a line of migrating whales. The faces of the human riders were every bit as glum as those at the riverside shrine had been. There was no way for a dolphin to properly comprehend the anguish of these land dwellers, she reckoned, but Fusa felt instinctively that something was going on in their world they'd rather was not — something from which they felt a need to escape.

The terrain down at sea-level was in an appalling state. Standing out from the flattened rubble, the few buildings that hadn't collapsed were the misfits. So high had the water been when it breached this section of coast that all manner of things now lay strewn upon the buildings' roofs. As well as the planks and the poles and the lumps of wall and the trunks of trees, some larger items now resided there, too. On top of one dwelling was a whole other dwelling, and on another was a huge metal boat that lay on its side, its barnacled underside facing the very ocean that had lifted it up and dumped it down where a boat had no business being.

Mako, whose eyes these days seemed to burn with shame at all hours, couldn't stand the sight of the devastation, had taken himself off to sift for flatfish in the sediment. Fusa spotted him some time later up at the surface, where he appeared to be interacting with the gulls. It wasn't clear at first what was so interesting about those wide-winged birds — they were simply doing what they did: swooping and cawing as they scrapped for a bite. But when she went up and saw what their meal actually was, Fusa understood why the youngster was so preoccupied.

In the water, face down and inflated like a pufferfish, was a lifeless human. Its body was beginning to come apart where the gulls pecked at its bloated flank. Mako was slapping the birds away with his tail, trying his best to get them to move on. But gulls with a taste for meat would linger until it was all gone.

Although he was trying not to show it, Mako was obviously upset. For some reason, he seemed to hold a deep affection for the flat-faced land creatures, and the discovery of this dead one had sickened his heart.

She felt it herself. There was something terribly sad about the sight of a human in this state, with its foot caught beneath a solid block. She tried not to dwell on the macabre circumstances that had caused the life of this individual to end in such a way, but from the evidence, it was clear that their foot had become trapped right as the surge washed in.

Kikuko, for her part, was largely unfazed by the plight of this poor human. The girl looked upon the carcass – and, indeed, upon the whole clean-up operation unfolding in the ruined town – with curious indifference.

'You don't care for those creatures very much, do you?' Fusa asked.

Kikuko gave a click. 'Humans? Not really. Their world and ours are so different. I don't see any reason for us to mix.'

Mako, having now succeeded in driving the birds high into the sky, glided over to where the others were resting. He gave Kikuko a searching look, then quietly chirped: 'Is it true you don't travel with a pod?'

'It is.'

'Why?'

Kikuko performed a tight somersault in the water and blew out some bubbles. 'It's just always been that way.'

'Don't you have any friends?' inquired Fusa, before quickly pressing her fin against her. 'Other than us, I mean.'

'We cross paths with a few other families from time to time, yes. But I like to play with other creatures, too. Not only dolphins.' Kikuko pulled away from Fusa and turned back to face the pair, and when she next spoke there was an authority to her voice. 'Now,' she said. 'In case you haven't noticed, while we hug the coast like this we're swimming against the current. This is costing us pace and energy.'

The others eyed each other fretfully. It was true. They *had* to get into the south-flowing currents — which meant heading into deeper ocean.

Fusa looked ahead to where more human carcasses were drifting in the shallows. Moshiri had been tolerant of the trio's journey so far, but if the trout-god was aggrieved by Mako venturing further offshore, there stood to be a whole lot more death and destruction — and perhaps an even greater number of bodies in the water.

13

ATTACK OF THE SHADOW

WITH EVERY THRASH of his tail, Mako worried that some thunderous quake was just a moment away, prompting an angst so heavy that his body seemed to lose its propulsion. Listlessly trailing the other two, he experienced the marine environment as Fusa did: blindly, and filled with an ever-present sense of dread.

Guilt clung to him like a scar as he surveyed the land. The echoes that bounced back told a story he simply couldn't bear. The world of the humans was truly annihilated; it was likely Moshiri had inflicted a greater blow upon them than he had the creatures of the ocean, when they'd done nothing to deserve it.

As they swam ahead of him, he listened to the other two chattering away. It was clear a bond was developing between the pair.

'I wish I'd seen as much of the world as you, Kikuko,' Fusa was chirruping. 'Especially the far south. The seniors of my pod say the warm waters there are so packed with fish that a dolphin only has to open her mouth and a meal will swim right in.'

'Free advice, auntie. Ignore those old dawdlers. They've got krill for brains. Yes, the ocean down there is teeming with marine life. But I suspect your seniors squeezed one too many pufferfish if they think things will simply feed themselves to you.'

Fusa giggled. 'So you've been there?'

'Been there? I was *born* there. I stayed down in those waters until I could catch my own meal, then we journeyed all the way up the other side of the island. You know, this is actually the first time I've been on the east coast.'

'Does Moshiri thrash in those other places, too?'

Kikuko let up a bubble. 'The "backbone fish of the world"? Can't say I know an awful lot about him.'

'You don't pray to him?'

'Not as such, no. In fact—', Kikuko paused here, as though doubting whether she should continue, '—my mother and father say he's not even real.'

Although she was in front of him, Mako could just picture Fusa's eyes widening, precisely as his own had done. Kikuko might regret saying such an outrageous thing when Moshiri's colossal eye soon studied her.

'Not real?!'

'Keep your fin on, auntie. It was just a suggestion. Besides, we'll find out soon enough.'

Fusa's brow dipped in confusion. 'We will? How?'

'You're crossing the western sea, aren't you? When you come back, you can tell me whether or not you found him.'

With the coast curving around a headland, the trio were now moving away from the human settlements, muting the din of activity on the shore. For Mako, this was a relief: not only did distance from the human world lessen his feeling of guilt, but it reduced the chance of bumping into any more of their kind bobbing lifelessly in the ocean.

Fusa and Kikuko remained ahead of Mako. His anguished thoughts had deafened him to their chatter, but when Kikuko gave a sudden whistle, he snapped back into focus.

There was excitement in her voice. 'Look!' she was squealing. 'On the rocks! Come on!'

Mako threw out a scan and waited for the echoes, which located creatures at rest on a promontory. He made to enquire, but Kikuko was already on her way to the shore, spiralling and chirruping with uncharacteristic abandon. Her enthusiasm saw to it that Fusa raced to catch her up, and Mako himself was curious enough to pursue as they approached the rocky headland.

The three dolphins went up into a spyhop to see a colony of sea lions sunning themselves.

'Hi!' Kikuko called out, before spitting a jet of water into the face of the nearest animal.

Fusa, clearly alarmed by her friend's behaviour, drew back close to Mako. He too felt a frisson of nervous energy, but it turned out there was nothing at all to fear: right away, the youngsters of the colony dropped into the sea and began to gently wrap themselves around the dolphins' bodies.

'These are my friends,' clicked Kikuko. 'They're so much fun! Watch this.'

At once, Kikuko propelled herself downwards, leading the curious creatures on a frenzied chase.

Fusa held back, though. 'My last encounter with a sea lion ended badly,' she cheeped, sadly.

Mako tilted his head to her. 'What happened?'

'It wasn't the sea lion's fault – it was me. I caused an accident that led to my dad leaving our pod.'

'He'd have gone anyway,' said Mako, but before he could finish making his point, a fat pup glided across to Fusa and held its whiskered nose to her beak, and she giggled with glee and sped off with the rest.

The older animals lolling around on the rocks were clever, and very friendly, but Mako's attempt to communicate was in vain. They weren't capable of any kind of language intelligible to a dolphin, so when his patience ran out, he dived back below the waves to frolic.

Why he hadn't played with the lithe, acrobatic sea lions before was a mystery to him. There'd been ample opportunities; sea lions frequently followed the pod as they ventured through the ocean. His mother once told him that their eyesight was more powerful than any other marine species, but since they didn't have sonar capabilities, they relied on dolphins to lead them to food.

Intrigued, Mako wished to find out for himself if that was true, and paired off with a male he guessed was around his own age. In the folds of the seabed, he raced with his new friend – they were evenly matched in speed – and when that was concluded he went in close to the sea lion and demonstrated his sonar by sending out click trains.

The sea lion watched Mako intensely with its big eyes. Fronted, like humans, these dark orbs glistened with concentration, but the gentle creature lacked the means to mimic him and merely made a barking sound that seemed to come from deep within his belly. Mako gave a chuckle and dipped back into the trough to race again, but the beams he'd sent out in his demonstration returned with a very strange, and unexpected, echo: a lone dolphin was ascending from out of the expanse. And something was fastened to its head.

He turned to find Kikuko, but she was already there, chirping next to him. 'You've got him too? Reckon it's one of that pair?'

'Could be,' said Mako, who was just starting to move away to investigate when a deafening chorus of barks roared out, and the sea lions, moving as though they were a single body, darted up to the surface and vanished onto the rocks.

Summoning Fusa wasn't necessary; the cow, startled by the cacophony and the swiftness with which the sea lions vacated the water, wasted no time nestling between Mako and Kikuko.

The sea lions were now running away from the

lapping waters. How strange they looked, galumphing like that across the rocks! The flippers they'd used so gracefully to slice through the waters were now angled out to the sides, their heads stretched back to allow them to see ahead of themselves. They were clearly better suited to water, but it was surprising how quickly they could traverse solid ground. Mako felt a flush of envy: why couldn't *he* do that? He began to imagine what tricks he could perform for the humans if he were more like a sea lion. They gave him fish just for doing the things he ordinarily did; what treats would they gift him if he could perform on land as well?

Before he could indulge this fanciful notion any further, however, Kikuko let out an anguished clicking, and Mako realised he ought to have paid more attention to the oncoming individual. By now, this stranger was visible to their eyes, confirming that he was indeed wearing a contraption on his body. But there was no time to study the item – the dolphin, moving at a speed Mako never dreamt possible, arrived with a fierce clap of his jaws and slammed right into his side.

He was attacking.

Kikuko and Fusa squealed, and peeled away. The force of the blow had winded Mako and, unable to expel bubbles, he was beginning to panic. This aggressive loner, who himself wasn't yet fully grown, still looked as though he had plenty to prove.

With incredible force, the dolphin swung his body around, revealing a long scar across his side, and slapped Mako full in the beak with his tail. The strike was stunning, but even in his dizzied state, Mako felt extremely grateful that only one of the flukes had connected; had he been hit with both, it was almost certain he'd now be sinking down to the whalefalls on the ocean bed.

Still the crazed dolphin came at Mako. What was his problem? This couldn't have been his territory – he was nowhere near here while the trio had been playing with the sea lions. Desperate now to expel a full breath, it crossed Mako's mind that this animal's entire nature had been somehow changed. No dolphin he'd ever met had brought such violence to an initial meeting. Warnings were one thing. But an outright assault was unheard of.

Kikuko joined the fight. She came charging in, shielding Mako from the next attack, and for doing so earned herself a powerful shunt to the underside. But the distraction was enough to allow Mako to make a retreat and regulate his breathing.

The dolphin gave chase, but Mako, charged now with adrenaline, stayed ahead. The pursuer then did something surprising, however: he flipped back the other way, and locked his eyes onto Fusa.

Mako's innards rippled. Fusa, bobbing vertically, had frozen.

Ignoring his pain, Mako raced forward to stop this crazed dolphin hurting her; with as hard a thrash of his tail as he could manage, he accelerated after him. 'Hey!' he quacked. 'Who gave you that scar? Your ugly mother?'

The attacker was undeterred, but still Mako went on with the insults. 'I bet your mother took one look at you when you were born and wished she'd never met your walrus of a father. You hear me, Scarside?'

But the attacker kept on, a dart aiming squarely for Fusa's centre.

Desperately, Mako whistled to Kikuko but she, too, was too far back to prevent the coming strike. Poor Fusa was done for. With her underside exposed like that, this creature's snout was going to turn her organs into jellyfish.

And then it was over: the attacker had got to her.

Yet he didn't strike. He simply hung on the spot, looking intensely upon Fusa.

Mako and Kikuko frenziedly scrambled to reach them, and were soon beside the young cow.

The trio, in a tight semi-circle, faced off against the attacker. There was hurt in this dolphin's eyes. Did trauma explain its behaviour? Mako cast an eye over the harness around its head, and at the strange device attached to it which was connected to a metal plate. All of this weird stuff was of the human world.

Time seemed to disappear as they waited for the dolphin to make its move. Why didn't it just savage her and get it over with? Fusa, for her part, was doing a very good job at being brave. Perhaps it was that she knew there was little point to protesting; if this out-of-control animal wished to kill her, nothing she could do would prevent it.

Finally, the dolphin, who had never once taken an eye off Fusa, clicked a single word.

'Blind.'

Fusa gave a gentle nod of her beak.

And that was that. The terrifying assailant sped down into the vast depths.

∼

How the sea lions had known was a mystery to Fusa, but they'd done well to make themselves scarce before that *thing* arrived.

They'd encountered it before, perhaps. Suffered its same needless violence. Or else those whisker-nosed creatures acted swiftly on some warning the trio had mistaken for a simple bark. However the sea lions had done it, it was to the dolphins' own great misfortune that they themselves had not.

Behind the headland of a nearby promontory, within a labyrinth of shallow caves, Fusa was trying her best to find something for her injured companions to eat, but with her sonar-blindness, hunting had taken on an entirely different character.

Unable to locate prey in the echoes of her click trains,

Fusa had only her eyes to rely on – and pure luck. In clear waters, her vision was strong enough that nearby fish could be easily sighted. But without the vital readings in her sonic field, she couldn't know the location into which they were about to move, and as such, by the time she reached one, it was already too late. Of course, there'd been occasions when food simply drifted by, gifting Fusa the chance of snatching a meal away without any effort at all. Those occasions, however, were few and very far between.

Snuffling through the sediment that blanketed the hump of a seamount, she swallowed a few flatfish and a heap of crustaceans, saddened by the thought that much of her life's diet would be the things that scuttled along the bottom. When she was satisfied she'd gathered a sufficient meal, she went back up to the shallows where the adolescents were resting, and gave a whistle. 'Ready?'

Kikuko turned, with a laboured effort, to gingerly pluck away the flailing prawns as Fusa released them from her jaws. Mako, however, couldn't be tempted. The poor boy had come off badly, and was likely to need quite some time to recuperate. The sight of blood spilling from his mouth was worrying, not only because of its volume but also because of its potential to attract sharks. Luckily, he'd retained enough presence of mind to shut off the blood supply to his face, stopping the stream from pouring out any further.

With a tender chirrup, Fusa moved along Mako's side. 'You can't even manage one?'

'No, thank you, auntie.'

Fusa drooped. She wanted him to eat, if only because it gave her pleasure to know she could still do something useful for another dolphin. But Mako simply wasn't interested.

By now, the sun had dipped into the lower half of the sky, and the afternoon rays carried with them just enough warmth to suggest the season had changed. Fusa pictured Squid Hood Bay. It was easy to see why Wakko Totto loved going back there each year, and although her heart ached at the absence from her pod, it cheered her spirit to picture them all there now, strand fishing on the soft sands of its coves, Misa playing in the kelp forests that clung to the coastal shelves like vast anemones.

But the thought of the boiling poison in the northern waters quickly destroyed the daydream. There was no doubt it was spreading – the hordes of arrivals at Snow Crab Lagoon confirmed it – and the worry of that infectious, choking substance making it across the strait to pollute that glorious bay was torture to her.

Mako, who'd barely said a word since the assault, suddenly gave an inquiring quack. 'How's your belly?'

'Feels great,' said Kikuko. 'I wish I got walloped by a deranged dolphin every day.'

Mako let out the faintest of chuckles. 'He was strong. When he got me with his tail, the light went out. I thought he'd crushed my head.'

'You were so brave, Mako,' said Fusa.

'Me? Kikuko was the brave one, auntie. She only got hurt because she tried to stop him getting to me.'

The trio fell into quiet contemplation and Fusa, forced by the strangeness and savagery of the event, replayed it over and over in her mind.

The silence was eventually broken by Mako. 'What *was* he?', he said, rolling his flank around as though testing he still could.

'I can't figure it out,' said Kikuko. 'But I'm pretty sure he's been following us for some reason.'

For Fusa, there was something even more curious. That vicious animal was readying to end her life, yet he stopped before he hit her. 'Why did he swim off when he realised I was blind?'

Mako let up a bubble. 'I think it was sympathy.'

'Sympathy?' clicked Kikuko. 'I've heard of pointer sharks with more sympathy than that thing.'

'Maybe not sympathy, then. But pain resided within him.'

Fusa swayed her beak. 'And sickness, too. My guess is he's had a hard life.'

'Find me a dolphin who hasn't,' said Kikuko, coldly. 'We're going to need to be careful.'

'Even *more* careful, you mean,' said Fusa, glancing across at Mako. Ever since he'd agreed to go in front of Moshiri, a permanently worried look resided in that boy's eye.

'We should rest now,' Kikuko chirped, and with that they slowed down their hearts and nestled close to the soft algae that carpeted the caves, remaining still and silent until the ocean grew inky with the darkness of night.

And when Fusa next opened her eyes, she discovered with a squeal of fright that Mako was no longer with them.

Facing Moshiri, it seemed, was simply too terrifying a prospect.

14

LURKERS IN THE DEEP

IN THE DEAD OF NIGHT, with Fusa and Kikuko resting silently at the surface, Mako's anxieties got the better of him.

His face was tender from the rogue dolphin's attack, and his belly bruised, but nothing pained him more than the thought of what might be coming.

Fusa had *seen* things. She claimed not to be able to comprehend much of the visions, but Mako suspected otherwise.

Just how bad was what she'd seen? Did Moshiri simply swallow him whole on arrival? Or did the trout-god thrash with enough force to collapse the world entirely? Whatever Fusa had glimpsed, it was appalling enough that she'd been compelled to conceal it.

The noise in his mind was as ceaseless as the thrum that carried over from off the nearby shore, compelling Mako to leave his companions for a while. He glided off in the direction of the human habitations, longing for nothing more than the cheerful attention they so liked to lavish upon him, and as he swam, he hoped that some time among them would earn him both distraction and that very special kind of comfort.

At a small harbour, he nudged up through the surface

and held himself in a spyhop, expectantly. The humans on the shore, however, were anything but cheery.

As they worked their nimble hands, the pair tossed words around as rapidly as they did the lobsters from out of their cages.

'See the last bulletin?'

'Been on the boats all day. What's being said now?'

'The situation up at the Fukushima plant has got worse.'

'Please don't say the other reactor's blown.'

'Not yet. But they're increasing the evacuation radius.'

'This is too shameful. In the eyes of the world, we'll be seen like the Soviets after Chernobyl.'

'Have faith. The engineers are working hard. Disaster may still be averted.'

Mako let out as happy a quack as he could muster. The humans turned, their eyes straining in the gloom to spot him, and a fish came hurtling through the sky beside him. But it wasn't food he craved from the humans, it was their affection – and this was not forthcoming.

Forlornly, he swam around the harbour and read his scans. A blip was approaching from the open water, prompting a cold wave of panic. But it wasn't the crazed dolphin. It was just Kikuko.

∽

'He won't have gone far, auntie. You rest here a while longer, and I'll check out the coast.'

Fusa's heart constricted. She *really* didn't want to be left alone in the dark, but she knew Kikuko was right: somebody needed to stay here, or else Mako wouldn't know where they'd gone when he returned.

'Don't fret,' chirped Kikuko as she headed off to find Mako. 'I'll be fast.'

The instant she was alone, Fusa was overwhelmed by the depth of the gloom; able to see nothing, she concentrated instead on her hearing. Distantly, waves were breaking rhythmically on the shore, evoking memories of her lessons to Misa and the podlings where peeling tubes broke upon the surf.

Buoyed by these happy recollections, she began to grow hopeful about the future. This distressing experience would all be over one day; when she was as knowledgable as Kikuko, she could teach the calves about all kinds of exciting things. And even if she didn't learn another thing the rest of the way, the account she'd give of coming face to face with the great Moshiri was sure to earn the respect of the entire pod.

Perhaps even Toshi would enjoy hearing about that. Who knew – maybe it would impress him so much that he'd want to stay with her and the pod after all?

But the lightness of Fusa's mood quickly ebbed away. From somewhere out in the expanse, stilted transmissions were beginning to arrive.

Orca were coming in.

For just a moment, Fusa froze, before realising failure to act could get her killed. She threw out a scan towards the coast, then remembered that, with her sonar-blindness, she could wait until dawn and still wouldn't be able to read them.

Left with only one option, she sucked a huge breath of air into her lungs, and dived down to the seamount.

∼

'There you are, pretty boy!' chirped Kikuko. 'We thought for a moment you might have changed your mind about going to see the trout-god.'

Doing his best to conceal his shame, Mako turned away. 'I couldn't rest, that's all. So I came here.'

Kikuko swept her head from side to side as she threw out a train of clicks up onto the land. 'You've really got a thing for humans, haven't you? What's the appeal, anyway? They can't even swim.'

Mako, affronted by this, gave a clap of his jaws beside Kikuko's face. 'What are you on about? I just wanted to—'

'You're mistaking their curiosity for love,' creaked Kikuko. 'And you'll regret it.'

Readying to argue, Mako spouted. But just then, three objects appeared in his sonar field that caught him by surprise.

'Where's Fusa?' he squealed.

'I left her to come find you. Why?' Her eyes suddenly widened as her own echoes returned to her. 'That's orca! They're coming in quick!'

Side by side, the pair thrashed out from the shallows of the harbour and into open water, rounding the shore to get back to the seamount's ridge.

But Fusa was nowhere to be seen.

Frenziedly, Mako and Kikuko scanned the steep face of the ridge as they raced down it. But as pitted with craters and crevices as the seamount was, their sonar was largely useless.

Mako let out a groan. Fusa really was in trouble now, and not merely because of the difficulty she faced finding a meal by herself; with the absence of her sonar, amid darkness as total as this, she simply wouldn't know which way she was going. There was every chance she was travelling out into the expanse this very moment, moving ever closer to the currents favoured by the migrating orca clans.

One after the other, Mako investigated the cave mouths, only to be disappointed. Returning echoes revealed a shelf of rock so vast a dolphin could spend his entire life surveying it and still not find her. Down and down the shelf went, right to the deeps of the east, to the very roots of the big island. But still he weaved, this way and that, tirelessly searching each and every hollow which might conceivably house Fusa.

Eventually, he came to an opening in the shelf, a fissure that extended further into the rock than he was willing to go alone. Conserving his air, he hung near its entrance and waited for Kikuko, and when he saw her at the surface, he went up to join her to tell her of this deep rift.

In a spyhop, the pair steadied their nerves. The high winds whistled across the waves with such force that he wondered how the large ships passing on the horizon stayed afloat. They were very brave, humans, to conduct their business this way when conditions were so very hazardous.

As they rose and fell with the swell, Mako gave a quack. 'We'll need to stay together where we can.'

'Agreed,' clicked Kikuko. 'Orca will be too wide for a fissure like that. But sharks won't.'

In unison, the pair arced into the water and dived until they reached the crevice. It was too narrow to swim abreast, so they proceeded inside with Mako above and Kikuko below, scanning incessantly as they moved ever deeper into the rock. But nothing organic at all seemed to dwell within this great rift. It was a forgotten place, an empty, lifeless world suited only to a creature whose life was so shameful there was nowhere better for him.

His body deflated in a sad droop. It was just the kind of place for *him*.

Soon the narrow gap began to open, and the pair found themselves in the centre of a chamber whose appearance was like that of a huge bubble which had exploded within the rock itself. The main fissure carried on ahead, but two separate channels forked out to the left and right.

Kikuko let a bubble out from her mouth. 'Any preference?'

'I'll take the right side.'

'We'll meet back here, then,' said Kikuko. 'Don't head on up into the main fissure until we're together again.'

Mako swayed his beak, trying his best not to let his nerves show. 'Be careful.'

'You too,' said Kikuko, as she glided out of sight.

Inside the right fork, Mako took care how he held his body, yet still his tail caught the side of the crevice, sending down dislodged chunks of rock. Echoing as they tumbled deep into the coastal shelf, Mako was dizzy with dread. The trout-god wouldn't take kindly to being pelted with missiles in such a way.

Another mishap like that was more than Mako's thundering heart could take, so he moved as slowly as possible to avoid a similar collision. Gliding further into the fork, his echoing clicks told him the sheer walls ahead were pocked with craters. His mind began to torture him with thoughts of some monster's ambush, but he didn't fret. All panicking was good for was burning through his oxygen faster.

He threw a scan directly ahead. For the first time, an echo returned with something living. But with barely the tip of whatever this was protruding out into the fork, it was almost entirely concealed within the cave. It was an octopus, perhaps: one tentacle left carelessly unattended. Or a squid. Mako's stomach gave a growl. A squid would go down rather well right now.

Closer, he advanced. The object began to gently sway. It looked like… was it a tail fluke?

Cautiously, Mako glided along the fork until he came right to the edge of the crater. He was too afraid now to emit any sonar signals, lest this thing become startled, so he waited to see what he could make out with his own eyes.

He edged his snout around the rim, advancing haltingly until, finally, his eye took in the hollow.

A dolphin was inside.

But it wasn't Fusa.

This was a male.

And with the wide scar along his side, and the strange box fastened to his head, Mako knew *exactly* who it was.

∽

Despite her fatigue, Fusa thrashed as powerfully as she could until she reached the foothills of the seamount. Then, where the slope began to level, she followed its line, hoping to find a trench into which she could shield herself against the orcas' sonar scans, which would soon have her as a blip in their predatory brains.

She reached a section of rock beset with long, horizontal grooves – like the underjaw of a humpback whale – and could hardly believe her luck. Spoiled for choice, she swung into the first depression she reached, and steadied her heart rate before continuing along the softly zig-zagging gully.

Rationing her air was critical; all this hiding would be for nothing if she was forced to the surface now. She ducked in as close to the trench's side as she could, the vast volume of water above her sickeningly dark, and, closing an eye, she allowed one half of her brain to nap.

Just as she was beginning to feel confident that she'd evaded the orca, Fusa heard an animal sound. It consisted of clicks and chirrups, yet differed from the language she was used to hearing.

She halted. Whatever was making that noise was inside a crater further along the gully. Being almost blind in water this lightless, all she could do was wait.

And then she felt it. Somehow, the thing had got behind her.

A dolphin was moving alongside her body, investigating her, his rope-like adornments scraped gently against her skin. No scar marked this young bull's side though: this was not Mako's attacker.

Frozen in terror, Fusa endured his curiosity a few

moments before letting out a few timid squeaks. 'Hello. I'm Fusa.'

'Fu-sa,' echoed the dolphin.

'What's your name?'

'Name... Zhe—bi.'

Zhebi? That was a funny-sounding name. He must have come from far away.

She strained to make out the vague shape of the odd box-like thing attached to his head. There was a kind of whale in the cold waters north of Wakka Totto's ancestral homelands that was known to have a long tooth that protruded from out of its head. But *this* was definitely not a thing that nature had put there. Humans were the only beings she knew of that dealt with such precise lines and angles – and why they possibly wanted to put their devices on a dolphin was a mystery to her.

Still, she felt it better to keep quiet and let this solitary creature take the lead. Having seen how Mako had nearly had his beak broken, she didn't much fancy finding out whether this one had a temper.

'Friends,' he wheezed. 'Boy and girl. Where?'

Fusa bristled. What business did he have with Mako and Kikuko? 'They're gone now. Very far away. What about your friend?'

The male said nothing.

'The dolphin with the scar down his side,' said Fusa, her heart pumping so hard with fear that her oxygen was rapidly running out. 'Where's he now?'

'Sick. Zhao is resting.'

The dolphin's voice was ailing. An unmistakable illness had resided in the eyes of Mako's attacker, too; something had evidently stricken this peculiar pair.

'Fusa and friends going some place. Where?'

Awkwardly, Fusa shifted. 'We need to see the trout-god. He's upset. He rocked his giant scales against one another, and caused a terrible rumble.'

'Rumble. Yes. Zhebi and Zhao, we see rumble. In north.'

'Have you been following us, Zhebi?'

'Not follow. Escape.'

'Escape? What from?'

'From west. Human very bad to us there. We come east through strait. Safe there. Then the wave bring poison in the water.'

'You saw the wave, too?'

'Make us sick. Zhao is bad sick.'

Fusa let up a bubble; her lungs were just beginning to ache. 'That's why we need to see the backbone fish.'

Even though she knew it was rude, Fusa was just too curious to let it go, and nudged at his contraption with her beak. 'Why do you have this?'

'Human put it on us.'

'But what for? What does it do?'

'Human take away sonar from Zhebi and Zhao. Then they give us human sonar.'

∽

Though the creature in the cave was unmistakably the animal that had hurt him yesterday, Mako felt no fear.

Not even a prawn would be afraid of this individual.

A rush of violent energy coursed through Mako's body as he stared at the dolphin at the crater's rear. Kikuko, who'd quickly come to Mako's aid, was glowering, too. This thing had nearly killed them both, and now it had cornered itself. They should smash him.

Yet this dolphin was obviously nearing the end of his life.

Sympathy cooled the heat of Mako's temper. He imagined this was him: a lonely young dolphin, far from his family, without a mother to comfort him or friends to cheer him up. Was there any worse predicament for a creature to find itself in?

Kikuko was obviously moved to pity, too, and went forward. 'Are you alright?'

The dolphin gave no reply.

'He sounds like he might be dying, Mako. He needs to breathe.'

Nudging the stranger with her beak – how brave this girl was! – Kikuko's soft words were nevertheless commanding. 'Come on,' she said to him. 'Come with us up to the surface. You must get air.'

'No,' replied the dolphin. 'No air. Zhao finish now.'

Kikuko turned to Mako with distress. 'He's got to spout, Mako! Help me get him to the surface!'

'Ma—ko,' whined the dolphin. 'Mako forgive Zhao. Human do this. Human poison Zhao.'

Kikuko gave an urgent whistle. 'Come on, Mako! Help me! He's going to drown!'

The ailing creature gave a weak nod of his beak. 'Yes. Zhao drown now.'

Although Mako's heart grew sick to witness it, he understood that a dolphin's choice to suffocate was his own. It didn't happen very often, but several members of his own pod had, at various times, chosen simply not to go on, and had taken themselves down to drown. One such dolphin was a cousin of his father's who had become ill and, rather than slow the pod, he descended to the huge, exposed skeleton of a whalefall and let the life fade out from himself.

Kikuko held herself tightly against Mako in a state of distress. She looked as though she might be contemplating drowning herself, just to put an end to the anguish of watching this happen. Mako pulled away from her and went closer to the dying dolphin, holding his eye next to his.

'It's alright,' said Mako. 'Don't be afraid.'

'Ma—ko, please forgive Zhao.'

'I do, Zhao. I do forgive you.'

A rattle sounded inside the chest of the dolphin,

followed soon after by a terrible gargling in his throat that made Mako's blood turn cold.

'Human,' said the mysterious dolphin, his voice a thin, strained whistle. 'Human… no friend.'

And with that, Zhao's eyes closed.

Mako and Kikuko drooped. They remained like this for a time, their sadness a raw, open wound. Above the waves, the sky was just beginning to brighten with dawn. How strange it was to think that Zhao would never see another day.

Ready now to return to the surface for air, Mako held his flipper against Kikuko, whose crushed spirit was as plain to see as the fin on her back. Together, the pair backed out of the cave – and both let out a flurry of bubbles as they clattered into Fusa and another male, who looked just as shocked as they were themselves to be meeting in such a way.

15

A GIFT FROM THE FALLEN

Grief numbed them.

With Zhebi down in the gloom beside the body of his friend, Fusa hung with Mako and Kikuko at the surface, watching embers of sunlight brightening the east.

So awful was their description of Zhao's self-drowning that Fusa was thankful not to have seen it. She couldn't help but picture Misa in some future time, who's path had inexplicably twisted from that expected for her. Far from the happy, loved individual Fusa hoped she'd be, she was instead solitary and wretched, a girl who hid herself in the darkest of canyons, whose very life meant so little that she chose one day to take no more air.

How lucky Zhao's own mother had been to have missed this sad event. Her heart would have shattered at what had become of her baby.

Zhebi, though, was curiously detached. Perhaps his heart was made of different stuff? He didn't even seem sad; though, he didn't really seem much of anything at all. In the short time Fusa had been with him, that dolphin proved impossible to figure out. It wasn't that he was closed, as such – he answered whichever questions she felt brave enough to ask – yet the nature of his life, as undeniably painful as it had been, was shrouded in a kind of mystery that not even she, with her endless nosiness, wished to venture near.

The trio waited and waited, but still Zhebi failed to appear, and when the spectre of the scene below became impossible to ignore, they went down to check on him. But the deeper the trio dived, the more Fusa filled with dread. Had he, too, chosen not to take another breath?

Thankfully, they found Zhebi as they'd left him, within the wall of the gully. The gentle swaying of his fins reassured them he was still alive, but he was motionless – lost, perhaps, in what may have been thoughts.

As Fusa wondered whether this dolphin was even capable of thinking about things, she noticed just how weary Zhebi's eyes looked. His sickness prompted another ripple of anxiety in Fusa. By the time the rising sun fell once again, it was possible that two dead dolphins might occupy this forlorn hollow.

Mako was fascinated by the device on Zhebi's head, and had moved closer to study it. 'So, it's a kind of sonar? Why isn't it doing anything?'

As though roused out of a slumber, Zhebi became suddenly animated. Speeding up without warning, he called out: 'human sonar is different.'

The others followed, and lingered with him just below the surface where he positioned his machine in front of them. 'Human sonar only work in light,' Zhebi said. 'At night, or in deep water, sonar is silent. You watch now.'

The first rays of direct sunlight were beginning to shine. To Fusa's amazement, part of the box suddenly blinked into life, and a pattern of squares appeared on the glass in front of them. Zhebi moved back from the trio, then sent a click train in their direction – and three tightly packed dots flashed at the bottom of the glass face.

'That's us!' chirruped Kikuko. 'His machine echolocated us!'

'But we're only dots,' said Mako, moving closer to

Zhebi. 'How do you know *what* we are? We could be anything.'

'Like boats,' suggested Fusa.

'Or fish,' added Mako.

'Or orca,' said the three of them, in unison.

Zhebi turned towards the coast and fired a long click train at a lower frequency. 'Human sonar not strong like biosonar. Look. Mako, you scan too, same like me.'

Mako did as instructed, and all waited for the echoes to return before Mako began to describe what appeared now in his mind. 'There's a ship out there. A big one, made of metal. It's moving from north to south.'

A dot appeared at the top of Zhebi's glass. It was bigger than the ones that represented their own bodies, as a ship was, and it was moving along a north/south axis, as this ship was.

Fusa looked at the others, urging them with her eyes to interrogate him, but her young companions remained silent. Zhebi surpassed all three of them in physical prowess, and it was clear in the lines of his muscles that he was more powerful too. But he wasn't going to hurt them just because they showed a bit of curiosity.

In the end, she asked it herself. 'Zhebi,' she cheeped, 'who *are* you?'

~

While the sun rose higher into the morning sky, the trio listened as Zhebi recounted what he remembered of his own history.

Fusa struggled at times to follow along. His speech, either because he came from a different part of the ocean or because the events he described had prevented his mind from fully developing, was jarring and awkward. But the story that emerged was coherent enough that, by the time he was finished, the three of them had grasped the essence of his life story.

He was born "across the sea". As a podling, Zhebi and his friends liked to catch cuttlefish along the coast. Playing in the shallows was always great fun – the humans liked to wave, and they sometimes threw fish into the water for them – but as his pod migrated north along the shore, they noticed that something odd had happened on the land, as though some invisible line existed upon it that had created two quite distinct worlds.

Beyond that line, the land folk were different. For a start, their environment had changed: instead of the shiny, tall towers and the long promenades lit up prettily at night, their buildings became shabbier, like they might fall down at any moment. But the creatures themselves had altered too, in a way that was noticeable even to the calves of the pod. The humans north of that invisible line were like their buildings: faded somehow, on the brink of collapse. These ones didn't wave or throw fish – in fact, they'd just as soon take a fish from a dolphin than share one of their own.

One day, when the podlings were mature enough to entertain themselves for an afternoon, Zhebi and his friends encountered a most unusual kind of boat. Normally, boats trailed nets in which shoals of fish and other marine life were caught. This one, however, moved under the water.

Under the water. That was what he said. Fusa wanted to inquire if he'd spoken mistakenly, but Kikuko confirmed that she'd seen something like that once, too: a wide, metal vessel which, to an elderly dolphin whose senses weren't so sharp anymore, must have looked like a very strange whale.

His friends had wanted nothing to do with it. But Zhebi followed the mysterious underwater boat around the bay and out into open water, where he suddenly found himself tangled up in a net.

The next thing he remembered was waking up alone

in a pen. It was so small that there wasn't even room to turn around. Above him, on walkways, humans stomped around, passing their odd language back and forth.

Day after day, Zhebi remained in this pen, becoming numb to the pain of the barbed sticks the humans pricked him with, and half mad with lack of stimulation. It was as though he were dead, only it was worse than being dead. Dead dolphins didn't have to wonder why the life they knew had come to an end.

When the humans pulled him out of his enclosure, that was when he learned that being confined to a tiny box was the better option. They took him *inside* one of their buildings – Fusa recoiled at the very notion of that – and placed him in a tank on the floor. To keep himself calm, he took in as much as he could of his surroundings, noticing how the humans' coverings matched one another's, and how the hats they wore on their furry heads were adorned on the front with a shape like a starfish. But that was just about all he could remember of that, because he'd soon fallen asleep again, and when he woke up, he was sonar-blind.

Thankfully, the pen they returned him to wasn't so confined, and this one they allowed him to leave now and then. Still, it wasn't open water; his new enclosure was merely set within a much bigger expanse.

It was here that the humans played with him. Mako had inquired then if, by played, he meant like hide and seek. And it turned out that was exactly what he meant. For successfully avoiding being sighted by another of the enclosure's dolphins, Zhebi was treated with a fish. But if another dolphin found him too easily in the coral caves, the humans shocked him with a stick that crackled on the end with a kind of lightning.

He got better and better at this game all the time. Which was how he earned his nickname, Zhebi, which meant "hide". Fusa had wanted to know what his real name was if Zhebi was just a nickname, but the poor dolphin had no recollection of what his parents had called him.

The same applied for Zhao, only his nickname meant "seek". The humans housed Zhao in the pen opposite from Zhebi, and his work was different in nature: instead of remaining hidden, he was rewarded for attacking things.

Each time the humans took Zhebi and Zhao out of their pens, it was to fiddle with the devices on their heads. Sometimes they took them off and replaced them, other times they merely probed them with their tools. Once, they ran a kind of rope from it into Zhebi's box, and when they did that the most unusual thing happened: everything he looked at was captured on the box's glass window.

Then, one day, a new activity emerged, and that was when many of the other dolphins started disappearing from the enclosures. The humans had begun killing their pen mates. This they did by attaching an object around their neck and, when the dolphin was in just the place they wanted it to be, the object exploded and blood rained down over the lake.

The sound of the explosions made Zhebi ache each time. But it was also how he and Zhao came to be free, since one day a captive dolphin managed to get back to her enclosure before the humans could make her burst, and she killed them. The explosion caused the gates of the pens to open, and even though Zhao got badly scratched along his side as he squeezed his body past jagged metal, the pair managed to flee.

After many days of swimming, they crossed the western sea and came to the big island. They passed through a strait – Fusa grew excited to realise this would have been the very one she crossed to reach Squid Hood Bay each year – and travelled down the coast. But then the seabed shuddered with a tremendous force, and the ocean pulled them up to the surface momentarily before shoving them back down again. It frightened them both, but they remained focussed on getting as far away as they possibly could from the humans in the west.

Things were going well for them; they were even beginning to relax into the idea that they might finally be free. They found a small inlet near a large human structure and stopped in it to rest. But then the structure exploded, and the inlet flooded with water that was full of impurity.

Of course, Fusa and her companions knew all about that. But Zhebi had then explained to the trio that it was a kind of pollution familiar to he and Zhao. Back west, where they were captive, humans used to sometimes play with objects that turned the water tingly with a similar kind of toxic pollution. One of the other captives even claimed to be able to see it where it hung in patches, describing it, very mysteriously, as a kind of shimmering force.

Ever since the explosion, Zhebi and his friend had grown ill. Zhao, who'd been poisoned by this stuff while in his pen, fared especially badly; as his health worsened, his behaviour started to change. It was as though all the things the humans had done came alive inside his memories, and the aggression they'd encouraged in him now took over.

Late last evening, when Zhao was too exhausted to move, Zhebi had left him in the crevice to find him some fish. But really he knew there was no point.

∽

Fusa now understood the final words poor old Zhao had spoken to Mako. The land dwellers were indeed no friend of dolphins.

Yet as sad a story as his was, she supposed the type of human he'd described wasn't the same as the type she and Mako knew. How could they be? All the ones they'd encountered themselves were kindly and filled with joy. It was like marine life, perhaps. Orca were vicious, brutal beasts. Yet they too were a type of dolphin, who loved their calves and sought out fun.

Kikuko had gone back down to the coastal cave with a quizzical look in her eye, and Mako was taking a moment to rest, so Fusa turned to Zhebi, who was already facing her.

'What is backbone fish?' Zhebi asked.

'The great trout, Moshiri,' replied Fusa. 'The fish-god, on whose enormous spine the entire ocean rests.'

'Why you go to him?'

'Because we need to explain that Mako didn't mean to offend him. We have to plead with Moshiri to settle, because he doesn't know just how much damage he's causing. And then I can go to Squid Hood Bay, and be with my daughter again.'

Zhebi's usually blank face appeared suddenly expressive. 'Where is backbone fish?'

'Excuse me?' cheeped Fusa.

'Moshiri. Backbone fish. Where is he?'

Fusa went suddenly bashful. 'Well... we don't exactly know. But if we keep going west, we'll eventually come to his head.'

Zhebi seemed to lighten somewhat then. 'You mean west coast, of big island.'

'No,' stated Fusa. 'True west. The very edge of the sea.'

Zhebi's eyes widened. He began to thrash in the water, causing Fusa to dart around to the other side of Mako.

What was going on? Could it have been his illness? As Zhebi said, Zhao had lost control of himself in his last days – and Mako still had the bruises to prove it. But this wasn't the symptom of some sickness they were seeing. It was agitation of the most normal kind: Zhebi had become suddenly very afraid.

Fusa moved closer to him. 'What's wrong?'

'Fusa and friends cannot go across sea. Moshiri not there. Only human. Human will put you in pen.'

Fusa looked first at Mako, whose eyes were clouded now with distress, then back at Zhebi. 'I'm sorry,' she whistled tenderly. 'But we must try. The trout-god has hardly begun to move yet. I think, when he's finished, there'll be nothing left. And I can't bear the thought I did nothing to try and stop it.'

Right then, Kikuko burst through the surface. 'Pardon me. I just ruined a moment between you, didn't I?' She turned to Zhebi. 'Sorry, Muscles. Could I borrow you for a while?'

Zhebi gave his beak a confirmatory sway, and disappeared with Kikuko back below.

Mako pulled in closer to Fusa, and looked at her with sad eyes. 'You had the vision last night again, didn't you, auntie?'

Fusa cast her gaze downwards, embarrassed.

'I was going to wake you, auntie, but I felt I shouldn't. Was it the same again?'

'More or less.'

'The boats, and the horrid noises, and the terrified dolphins?'

Fusa nodded.

'And you really think Moshiri is trying to show you something?'

'I do.'

'What, though?'

'I don't know, Mako.'

'Was there anything new about the dream?'

'Some things are a little bit clearer,' said Fusa. 'But it's still all very strange.'

Mako's eyes narrowed. He appeared suddenly agitated. 'Was I there, auntie?'

Fusa turned away. It felt wrong to lie to somebody who'd cared for her as much as Mako had. He was like family, and deserved better. But at the same time, there seemed little point causing him needless distress. 'No,' she said. 'They're just strangers.'

Mako, who was straining to hold back his emotion, was eventually overcome and let out a piercing quack. 'The western sea sounds like a bad place, auntie,' he said. 'We're going to be in a lot of danger.'

'We are, Mako.'

'And do you think Moshiri will hear me this time? If we find him, I mean?'

'I don't know. But what choice do we have? We can either do what we feel is right, or allow the whole world to suffer.'

'That's no choice at all,' whistled Mako.

Fusa was about to commend her friend for being so brave when Kikuko and Zhebi reappeared at the surface with a most surprising sight. Perched gently between Kikuko's teeth was the box that had been fitted to Zhao's head, its straps swaying in the current. 'Here,' she clicked. 'It might not be perfect, but it's better than nothing.'

Fusa recoiled. 'You want to put that thing on me?!'

'Why let it go to waste?' asked Kikuko. 'It might give you half a chance of becoming independent, if you can figure out how to use it.'

Mako smiled broadly and helped Kikuko negotiate the straps around Fusa's upper jaw. On her left side, Zhebi appeared overcome with tiredness. Recounting his history had obviously exhausted the poor thing.

'What about you, Zhebi?' asked Fusa. 'What will you do now?'

'Zhebi stay here.'

Fusa gave a cheep of surprise. 'Here? For how long?'

He replied with blankness. 'As long as it takes.'

The trio looked at one another. 'As long as what takes?'

'Zhebi can remember time before human take us. Pod

leader, she say dolphin go to good place after life finish. Zhebi wait now for Zhao to begin journey from ocean to sky. Zhebi hope sonar work good for Fusa.'

Kikuko spouted and turned to her companions. 'Come on,' she clicked. 'If the currents favour us, we'll be at the strait this time tomorrow.'

With a beat of their tails, the trio pulled away. But just as they set off on their voyage south, Zhebi called out after them.

'Fusa and friends, take care. Backbone fish not in west. Only human.'

16

THE HERDING

MAKO WAS SLEEPING PEACEFULLY when a rumble below made the seameadow quiver. His spirits, which over the course of the morning had been bright, were cast at once into shadow.

The rumbling soon faded, but even while he chased some spidery cuttlefish, he kept one apprehensive eye on the seabed, convinced that the entire sheet of rock was about to split apart.

Nearby, at the surface, Kikuko was floating belly up. Snow, falling in a constant, though weak, flurry, was landing directly upon her, and she was fascinated by it. He sent a whistle up. 'I still can't believe you don't have snow in the south.'

Kikuko spat a jet of water up into the air. 'Weep for us, pretty boy. All we have is plenty of food and clear waters every day. My parents told me about this *snow* stuff, but it's the first time I've seen it with my own eyes.'

With a burst of power, she leapt up out of the surface and caught some flakes in her mouth before reentering the shallows. 'I thought it might taste like krill,' she said. 'But it doesn't taste of anything.'

Fusa came across the meadow to join them. 'Are there

fields like this where you come from? I just love the seagrass.'

'Sure,' clicked Kikuko. 'But if you like these, wait until you see the reefs in the south. They're amazing. Whole gardens of coral. Every type you can imagine growing together in great clumps. They're losing some of their brightness now the water's getting warmer, but they're really pretty.'

Mako wondered if the odd prickling stuff that sullied Snow Crab Lagoon had anything to do with that, and, once again, he fluttered with angst. But he forced his mind to stay focussed on the future. 'When Moshiri forgives me,' he chirped, 'that's where I'm going. The coral gardens. And I'm going to play all day, and eat when I want, and when I have calves of my own I'm going to tell them all about the time I upset the great backbone fish of the world and how I put everything right again. They'll call me brave Mako, the saviour of the ocean, who saved the world from splitting apart and stopped that horrid impurity from infecting everything.'

Kikuko gave a musical squeal. 'You are a pretty boy. But you've got the brains of a sea cucumber. "*Mako the brave, saviour of the ocean?*" More like: "*Mako the big-head, bringer of trouble.*" Now come on,' she chuckled, turning to Fusa, 'the sooner you figure out how to use that machine, the sooner we can be on our way. We're getting near the bridge now. You two will be through to the other side of the island in no time.'

Fusa appeared suddenly glum. When she spoke, it was with a beak that dipped downwards. 'What about then?'

'Then,' replied Kikuko, 'you two will be away across the sea.'

'Not us. You. What will you do?'

'I'll be joining my parents in Lobster Claw Harbour, and then we'll journey on to Oyster Cove. But you already know that, don't you, auntie? Now, are you going to be brave and test out your new toy by yourself, or are you just going to waste the morning here with us?'

Mako held an intense gaze on Fusa. Hope was so rare in his heart during these trying times that he almost didn't recognise it, but there was a chance their encounter with Zhebi and Zhao had changed everything. Conceivably, Fusa was now on the brink of regaining some independence, and this, in turn, would give him more of his own time back, freeing him up to wander and play and, when the fancy struck him, to perform clever tricks for the amusement of the ever-affectionate humans.

He let up a bubble of air. 'Kikuko is right, auntie. You can't practice while we're here to help you out.'

'But what if—'

'What if orca come in for you again? We won't let them. Kikuko and me will keep watch while you navigate in the shallower waters. Any sign of trouble, and we'll get you.'

Fusa looked across, her eyes a jumble of worry and panic – and determination. She gave a nod and pulled away, and as she vanished, Mako felt his heart swell with pride.

∽

In the bright upper depths, Fusa marvelled whenever returning clicks flashed upon her screen. The future had seemed so very murky, but now, like the dots on the glass, it was snapping into clear focus. With this device, she was going to survive. Her machine meant freedom itself.

Now, she could lead Mako to Moshiri, rather than the other way around. And after she'd proudly delivered her plea and made the trout-god understand it all, she could begin the long swim back to Squid Hood Bay, choosing any route she fancied.

It was just a shame her good fortune had come at the

expense of poor Zhao. Taking his box would never have occurred to her, but Kikuko was right: they couldn't let it go to waste. A rusted gadget on a dolphin's bare bones helped nobody.

Firing a sonar beam from her head directly out in front of her, a dot, wide and narrow, appeared. It was a ship. Wasn't it?

Thrashing her tail hard to catch the thing as it passed, her blood whooshed with excitement on confirming the sighting. This machine was a poor replica of the sonar she'd been born with, but she'd get better and better all the time at reading the dots on its screen. With a little luck, it might even allow her to distinguish friend from foe – and what a difference *that* would make to her life!

Confident now that she was able to read navigation information, Fusa went back to the others, who greeted her with a cheer of quacks and clicks. They swallowed down a hearty meal of amberjack and squid – competently echolocated by Fusa – and set off.

Side by side, the trio swam slowly against the currents as they went around the headlands. Then, when late afternoon had become evening, they followed the inclining continental rock back to the waters of the coastal shelf, where, to Fusa's delight, Mako devised a game.

'You tell us what you see,' he whistled, 'and we'll tell you if you're right.'

Fusa chirruped with pleasure. 'What do I get if I am?'

'You get to see your daughter again, auntie. And pretty boy and me get to stop worrying about you all the time.' It wasn't quite what Fusa was hoping for, but Kikuko's answer was fair.

Holding herself above the surface in a spyhop, Fusa fired her scans at the shore and began relaying the information. 'It's busy with activity. There are a lot of boats over there. The marine life seems denser, too. I'm getting a lot of blips.'

'It *is* busy,' agreed Kikuko, with just a hint of concern on her voice.

Mako, though, was jubilant. 'I knew you'd figure it out! Just think,' he quacked, performing a tight somersault beneath the waves, 'you'll be independent in no time at all!'

'No longer your problem, you mean,' chirped Fusa, poking him playfully with her beak.

Mako gave a giggle. 'Old Mako, explorer of the western sea! Venturing anywhere the current takes him!'

Just then, the low sun was blocked by a cloud made heavy with rain, and Fusa gave a sudden squeal of dismay.

'What is it?' said the others, gliding up either side of her.

'The dots on my machine just blinked off. I'm blind again!'

Mako twisted in closer. 'Remember what Zhebi said? It's the cloud, auntie. The machine won't work unless there's sunlight on it.'

As if to prove his point, the cloud then rolled away from the sun's face, and dots once again began to show.

Fusa let out a soft whine. 'It's very dim, though, isn't it?'

'It'll be night soon,' said Kikuko. 'Perhaps we ought to rest here?'

Mako gave a creak of disappointment.

'What is it, pretty boy?'

'Nothing,' said Mako. 'It's just, I sort of hoped we'd reach the bridge today and start the journey through to the island's west side. I didn't like the rumbling in the seagrass meadow earlier. That was Moshiri. He's getting restless again. The last thing we need is for him to spit out the ocean like he did before.'

Kikuko flicked her beak dismissively. 'I'm sure the trout-god won't mind waiting a while longer to smash the world apart. Besides, it'll give Fusa more confidence with her machine. And that's in your interest, isn't it, old "Saviour of the Ocean"?'

Mako rolled over and shyly chuckled, then spat a jet of water up into the dusky sky. 'I don't know *what* you're talking about. Fine, let's rest. But no more stops until we make it to the strait. I can't wait to see the bridge the humans built! Is it really as big as you say?'

'It's a bridge, Mako,' clicked Kikuko. 'It's no more or no less interesting than anything else in their world. Now, let's close an eye. We have a big day ahead of us.'

'Don't even talk about that,' whistled Fusa, sadly. 'I can't bear the thought you'll be leaving us so soon.'

∽

Fusa and Kikuko were both sleeping, but within Mako, a temptation was burning.

Boats were close by, and he wondered what business was occupying their riders. Their kind seemed to work so very hard. It was never play that kept them busy, always some kind of toil. Perhaps these ones might like a dolphin for company? They were always so amused when he imitated the way they walked.

His stomach growled as he considered the fish they'd throw to him, and he turned to head off for them. No sooner had he pulled away, however, than a train of clicks reached him from behind.

'Where are you going?'

Kikuko had been waiting to catch him in the act.

'Aren't you hungry?' asked Mako. 'I'm dying for a snack.'

'There's anchovies over there in a baitball. Go get those.'

'I thought I'd see what the humans are having.'

'Do I really need to remind you that it was because of your wandering that we nearly lost Fusa?'

'Will you relax? You sound like my mother. Look how

many boats there are around here. Every one of them is loaded up with fish for us, I bet. Look there, closer to that cove. That's a dolphin herd. They've got the right idea. Why waste energy when there's humans around to share a treat!'

'I'm not going near them, pretty boy. You heard poor Zhao's last words.'

'Zhao was talking about some other creature. Humans aren't all the same. The ones on this ocean love me. You can ask Fusa.'

'Don't even think about waking her! Today's been exhausting for her.'

'But they do, though! They're always so pleased to see me. And I *always* get a treat. If you don't want to come closer, that's fine. But just watch. You'll soon see there's nothing to worry about.'

The look in Kikuko's eye suddenly flashed from mild annoyance to deep concern. 'Zhao wasn't the only one to warn us, though,' she said. 'My parents did, too. Remember? "*Humans are the most dangerous creatures you will ever encounter*".'

'Humans have saved my life twice already,' quacked Mako. 'And they've given Fusa her sight back, too. Just watch, will you? This trick of mine is the best.' And with that, Mako swam off.

The boats were arranged in a crescent shape. With a big smile, he came up out of the surface at the middle vessel, holding his body out of the water to mimic the clumsy way they walked.

But the riders didn't wave. And they didn't throw a fish.

'Great trick,' said Kikuko, whose voice travelled to him through the ocean from afar. 'Got any others?'

Mako dropped back into the water. How embarrassing! Perhaps a different trick was in order? Speeding beneath the boat to its other side, he took a big run up and leapt out into a perfect somersault.

The humans were smiling now; Mako held his gaze upon them expectantly. But he soon noticed that their's weren't happy smiles, as such. One of the individuals lifted a sharp-looking stick – for a moment, Mako wondered if it was a different kind of snack – but another one intervened and pulled his arm back down again with a yell: 'No! Too handsome.'

Mako turned back to face Kikuko, ready to begin gloating. But then he noticed something odd. The arc of the boats had drawn closer together. Now just within the shore's natural harbour, the boats were surrounding him on both sides, manoeuvring ever closer to the cove.

Racing across the seabed below him, at maximum speed, was Kikuko. Whatever was she up to?

Mako turned to face the shore, and threw scans towards the deepest recess of the cove, where two high cliffs stood facing each other, adjoined by long lengths of something delicate and billowing.

His returning echoes revealed a large number of dolphins making their way out towards him. Then his eyes picked them up, and suddenly the ocean was a frenzy of clicking.

The dolphins from the cove were in a state of panic.

Mako called out to them. 'What's wrong?' But the dolphins scattered without answering.

Suddenly, Kikuko was back in his field of vision, down in the folds of the seabed. 'Mako!' she whistled, her voice as tense as it was urgent. 'Come deep! Listen to me! You have to come deep!'

'Why, Kikuko? What's going on?'

'Come deep! They're lowering their nets, Mako! Can't you see? The humans have herded those dolphins!'

He craned his neck to the left. A pale-skinned calf was becoming separated from its mother, unleashing an anguished squeal from the cow. Kikuko went across to the tiny thing and shunted him down to the lower depths. 'Mako!' she cried out again. 'You need to dive! Now!'

Mako poked his head above the surface to see the humans. They were now wearing grins which stretched from one ear to the other, and one of them was holding aloft a fish in the dusky evening sky. Mako gave a chirrup of delight. 'I told you, Kikuko! They *do* love me!'

The fish came hurtling through the sky. Mako caught it in his open jaws. He sent a whistle over to wake Fusa up – she so loved to watch him winning snacks from the land folk – but to his surprise, Fusa was heading out north from the shore, thrashing her tail flukes like her life depended on it. 'What's she doing?' he called down to Kikuko.

'Exactly as I told her to – she's getting away from the cliffs! And you need to, too! Right now!'

Kikuko and the calf hurried to the surface, now beyond the tightened line of boats. Why was she being so rude? She was making no attempt at all to be friendly with the humans. In fact, she was swimming away south with the calf on her back, thrashing as hard and as fast as he'd ever seen her go. One of the boats was going after her. Even though her behaviour had been so poor, they wanted to give her a fish, too.

Mako, who was now closer to the shore than he realised, focussed his eyes on the lengths of fabric hanging in the sky between the cliffs, which rippled in the wind. Hadn't Fusa said something about such things? The dolphins were now directly underneath these coverings, and were emitting shrill, panicked, whistles.

But it wasn't only panic.

It was actual pain.

Mako's heart began to pound.

Perhaps Kikuko was right. This might not have been such a good idea after all.

He dived, but already he was so close to the shore that the waters here lacked any real depth.

Turning back to the boats, he saw that their nets were now fastened to one another, forming a long, unbroken barrier which was trailing along the actual seabed.

And when he saw that, he realised the truth of the situation:

The humans had trapped him.

17

SLAUGHTER AT BLOOD COVE

THERE WOULD COME A TIME, perhaps, when Mako would forget what he experienced in the cove that evening.

It was hard to imagine now, but some future might just exist in which his every waking thought didn't revolve around it. He'd be foraging among coral beds, maybe, nosing around in the sediment for flatfish, only to realise that his mind had simply been at rest awhile. Or it might be that he was playing with his grandchildren, lost in their leaping contest as he watched them soaring in the sky, a moment of stillness in a mind sullied by his trauma.

That time may – if he was very, very lucky – come. Tonight, though, there would be no peace at all. Tonight, every thought and every sight – all sounds, all memories, every sensation, dream, fear and regret – was tainted with the savagery of a massacre. And he knew, as certainly as he knew the tides will ebb and flow, that this experience was becoming a part of him, as permanent as the scar along Zhao's side.

It began the moment the boats sealed off the cove.

Acting on the sliver of hope still alive inside him, Mako swam the short distance over to the north cliff. But that towering wall of stone, which rose right out from the shallows, offered no caves or tunnels to retreat into.

He twisted sharply in an attempt to investigate the south cliff, but by now the humans had turned the open waters of the cove into an enclosed pool. The densely packed horde of bodies – mostly dolphin, but a few whales, too – blocked his way to it.

Humans were jumping over the sides of their boats and splashing down onto the sand below their feet. In the odd skins that wrapped their heads and bodies, they appeared curiously sleek, almost like seals. Yet no seal Mako ever saw behaved like this.

Only now he was part of the crush did it occur to him to quiz the others. Pressed against a cow, he whistled desperately: 'Why are they doing this?'

Blankly, the cow returned an answer. 'They're hunters, boy. We're their prey.'

He let out a squeal. 'Humans *eat* dolphin?' He tried to thrash, but with the space around him much diminished, there was nowhere to move into.

The cow began to speak again, but with the noise now ringing out it was impossible to hear what she said. He rolled his body around, hoping to catch a glimpse of the source of the commotion, wondering if this was another of Moshiri's sly attempts to get at him.

The humans had lowered metal posts into the water, which they were striking with heavy metal tools. If their intention was to overwhelm the captured animals, it was very effective: the sound carried through the water with such deafening force that Mako was losing the ability to even think.

The cow beside him gave a terrified wail as a pair of hands emerged from over the side of the boat and seized her around the tail. 'Let me go!' she screamed, but the instant the human had a hold of her, a second one jumped overboard and took hold of her beak, clasping it shut between his powerful fingers.

'What are you doing?' quacked Mako. 'She can't speak! Let her go!'

They did no such thing, however. Keeping her constrained, one of the humans then held up a long, thin pole tipped with a sharp point, which he thrust down into her with all his might. He gave this a twist, then wrenched it back out again, prompting a torrent of blood to flow down the cow's eyes and into the shallow water.

Mako pushed away as hard as he could from this terrifying scene – her blood was in his own eyes too, now – but he quickly realised there was simply no room at all to get away.

Now, it was just a matter of waiting for his turn.

The humans manoeuvred a piece of cloth beneath the lifeless cow, which was fastened on either end to a wooden pole. With this, they hoisted her up out of the water and threw her onto the boat, where she landed out of sight. 'Are you alright?' Mako called up, but she didn't answer.

A male dolphin was now beside him, a bull with a short snout. As before, Mako quizzed the individual, but the dolphin, whose eyes were misted over in a kind of stunned blankness, made no noise at all. Even when the spear was plunged into him, the bull remained silent, and as his blood rushed out into the cove Mako emitted a creak of fright.

A whale was next. Then another dolphin, this one with the appearance of a juvenile orca. Into their bodies the pointed pole went, and out spilled their blood. The waters grew opaque and foamy as the humans hoisted the slaughtered out from the cove and into their boats.

For a brief few moments, things got a little better. One of the humans called out to his friends — 'Too much blood!' — and the next dolphins to have the spear driven into them barely shed any blood at all; directly after puncturing them, the humans did something that stopped it from flowing. One of the speared dolphins managed to get his jaws apart to speak to Mako. 'I'm drowning!' he spluttered, then fell silent.

The tools continued to strike the metal poles as the boats' propellers whirred. But not even this was enough to block out the anguish of the dolphins, whose cries and squawks rose up to meet the long strips of fabric blocking out the sky.

Frantic with the trauma of the slaying, Mako turned his focus inward. When the spike eventually came down into him, he didn't want to be peering into the eyes of a human.

His mother's face appeared. Why had he made things so very hard for her? She'd asked him nicely to behave himself, and he ignored her. Then she tried to reason with him, but he shrugged it off as nagging. Even when she meted out a punishment for him, he continued to pile strife upon her. And yet she'd always looked so adoringly upon him. No mother was as proud of her calf as she'd been of him. He was the most handsome member of the whole pod, she said.

If only he could tell her now how sorry he truly was.

With a frenzied thrash, one more dolphin was pulled out from the cove, and suddenly hands were grasping onto Mako's own tail.

The humans were ready for him.

He shut his eyes: he was with his father now, strand fishing.

Human fingers clutched tightly around him, and he felt himself being hoisted towards the boat's rear. He thrashed, churning the waters violently once again.

Further inward he went. He saw his friends, surfing the wakes of passing boats, laughing as they misjudged the strength of the waves and went tumbling back into the water.

A different set of hands now clamped shut his jaws. How rough they felt against his sleek skin!

Still, Mako looked inside his mind. He saw Fusa,

brave auntie Fusa, who couldn't have tried any harder to warn him against this. How sorry he was to have doubted her.

The human at his front side held aloft his spear. Mako looked away. He didn't want to see the thing come down into him.

With his last thoughts, he willed Fusa onwards. May she reach the great backbone fish. May her protest stir Moshiri's heart, help him know the terrible pain he'd inflicted. May the name of his auntie be forever known among all the pods of the ocean.

Mako braced himself for the sharp pain of the spear. But the human stopped right before he thrust it down. 'Hang on,' he said. 'This is a pretty one.'

'Contender for display?'

'I'd say so. Won't fetch a price like that escaped albino, though. Still, let's bag him.'

Why were the humans delaying? Wondering if the deed may already have been done, Mako let his eyes come open. He hadn't crossed over into the spirit world: he was still here in the cove.

With a little more space to wriggle into, Mako was able to twist himself slightly to see behind. By now, the majority of the herded marine creatures were out of the water, but still the humans went on slaying those whose hearts beat with life.

A human on the boat was running a net over Mako's tail flukes, as though trying to catch him. What a waste of time, when here he was, already in their hands! The fine mesh of the net soon wrapped his body completely, and a human was promptly tying off the front, sealing him inside and bringing to mind the covering the folk at the shrine had used to lower him safely into the river.

How to make sense of it? Humans were so kind! Yet what he was witnessing now was cruelty on a scale that was unimaginable.

A contraption winched him out of the water, and he

found himself rolling over the edge of their boat, into the soft blanket of lifeless dolphins that covered the floor. He wasn't the last to be thrown into the boat, though: two more of his kind, their spear wounds plugged with wooden pegs, came crashing down on top of him, and with that the boat's propellers began whirring more forcefully.

The boat moved to the cove's beach. Eventually, everything went quiet. No more agonised squeals came from the cove. Just human voices, chittering on the shore.

With all marine life now in the boats, the massacre had come to an end.

Dull thuds began to sound overboard as slain dolphins were tossed onto the hard earth. Then, with just Mako left in the boat, it was driven up a river that fed into this cove of death.

The human at the back of the boat shouted out. 'Contender!'

'What is it?'

'Bottlenose. Male. Juvenile. I think it's the show-off. Any pens left?'

'One. It was meant for that albino calf though.'

'You still didn't get him? Pity. Now, winch this guy out, would you? I need to get warm.'

From out of the sky, a metal hand came down and took hold of the net bag enclosing Mako. He felt himself rise into the air, then, when he'd been swung across to the right, he began to fall back down again.

He lay motionless on a walkway that stood beside a floating pen. Doing his best to stay calm, he thrashed once as a human swiped a sharp blade of metal across the net. For a moment, Mako was liberated from the rope, but he barely got a second to enjoy it, since the same human then shunted him with his foot, sending him into the pen with a splash.

Glad to be back in water, Mako wasted no time investigating the walls surrounding him. They were solid, but apparently low enough to leap over. He went back to give himself a good run-up, but knew as soon as he left the surface that they were just the right height to keep him trapped inside.

Next, he dived. Although the river that flowed into the cove was deep, a thick rope floor prevented him from accessing it.

There was no mistake about it, then.

He was captive.

～

The sun was already high when the noisy boat brought humans back to the walkway.

Mako lifted his body out of the water to spyhop, but the height of the surrounding walls obstructed his sonar signals and bounced them straight back.

He went to the bottom, and lay on the netted floor. From here, it was possible to get click trains out into the river, and to receive the returning echoes – he wasn't *completely* shut off from the world beyond his pen.

But it didn't help him read what was happening up on the walkway. Nor to catch the fish swimming boldly by. His stomach gave a grumble, and he winced to recall the account of his grandfather, who got to eat only when his captors said he could.

As the humans passed their monotonous words back and forth, all Mako could do was listen, and hope. They'd singled him out by keeping him alive, but now, perhaps, the time had come for them to finish the job they started in the bloody waters of the cove.

'Good news from the north.'

'The power station is under control? Thank goodness! But how?'

'They cooled the nuclear reactors by pumping in tonnes of water from the ocean.'

'Excellent! But what will they do with all that contaminated water?'

'That's tomorrow's problem.'

The unseen humans carried on this way until a new set of feet soon joined them on the walkway.

'Another one for the pens? Who's this?'

'Long-finned pilot whale. Male, juvenile.'

'Great! We have a buyer lined up for one of them.'

'Who?'

'Ocean Planet Aquarium, Dubai.'

'Put him in, then.'

'Where? The pens are full.'

'Drop him in with the last one. Mr Show-off.'

Mako heard the metal hand whirr into life again. Then, as he pointlessly strained to listen, he fell into shadow, as though a dark raincloud had just passed in front of the sun – which was very nearly the case, since, in the sky above him, was a whale.

Mako flicked his tail and moved to the corner. This was a big boy coming in, and he didn't much fancy getting squashed beneath him.

With the whale now lowered into the pen, Mako caught the eyes of a human, sparking a conflict inside him. He was hungry, and here was an opportunity – perhaps the only one he'd get – for food.

Though he wanted nothing more to do with humans, there was really no choice in the matter. He made an upward thrust and came out of the water, where he held his body high. The humans looked in his direction – this was going well! – so Mako made a good show of "walking" along the surface. The whale, however, was right in his way, and Mako collided into him and fell back into the water, and the land creatures vanished.

Mako gave a sideways glance at his new pen-mate. What an odd-looking creature he was! The whale wasn't fully grown, yet he was already so long. His dorsal fin was curved back on itself, rather than upright, and his tail flukes were wide. But most interesting to Mako was the whale's face. Short and broad – he didn't really have a beak – his rounded head opened wide at the front to reveal two rows of perfectly-aligned teeth. His eyes were marked by an obvious sorrow, and although he shyly avoided looking at Mako directly, he could tell the whale was a friendly sort.

Mako performed a flip in the air. It worked exactly as he'd intended: the whale came out of the corner. 'I'm Mako,' he whistled.

'I am Roopam.'

Although the language was intelligible, the whale's voice was quite different from a dolphin's.

'Where are you from, Roopam?'

'West,' replied the whale.

'That's where we were going! Do you know Moshiri?'

'Moshiri?'

'The great backbone fish of the world. His enormous head can be found across the sea on the other side of this island. At the western edge of the world. My friend and I are going to see him. Hopefully he won't eat me.'

The whale gave a shy chuckle.

'What's funny, Roopam?'

'The western edge is that way,' said the whale, sending a sonar beam towards the endless open ocean to the east. 'Across the expanse. Is your friend a blue whale? I hope so, or you're going to be disappointed. Such a journey is beyond all but the very largest whales.'

Mako fell into a quiet gloom. This was hardly the news he'd hoped for.

Within the confines of the pen, he swam circles around its edge. It was only just long enough to allow for a single burst of speed in any one direction. Yet it was better for Mako than it was for Roopam, whose body took up over half its length.

Mako watched as Roopam investigated his surroundings and assessed his predicament. The whale was coming to the same conclusion; discovering that he was now a captive creature deflated his spirits even further.

Only when the sky had bruised with the full darkness of night did Roopam speak again.

'Where is your family?'

'I left them in the north,' whistled Mako.

'Why?'

He was just about to explain, but a sudden rumbling in the bed below answered for him.

'That's why.'

Roopam tilted his bulbous head to the side, unsure of Mako's meaning.

'I did bad things. I even stole from Moshiri. Now the trout-god is angry with me. It wasn't safe for me to stay near my pod.'

The whale took his time digesting this information, then drooped sadly.

'What about you?' said Mako. 'Where's your family?'

'Gone. The leader of our pod was made sick by foul water north of here. It affected her mind. She led the whole pod onto the shore. They died.'

An icy jolt hit Mako in the heart. 'That water. Did it make your skin feel prickly and your eyes burn?'

'Yes. And it tasted strange, like something metal. Have you been in it, too?'

'I was there when it happened. At Snow Crab Lagoon.'

'When what happened?'

Mako closed his eyes as a flash of pain ran along his spine.

How very foolish he'd been.

'Humans,' he clicked. 'Their buildings burst apart and sent smoke high into the sky. Then this horrid stuff began to poison us. I thought Moshiri had done it, but now I wonder if the water was fouled because of their business.'

Roopam kept an intense eye on Mako a while, then twisted away to face the back walkway, from which a tall, thin figure was casting a shadow into the pen.

Mako kept his eyes on the land creatures too, who appeared to be studying the imprisoned pair. While they went to and fro across the walkways, they made their funny sounds.

'So?' said one. 'Any sign of the albino?'

'Not yet,' said the other.

'That was a twenty million-yen price tag we let get away.'

'Relax. We've got people trailing him. And the female who took him.'

18

THE MOURNING OCEAN

THE WORST NIGHT of Fusa's life was, at long last, nearing its end.

So rapidly had she fled on Kikuko's command, she'd simply swum off, out into the expanse. But the sun had fallen fast, and her machine blinked off, and with her location a mystery to her, she was left to suffer the dark hours lost and alone, hanging below the waves in a state of alertness, ready to bolt.

It passed frightfully. From out of the abyss, tormented groans rose and fell. These odd lowing sounds were so distant she wondered if she were going mad. Every kind of anguish existed in her lonely mind – not least the matter of where her young friends had got to – so why shouldn't it have dredged up such harrowing calls?

With the nearing of dawn, the eerie sounds began to change. While the first of them had come in on a deep frequency, and lasted just a moment, here at the transition between night and day, the pitch was going from a low note to a high, elongated one.

The faintest of smiles grew on Fusa's mouth. Her fears had all been for nothing — the travellers in the deep were just whales! Yet something had clearly come into their world against their wishes, and they howled and bawled with a mournfulness that was contagious.

By the time the great groans of the whales had grown distant enough to be lost to the din of the current, the crown of the sun was peeking over the horizon and her machine, finally, bleeped into life. 'Yes!' she cheeped to nobody, before firing out a long click train to her left side.

Chasing crude sonar returns, Fusa banked sharply, and soon arrived at a stretch of coast, hopeful that she'd soon find Mako and Kikuko hanging together. To her surprise, the waters here were ruined: all that resided in these parts now was a vast litter of debris.

She spyhopped to see fires burning on the shore, on what once was a promenade. The colossal surge had devastated these human habitations: many of their things were upside down where they lay scattered. The territory of these poor beings had all but ceased to exist.

Although she'd have liked to remain where she was in these shallows, she knew they were inhospitable to prey species, so Fusa tracked the line of the sea wall in the hope of finding food. Her sonar machine began to bleep once again when the opaque surf grew gradually less murky, and she followed its signal until her eyes picked up a plump pair of barracuda with their backs to her.

Distracted by their own meal – they were pulling chunks away from the carcass of some animal floating face-down in the water – Fusa darted in to grab the larger fish. The second barracuda sped away the moment her ambush was revealed, but she gave chase and, with her superior pace, was able to knock it off course during the pursuit. With its sense of direction momentarily disrupted, she took it in her beak and reunited it with his friend.

As the sun made its way up a frozen sky, Fusa watched the echoes carefully as they bounced back to her device. A large dot moving along a straight path indicated a shipping lane out in the currents. She wondered if Mako might be out there with the boat, riding in the wake of its bow waves. That would just be typical of him!

To Fusa's frustration, the screen on her device began to act erratically. Though the light in the sky was pale and flat, it seemed plenty bright enough to power her machine. It must be faulty; what other explanation could there be for a lone dot which was there one moment, faintly visible in the folds of the depths, and gone the next? She made a quick dive to scrutinise the shelf with her own two eyes.

As it sloped away, the rock began to scar with long depressions. It was just the kind of environment where she'd found Zhebi hiding. It was possible he was down there now, but this wasn't the time to check.

Right now, the only thing that mattered was rejoining her friends.

~

All day she'd searched, yet nowhere along the coastline had Fusa seen a single sign of Mako and Kikuko.

She wasn't giving up yet, though. Not while there was still light in the sky. The sun was now touching the bottom of the cliffs where they towered ahead of her, as though sitting to rest before making its final descent over the horizon, and very soon, her machine was going to fall silent.

From a spyhop a safe distance away, Fusa was watching a fleet of fishing boats. They were fanned out in an arc and, as they'd done last evening, were tightening as they pushed their way back between the cliffs of a narrow cove.

Her eyes fixated on the sheets of fabric quivering distantly in the breeze, rippling lengths so like the ones in the visions beamed into her sleeping mind by the god of the seas and storms.

Defying the instinct to stay back, Fusa edged slowly ahead. Smaller blips now appeared on her screen. Unlike the controlled, steady movement of the boats, these ones skittered, as though in a state of panic.

Still she crept closer, until the dots grew more defined. Then, with a shock of terror, she saw that they were dolphins. Just like in her sleeping vision, they were crying out in fear and pain.

Kikuko had been so quick in commanding her to flee last night that Fusa had no chance to observe what was happening. But now she saw it all clearly:

Humans were wrangling the dolphins into the shallows of the cove.

She let out a squeal.

Mako and Kikuko had been *hunted* by the land creatures!

Her heart flushed cold. She ached to approach the cove, to be certain there was nothing she could do to bring her friends back. Yet revealing her presence to the humans would see to it that she got captured herself.

Only the upper half of the sun was visible now, a jellyfish hood peeping over the land. The image on her screen dimmed; within moments, she would be plunged into another night of vulnerability. And there could be no more vulnerable a spot than right here on the edge of something so utterly ghastly that she couldn't fully believe it was real.

She had to leave, at once.

Thrashing her tail, Fusa took off to the north. She swam straight a while, then came in on a diagonal approach towards a shore indented with bays. Any of these would do for the night, but while there was still enough light for her screen to display her returning echoes, she was compelled onwards.

Taking as much air as she could into her lungs, Fusa

dived into a valley, its sides covered in softly swaying vegetation. Down the slope she went, into the gloaming, until her machine blinked off when she reached a seagrass meadow.

Hovering vertically, she took in her surroundings while the dim dusk allowed it, and settled her heart rate. Here was as good a place as any for a night's rest — near enough to fresh air, yet tucked away from predators and humans. What was more, a thick layer of sediment carpeted the bottom, in which flatfish would almost certainly be hiding.

With her left eye shut, the right side of her brain powered down. A few minutes passed in which her thoughts went quiet, and for just the briefest of moments she achieved a state of something resembling relaxation, until a flash among the swaying grass caught her right eye.

She woke. Remaining perfectly still, Fusa fixed her gaze on the meadow. It wasn't a dream: something was moving inside it.

And it was watching her.

Letting her jaws come open to signal aggression, Fusa waited for the spy to make its move, but it did its best to remain out of sight.

Only the tone of its skin was visible. It was bright like the snow covering the hills above the waves. Might it be food? She'd intended to wait until after she'd rested to snuffle around in the sediment, but if some foolish thing had misjudged her ability to snatch a snack, it was about to pay with its life.

A single swish of her tail flukes sent her creeping forward. With the aquatic world now all but dark, the bright pallor of this lurking entity was the only visible thing in the whole meadow.

Forward she went, ready at any moment to lunge. Then, just a heartbeat from thrashing her tail and attacking, she felt an almighty slap across her head and the frantic outcry of a newly-arrived dolphin.

'You stay away from him!'

Stunned by the slap, Fusa reeled as she span.

A familiar voice came through in a click. 'Auntie? Is that you? I'm so sorry!'

Fusa let her dorsal fin do its job, and was soon righted again. Seeing Kikuko's face, she gave a squeal of emotion. 'You're alive!' She raced forward to feel the girl's body against her own, but just then a chuckling within the seagrass startled her ear. Immediately, she assumed it was Mako. But the voice was too infantile. 'Who's that?'

Kikuko gave a whistle. 'Come, Kiyo. Come and meet auntie Fusa.'

Emerging from out of the swaying grass, giggling with glee at the scene he'd just witnessed, was a small calf, who went straight to Kikuko's side.

Fusa was confounded. What was going on? Who was this? And why did he seem so familiar to her?

'Humans are looking for this calf,' Kikuko clicked, anticipating the flurry of questions ready to fly from Fusa. 'They've been chasing us around all day. I just left him a moment to check that the boats had finally gone into the cove and when I came back and saw you, I thought you might be about to attack him. I didn't know it was you, though, Fusa.'

'But who is he?'

Kikuko looked at the calf with a sorrow that was unfathomable. 'Kiyo survived the massacre. The humans up at the cove are slaughtering anything they can capture. They got his whole family.'

Though no less marked with melancholy, the girl's eyes then took on a guilty quality, and she looked shyly away.

'What is it, Kikuko?'

As though the entire ocean had grown immediately heavy with some unseen force, the weight of the question that sat now on Fusa's mind suddenly crushed her. 'Where's Mako?'

Kikuko groaned miserably; in its tortured pitch, Fusa at once understood the truth of the whales' song. She went to her friend and, side by side, the pair hung silently against one another, stupefied with grief.

∼

Nestled in the valley of the seagrass meadow, they slept until the gloom of night reached its peak.

Fusa came awake first, but, not wishing to disturb Kiyo, whose small body was wedged between herself and Kikuko, she remained as she was.

Questions crashed into her consciousness like waves upon the shore. One after the other, with a relentless rhythm, they took shape, but no sooner did they distinguish themselves as individual things than they collapsed once again back into the ocean of grief that was Fusa's mind.

Amid the dark, time seemed to pull forward more slowly, but the call of gulls above gave her hope that she wouldn't have to wait too much longer for this interval of sonar-blindness to come to an end. Her machine had become as important to her as the fin on her back or the flukes of her tail, yet unlike those appendages, this one was anything but natural, and in light of Kikuko's account of what the humans had done in the cove, she felt curiously hostile towards it now.

Not once had Wakka Totto or any of the pod's elders described humans truthfully. Like Mako, her own kin were so fond of that species that they saw only what impressed them: their tools; their language; the culture with which they probed the deepest questions of all. Yet the brutality of humans had been in front of them all along. The dolphins of her pod had proven themselves to be as blind to their true nature as Fusa was to the world beyond the reach of her eyes.

Yet facts were facts. Their machine *had* given her a chance at life. And without their intervention, her body would no doubt still be stranded where the wave had washed it in.

Involuntarily, a sad clicking escaped her: as her beak drooped, she wished she were a little more worldly – just experienced enough that the maddening fickleness of humans might actually make sense.

Roused by Fusa's frustration, Kikuko opened both eyes and turned to her. 'He just wouldn't be warned, would he?'

Fusa ached with the urge to defend her captured friend. 'It wasn't his fault. He missed his pod's love. We mustn't blame him for what he couldn't control.'

Kikuko let out a bubble and ran her snout along Kiyo's tiny sleeping body. 'I just want him back, auntie. But I know that's not going to happen. We should head back north and reunite you with your daughter.'

'I'm going to see the trout-god.'

'You still want to do that?' Kikuko twisted away, but she was unable to hide her bashfulness. 'Is there any point now? I mean—'

'I'm going to see the backbone fish.'

'My parents will be in Lobster Claw Harbour by now. They'll adopt this one, I'm sure of it. And you can swim with us too, if that was what you wanted.'

'We'd be sisters,' cheeped Fusa.

'We're sisters now, krill-for-brains,' said Kikuko, taking Fusa's flipper beneath her own. 'Listen to me. Moshiri got what he wanted, didn't he? As terrible as it is, Mako is—'

'I'm going to see the backbone fish.'

'But what for?' clicked Kikuko, crossly. 'What is there to say to him now?'

'"Settle down".'

'I won't, auntie! You need to help me understand—'

'No, Kikuko. "Settle down". That's what I'll say to him. "Settle down, great trout, on whose mighty spine our watery world sits, for in your wrath, you're only hurting the innocent".'

Kikuko tipped to her side as she held a quizzical look upon Fusa. 'Innocent? What about Mako and the things he's done? The little calf snatched by orca? The shrine?'

'I'm not sure any of this is about Mako,' said Fusa. 'The filth that filled up Snow Crab Lagoon, the blood spilling into the shallows at the coast. That's coming from the human world. I wonder if it's *them* Moshiri is angry with. But it's not the time for such questions. Tell me about that cove. Did you see anything that might help us?'

'It all happened so fast,' said Kikuko. 'But I mapped a river running into the cove's beach. It was very hard to tell, but I thought I heard dolphins up there.'

Fusa swayed her beak. 'Do you think it's possible the humans have enclosures on the river?'

'It's impossible to say for sure.'

'If they did, they might have put Mako in one.'

'Why, though? Why would they do that?'

'They put Zhebi and Zhao in pens, didn't they? I know it's just desperation, Kikuko. But I need to be sure he's truly gone before I cross the western sea.'

'What are you saying, auntie?'

'I'm saying I'm going into Blood Cove.'

'*Into* it? You'll be slaughtered!'

'I won't. Humans rest during the dark hours.'

Kikuko held an intense gaze on Fusa. Kiyo, in an attempt to find milk, was butting at her underside. 'They want this little one, auntie. If they're out on the water looking for him, there'll be trouble.'

'Then we keep him here while we investigate.'

Arcing her back in a stretch, Kikuko gave a whistle.

'Alright. But if dawn breaks, we'll have no chance. We go now.'

'Milk,' whined Kiyo.

Kikuko held her face against the calf. 'You must be very brave while your aunties go for a swim. Stay here in the grass. Milk later.'

∼

The waters of the cove tasted metallic, and made Fusa's eyes sting. Although her skin didn't prickle, it was hard not to think about the pollution they'd had to endure during their time in the lagoon.

Nevertheless, their relief at finding the cove free of fishing vessels was overwhelming.

Blind for the darkness of night, Fusa gave full attention to her hearing; no sound came from the beach itself, but beyond it, where the sand firmed up into soil, human voices echoed up the faces of the two steep cliffs.

Keeping close to the rocks, the pair swam in past tethered boats. Fearing a trap, they glided with patience and care until they felt the tingle of sand beneath their bellies. They studied the environment intensely the moment they got into the surf: the beach was cut into two sections by a river flowing from inland, and a wall jutted out beyond one of the banks, channelling the river's current into the foot of the northern cliff.

'What are you seeing?'

'It's hard to be sure,' replied Kikuko, reading her sonar scans. 'But around this wall are things that could be enclosures. Wait! What are you doing?'

'We have to be sure, Kikuko. I'm just going to poke my head around far enough to get my voice through the water.'

Nearby, humans were laughing. If their eyes worked as well as a dolphin's in low light, there was every chance they would spot her, but this had to be done.

She beat her tail, once, and glided forward up the river. 'Mako!' she whistled. 'Mako!'

Nothing came back.

'Mako!' she called again.

Faintly, a chittering of clicks carried down.

They were words.

'Auntie!' they said. 'I'm here!'

∾

Not even Kiyo's crying could spoil the mood when Fusa and Kikuko returned to the seagrass meadow.

To know Mako was alive was beyond their wildest hopes. Yet it didn't change the fact he was captive.

'There's no way we'll get past the beach without being sighted by the humans,' creaked Fusa.

A mischievous look sparkled in Kikuko's eye. 'There is a way: distraction. And I know just the thing for it. But I'm going to need a whole day to get organised.'

'A day?! They could kill him by then, Kikuko!'

'Yes, auntie, they could. But it's our only chance.'

Fusa gave a nod. 'Alright. I'll wait here in the seagrass meadow for you both to return.'

'Both?' gigged Kikuko. 'I don't think so. Kiyo's staying with you.'

And with that, Kikuko vanished into the waters of the north, whose depths, once again, were groaning with the sad lowing of grief.

19

A CHILLING TRUTH

ON THE ROPES at the bottom of his enclosure, Mako was woken from a restless nap.

Through the water, a violence of clanking was sounding as metal was struck against metal. With the light of day fading, the humans were returning with their latest hunt.

The agony of slaughter began almost at once. Recognising many of the piercing whistles from his own experience in the cove, Mako lifted his upper body out of the water. It went some way to lessening his distress – sound didn't reverberate so well in the open air – but he winced each time a shriek carried up into the valley.

Mako could see by the way Roopam kept his gaze fixed blankly on the ropes below that he too was suffering. He went over to the whale and placed his fin upon him, and together they stayed this way, trying not to hear as the dull smacking of bodies began hitting the ground.

A chill rippled through Mako as he considered how wrong he'd been about humans. Far from the amiable creatures he'd always taken them to be, they were truly the most dangerous beings it was possible to conceive. Especially haunting for him – it played in his head over and over again – were the words the cow spoke in the moments before they drove their spike into her.

'They're hunters. We're their prey.'

Was it so different to orca or shark, that humans ate dolphin? There were predators and there was prey, and Mako supposed nothing wished to be eaten by another creature – whether it was a mollusc on a rock, a sea cucumber lazing on the sediment or an intelligent, curious animal like a dolphin. Yet why did humans doing it seem *unnatural*?

Perhaps it was that they were taking from another domain. As landlubbers they ought to have everything they needed there with them. To plunder the ocean *as well* – in Mako's mind, that was as against the rule of nature as it would be for an octopus to grab a human child from the shore and devour it below the waves.

A sudden cacophony of footsteps on the walkway brought Mako out of his reverie, and he sank into the water. Finally aware of what humans really were, he decided he'd rather go hungry than perform for those cruel creatures again.

A sharp beam of light shone in, settling on Roopam's snoutless face. Mako followed it back to a device in the hand of the human who stood now on the walkway's edge.

'There you go, sir. Pilot whale.'

'Dubai wants a short-fin. That is a long-fin.'

'We can release him if you wish?'

'No. I'll be speaking to Lisbon soon. If I recall correctly, they're in the market for a long-fin for their new megatank.'

Mako watched as the point of light then came away from Roopam, and recoiled when the beam blazed into his own eyes.

'Pretty bottlenose.'

'Very. An entertainer, too. Good price tag on this one, I think.'

'Let's have a closer look at him, shall we?'

The human pair trudged away. Mako thought that might be it for them for today – the sun had just passed over the hill and thrown the valley and its river into shade – but just then he heard further noises, before a whiff which made his stomach growl caught his attention.

At the edge of the walkway, the humans were now holding a bucket full of fish. Roopam, too, shifted his long body around to investigate, but it was Mako they seemed interested in. From out of the sky, a single fish came hurtling; Mako caught it in his jaws, barely taking notice of the lifting machine presently lowering fabric down to the surface.

Mako swallowed another mouthful and gave a quack. 'What about my friend? Where's his fish?'

Suddenly, Mako felt his weight lighten. The humans, who'd worked the fabric underneath his body while he'd been eating, were hoisting him out from the water. As they lowered him onto the metal walkway, he turned to his right to see the fish-filled bucket.

The two humans crouching beside him glimpsed down with an intense expression of concentration. It seemed as though they were studying him.

'So, what do you think, sir? Display, or meat?'

'I must say, he's a little older than I'd hoped. My Florida buyer was very clear: he won't accept any dolphin for display that's over three years old. Still, he's a good-looker. And a good temperament, too. How's the quota looking for the year?'

'Good, sir. Very good. We should hit the maximum by the time the season ends in two weeks.'

'So you don't *need* him for meat then?'

'Bit too early to say for sure, sir.'

'I think I'll bring Mr Ito down tomorrow, then. It's possible we can pass him off as younger than he is, but I'd prefer it if Mr Ito sees him first. That will do for now.'

With bewildering suddenness, Mako then found himself back in the pen alongside a hungry Roopam.

Dusk set in soon after and brought an end to the commotion in the cove, and save for a few human laughs that sounded somewhere near the beach, the night passed quietly by.

As Mako and Roopam circled the pen, they consoled each other with stories of where they'd come from, attempting to work out whether they'd ever shared the same migration routes. After Mako explained his plan to appease the god of the seas and the storms – and just why it was necessary for him to do so – Roopam shared odd tales about his pod's beliefs.

Whales from his region attempted to communicate with many gods. They also, it seemed, held a mysterious idea that all things were united by some unseen force. Mako, however, still tormented by what had happened in the cove, found it too fanciful: if humans and dolphins were connected, then the slaughter they inflicted on the marine animals was really inflicted on themselves – and nothing would ever hurt themselves in such a way as that.

Beneath the darkness of the canopy, Roopam was just explaining how one of his pod's ancestors once came to communicate with some humans, when a whistle sounded in the water below them.

'Did you hear that?'

'No,' said Roopam. 'What was it?'

Mako went to the rope. 'I think I heard my name.'

Distantly, it came through the water again. 'Mako!'

'I did!' He poked his beak out through the netted bottom. 'Auntie!' he clicked as clearly as he could. 'I'm here!'

∼

No matter how hard Fusa tried, she couldn't get Kiyo to go to sleep.

His distress, she supposed, had less to do with Kikuko's absence than the loss of his own mother. Yet it was Kikuko he constantly cried for; he just wouldn't accept that, wherever it was she'd gone off to, the girl would soon be back.

To keep his mind off her, Fusa tried to nurse him. But what little milk she was able to produce seemed not to be palatable to him.

Next, she tried to find solid food. But even with biosonar, locating fish at this hour was a chore. She nudged in the sediment for anything that may be agreeable to a calf of his age – he was barely a single summer old – but the few spindly shrimp she located were unrecognisable to Kiyo even as food, and he simply bobbed next to them while he watched them flail through the seagrass.

After that, she tried wearing him out with games, but these merely excited him more. Still, his enjoyment of chasing was a welcome relief from his cries, and were it not for the fact Fusa herself was exhausted after a long day of looking for her friends, she would have gladly entertained him all through the night.

Unfortunately, however, she couldn't, and the calf grew irritable when her enthusiasm began to wane, and she in turn grew snappy with him; on one occasion, giving a more forcible nudge than was strictly necessary.

Now at the limit of her patience, Fusa remembered when Misa was Kiyo's age. She would become upset often, either through the pain of growing, or the fatigue of crossing over the strait, or sometimes for no good reason at all. At moments like that, it was the stories Fusa told her daughter that brought her most comfort, and she wondered if this might work for the poor calf here tonight.

'Did you know,' she said, over Kiyo's whining whistles, 'that a long time ago there was no ocean?'

The calf, still bleating sadly, looked across at her.

'That's right. The only thing that existed was a filthy swamp whose waters were so polluted that nothing could be seen. Just one creature lived in that horrid place, a vast trout whose enormous body stretched longer than the horizon from the east to the west, and his name was Moshiri, and it was on his powerful spine that the whole swamp sat.'

The calf, finally, began to settle. So Fusa went on, sharing the many stories told by Wakka Totto over the years, and Kiyo listened attentively. But as she told them, it occurred to Fusa that none of them really said very much about dolphins. In fact, almost every one concerned humans – how *they* were formed, how *they* came to put the land to use. Repeating the stories now gave her a curious feeling of discomfort.

But no matter. The tales had worked, and the calf, at last, was at rest, and Fusa, who'd been ready to drown him, was delighted.

The moment he fell asleep, however, when she was finally free with her own thoughts, an intense gloom enveloped her.

It was – all of it – as Moshiri had shown her in the visions.

With a boat approaching overhead, the time for considering just what that meant had already come to an end.

'Kiyo,' she whistled. 'Wake up.'

The calf came awake with a wiggle of his tail.

'You must stay very quiet. That boat is looking for you.'

To Fusa's horror, the vessel spluttered to a halt directly above. Was it possible the humans knew they were down here?

The answer to that question was right in front of

Fusa's very eyes. Humans possessed the means to see with sonar: she and Kiyo probably appeared right now as dots on *their* screen.

Very faintly, Fusa saw that a net had been thrown from overboard. A mild panic stirred in her, but for the calf's sake she concealed her distress.

What happened next, however, changed that.

With a splash, a human came *into* the water. With long flippers for feet – did they always have those? – and a hard covering wrapping its face, the individual began to descend into the seagrass meadow.

Before, Fusa's plan had been to conserve energy and remain out of reach. But the emergence of a hunter in the actual water prompted a change of heart.

She let out a squeal to tell the calf to follow, and Kiyo, more terrified of the gangly thing dropping down from the surface than Fusa was herself, was quick to obey. As they swam away, Fusa looked back to see the submerged figure heading back up, almost hidden behind a startling outpouring of bubbles.

As Fusa led Kiyo into open water, she kept her ears attuned to the environment. The sound of the boat was about the only thing that would give it away: sure enough, a put-putting at the surface confirmed the worst.

There was only one thing for it: they were going to have to go deep.

'Kiyo, listen to me now. You've got to keep as much air as you can inside you while we hide. We're going to go up and take great big breaths – as big as our lungs can hold. Do you understand?'

'Milk?'

'Milk later! Now, air. Lots and lots of air. Ready? Let's go.'

They sped upwards and leapt out of the water. Replacing their air as they spouted, Fusa noticed that the boat was almost on them, and hurriedly led Kiyo back down again to safety.

It was a minor victory, yet Fusa felt crushed by the weight of the responsibility. She couldn't do this! It was just about more than she could handle to keep herself alive!

Through her despair, an idea emerged, which quickened the pace of her heart. Perhaps there was a way they might see the sun rise after all. But it was risky.

Leading Kiyo ever deeper, she glided into the gloom of a fissure, moving along it as carefully as she could. The going was hard even when sun rays made it this far down into the network of gullies, but now, in the middle of the night and with no echolocation to guide her, all movement was pure guesswork.

She imagined this giant scar in the rock like a flash of lightning in the sky: the main channel along which they swam branched with infuriating regularity, with each fork itself subdividing into multiple dead-ends. Each time she slammed her beak into the rough face of the fissure Kiyo gave a chuckle, though eventually Fusa made so many wrong turns that even the calf grew frustrated.

'Go forward!' he whistled.

'It's not easy when you can't see anything — I don't know what *forward* is. Wait! Can you read sonar scans, Kiyo?'

'Yes, auntie.'

She gave him a pat with her flipper. 'Come ahead of me, then,' she cheeped excitedly. 'You're my eyes now.'

Obligingly, the calf squeezed between Fusa and the rocky face of the trench, and scanned ahead. 'Where?

'I'm not sure. I'm hoping to find another—'

'Look. He's like you!'

Fusa felt her organs turn into jellyfish. *'Who is?!'*

'That funny dolphin. Hey! Where did he go?'

'Follow him, Kiyo!'

The calf upped his pace as he led Fusa through the

gully, coming to a halt where, in a wider section of the trench, a friend was waiting.

'You're very hard to find,' Fusa said to Zhebi.

'Human take baby Zhebi and make him this way.'

With the first hint of dawn illuminating the upper depths, Fusa strained her eyes to take in what she could of her surroundings.

'Fusa make sonar box work?'

'Yes, Zhebi. I wish Zhao could know how grateful I am to him.'

'Zhao know this,' said Zhebi.

The calf, using Fusa to conceal himself from the muscular animal, edged forward. 'Come, Kiyo. This is my friend. Say hello.'

At the sight of the podling, Zhebi began to wave his beak with glee. 'Baby look like moon!'

'Zhebi, we need your help. Humans want him. They're chasing us.'

The young bull's expression grew serious. 'Human... want baby?'

'Yes. They got Mako already. They're holding him in a pen. I'm worried they're going to hurt him.'

At once, Zhebi's eyes bulged with rage. The sight of it was enough to freeze Fusa's own heart, so it was little wonder when the calf sped back around to her other side.

'Kikuko has some sort of plan,' she cheeped. 'But she won't be back until evening. Zhebi, I don't know what to do with Kiyo. He needs milk.'

Zhebi brought his beak close to the calf and held it against him tenderly. Just before he turned and sped away, he gave a gentle whistle. 'Fusa, baby Kiyo. You go sleep now.'

'Wait! Where are you going?'

But Zhebi had already vanished.

Fusa placed her fin across the calf's little back and hugged him into her. Overpowered by exhaustion, they fell asleep.

But Fusa's slumber was far deeper than she'd anticipated.

Suddenly in a dream, Fusa could hear, all around, the melancholy song of whales. Voices were sounding in the water, crying out in anguish. She could hear Misa, and Mako, and the stilted clicks of an animal whose language wasn't quite dolphin. A voice was coming out of her, too, but it was more like Wakka Totto's than her own.

She had no idea where she was; she was sonar-blind, as in her waking reality, but she could make out with her eyes a dark box, sinking away into the abyss of the ocean trench, all the way down to the whalefalls whose great ribs protruded from the floor.

And then, with great clarity, she saw a whole swathe of ocean as a great wall of fire: a scorched, choking impurity.

Moshiri was turning the clear waters of the coast back into the original swamp!

'Auntie! Auntie! Wake up!'

Kiyo was nudging Fusa with his beak. She opened her eyes to the welcome sight of more light in the upper depths, and saw, silhouetted in the faint dawn light, three dolphins approaching.

Zhebi had returned. And he'd brought two others with him.

A powerful bull and a mature cow came close to Fusa. She studied them intently: like Zhebi, they too had been adorned with human items. The bull had something that looked like an eye strapped to his right dorsal fin, while the cow was merely wrapped in a kind of rope onto which, perhaps, a similar device had once been fastened.

'Daeli,' instructed Zhebi, 'give milk for baby.'

The cow approached the calf and presented her underside. To Fusa's absolute relief, the starved little creature began to suckle.

Overcome with curiosity, Fusa moved with Zhebi up

out of the gully, and glided in a circle with him. 'Who are they?' she asked.

'Human take Yongsa and Daeli. Make them very good at hide and seek. But they escape, same like Zhebi and Zhao. And same like Zhebi and Zhao, Yongsa and Daeli hate human now.'

Her strange companion's words felt oddly menacing. But she wasn't going to dwell on them now, not when a long night of distress had come to an end.

Soon, the sun's light would power her machine, allowing her to properly survey the cove. And only then would she know just how impossible Mako's rescue stood to be.

20

HANGING IN THE BALANCE

Today was going to have to be a zero-mistake day.

The moment morning broke, Fusa ascended to the surface, where her machine came alive. But the pale sky offered such little light that the echoes returning to her screen barely showed at all.

Snow was drifting down in a steady torrent from the frozen clouds, muting the sound of a ship passing nearby. The stillness that hung in the air was both odd and unsettling.

Never in her life had Fusa faced danger like this. On these very waters, human fleets were scouring for dolphins; when they found them, they'd use a mysterious trick to herd them into shallow waters, to a beach that lay host to slaughter.

It was of the utmost importance she didn't fall for it.

Taking off in the direction of Blood Cove, she preserved her energy as best she could; not only was the day going to be a difficult one, it stood to be a long one, too. After a night caring for Kiyo, she was already depleted, but at least the calf was safe now, hidden from the eyes of hunters by the protective fin of Daeli.

As she swam, Mako lingered in her thoughts. He would be frightened, of course. But it wasn't his fear that saddened her as much as his confinement. Mako fizzed with life. Everything he did was with an enthusiasm that was exhausting to behold. His accounts of being in trouble with his pod weren't surprising at all: he had the energy of two dolphins, so keeping him safe from harm was a job that must have worn his poor mother out daily.

For Mako, the sense of betrayal would be impossible to comprehend. So certain had he been of their love for him that he never considered that humans may wish him harm. And for his naivety, it was likely he was going to pay the ultimate price.

That silly boy. He just couldn't help himself. But then, of course he couldn't: it was in his blood.

A few dawns ago, he'd told them about a dolphin who'd *deliberately* stranded himself on a beach. That dolphin was his grandfather. It was an act that cost the bull seven summers in captivity — and while he was lucky to be released at all, his natural life came to an end many years before it should have.

Coming now to a promontory, Fusa's sagging spirit began to slow her. It wasn't only Mako or his grandfather that were guilty of meddling in human affairs. Every dolphin she knew, it seemed, had some ancestor who'd been drawn to the land creatures, and as the ways of the human world crept into their lives, parts of their own identity changed as a result.

She spyhopped to discover the flurry of snow had abated, and observed the sun breaking weakly in the drab sky. Almost at the agreed meeting point, she sent scans in all directions, shuddering at the sight of a cluster of dots blinking on her screen.

Fishing boats were sailing out.

Today's hunt had begun.

Fusa remained at a cautious distance throughout the morning, biding her time in readiness for her peculiar new friends to appear on her sonar. And when they eventually did, there were three dots, not two.

Alongside Zhebi and Yongsa was a third bull, every bit as muscular as the others. Originally from the cold waters of the north, this dolphin, who called himself Flad, barely spoke at all; it seemed to Fusa that something had gone wrong inside him, since he jerked his head this way and that with a frantic intensity.

Zhebi took up the front, and in a tight unit the group slowly rounded the headland which formed the north cliff of Blood Cove.

Fusa braved a brief glimpse above the surface to see that the long strips of fabric hanging over the water were now blanketed with a thin layer of snow. She supposed the sight would be a pretty one, if not for the awful scenes that took place beneath them each dawn and dusk.

Keeping below the surface, the bulls read the environment with carefully directed click trains. Zhebi, taking his time, soon began to sway his beak.

'What is it?' asked Fusa. 'Is something wrong?'

'Human working on beach now,' he replied. 'Not safe to go.'

Flad, facing the open water, gave a whistle. The others turned in time to see the boats:

They were on their way *back*!

With an awful clanging of metal, the humans were herding a small cluster of dolphins into the cove, who thrashed their tail flukes with panic and confusion.

Fusa raced with the others back to the curve of the headland, out of the path of the returning boats. 'What's happening?,' she wheezed. 'Why are the humans making that noise?'

'Like waves inside water,' said Zhebi. 'It make dolphin so scared they go close together.'

Fusa furrowed her brow. 'Why don't they just swim away? Don't they know they're being trapped?'

'Noise too powerful,' said Yongsa. 'Make dolphin go blind, like us.'

Fusa shuddered – she was seeing her dream visions in a new light.

It wasn't that they were lost. They were disorientated! The awful hammering was disabling their biosonar!

'Net close around them now.'

Fusa flushed with a rage that surged from the flukes of her tail to the tips of her fins. The impulse to warn the distressed dolphins was so overpowering she forgot about the pledge to be extra careful today.

And before she even knew what she was doing, Fusa darted out into the cove, straight into the path of the oncoming boats.

∼

The snow had stopped falling, and the humans were returning to the walkways.

Mako's stomach growled, and he wished it would stop. Already he was connecting food with the land dwellers, and that was a dangerous arrangement. He may be a reckless young animal – and he was certainly an impulsive one – but with all that had gone on he was at last wise enough to know that a dolphin should eat only what he hunted.

Still, hunting wasn't an option, and was likely never to be again. The nature of captivity meant he ate when *they* chose. And it appeared they'd chosen not to feed him now, anyway.

The shortest of the three humans was speaking commandingly. 'What about the albino?'

'Our divers traced him last night, but he got away before they could net him.'

The short individual produced a humming sound in his throat. It seemed to Mako he was annoyed.

'Rest assured, Mr Ito, our men are still in pursuit.'

'They'd better be. So, this is the bottlenose in question?'

'Yes, Mr Ito. As I said, he's a little longer than we'd have hoped.'

'It's risky, palming off mislabelled merchandise to our clients. And Dubai is one of our top buyers. I fear the risk is too great.'

'You are right, of course, Mr Ito. But he's not far past three, if he is at all.'

'Show me him out of water.'

The short human's companions dipped their heads towards him, and gave a yell. 'Bring the winch over!'

'No!' snapped the shorter one. 'You said he liked to perform – let's see him stand.'

'As you wish, Mr Ito.'

Heavy steps pounded against the floor, and soon a bucket of fish showed up.

Mako gave a quack to Roopam. 'They *do* have food! Make sure you get your share this time.'

'You eat your fill, Mako,' whistled the whale.

'But we've been in here a whole day. Aren't you starving?'

Roopam's fins drooped as he turned away. 'It's alright. I'd prefer to go without.'

Mako kept his eye on the fish in the human's hand, issuing an annoyed chirrup when the individual refrained from tossing it into the pen.

'He wants you to go to it,' said Roopam.

Bringing the tip of his beak out of the water, Mako held his jaws open and waited for food to land inside.

But no fish came.

Roopam was right. They expected him to leave the water. So many times, he'd stood for them of his own free will. But now the very act felt like a betrayal to his kind. He was a dolphin, whose home was beneath the waves.

Yet hunger was a greater force than indignation.

He pulled himself up, and snatched the tossed fish out of the sky.

'That confirms it. Too long. Any other buyer and I'd

chance it. But we can't pass this one off as a three-year-old.'

Just at that moment, a cacophony of clanging sounded through the river, causing the humans t0 twist their heads back to face the cove. 'The boats are back so soon?'

'Some days are like that, Mr Ito. We'll get another hunt in after lunch.'

'Very good. The quota will be filled early this year, perhaps?'

'Quite possible, sir. Mr Ito, if this bottlenose is no good, should we take him down to the beach now? The next catch is coming in. We can process him with the others.'

But the shorter individual simply brought his fingers up to his lips, as though lost in his own thoughts.

∾

The moment Fusa reached the herded dolphins, the most awful commotion began from the boats.

The hammering of metal against metal was almost unbearable, even for her. She'd had many days to adjust to life without echolocation, but for dolphins who still relied upon that sense, this deliberate attempt to overwhelm them was devastatingly effective.

She lifted herself into a spyhop, observing that the arc of boats was now closing in as they drove the dolphins nearer the cliffs. With an urgent cheeping, she turned back to the panicking pod. 'Listen to me! If you let those boats push you into the shallows, you're going to die! You need to follow me over to the cliff, right now!'

With as hard a thrash as she could give her tail, she moved clear of the sweep of nets to rejoin the bulls at the headland.

But the poor dolphins had failed to heed her warning.

For them, it was already over.

Zhebi gave a whistle. 'Too many boats in cove now.

Cannot go to Mako. Must wait for human to come out again.'

Fusa twisted her beak away in frustration. Might there be a different approach to getting him? She was about to probe the others, but became suddenly distracted by the screeches of wounded dolphins.

The slaughter was commencing.

It was like being inside her dream vision all over again, each of those vile, tortuous sensations needling her. Unable to bear it, she swam off further around the headland, followed closely by the bulls.

Silently, she worked through ideas as to how they might proceed with their rescue attempt. But there simply wasn't a way, not while the boats were packed so densely in the shallows of the cove.

All they could do was wait.

∻

With the humans still standing at the edge of the pen, Roopam was keeping back at its opposite end, on the roped-off bottom, as far away from them as it was possible to be.

Mako, however, was spyhopping. He watched the intense expressions of the humans as their words went to and fro, keeping one eye fixed on the bucket that stood to their side.

The shorter individual had stood with his fingers pressed to his lips for some moments. When he eventually brought them down, he placed one hand on the other's shoulder.

'Keep the bottlenose here a while longer.'

'As you wish, Mr Ito.'

'He may not be a calf anymore, but with his good looks and acrobatic skills, I think I might be able to convince my Shanghai buyer to take him. I'll make a phone call after lunch.'

～

Though mere hours had passed, it was like a different day entirely to the one that had dawned with a flurry of snow. The sun's rays beat down through the mid-afternoon sky, yet the horizon was darkening with weather, and the wind promised to drive it into the shore.

The bulls had separated, leaving Fusa alone in the coast's shallow waters. Those mysterious males were fine in each other's company, but their need to be alone again was obvious, which was odd to behold. Dolphins, of every type she knew, were social creatures, yet these bulls – and the cow still down in the gullies with Kiyo – were solitary. They bore signs of physical abuse on their muscular bodies, but the scarring of their spirits was plain to see, too.

Hunting for rockfish, Fusa threw out scans until she eventually located three dots. With the bulls reconvening at last, she sped back towards the headland as quickly as she could.

'Human coming out again,' announced Zhebi. 'Beach empty again soon.'

The tiniest ember of hope brought warmth to Fusa's otherwise-frozen core. Whatever happened now, she could always say she did everything she could to rescue her friend. And she'd done it as an equal to bulls of unmatchable strength and fearlessness.

The foursome lingered in a tight huddle at the edge of the headland, studying the movement of the boats. Fanning out on the retreating tide, the vessels were on their way out into open waters.

Yet there were so few of them!

Zhebi gave a click. 'Problem.'

Half the boats were still in the bay. And of these, many were up on the beach where the tide had pulled back.

Access to the river appeared now to be blocked.

Fusa led the bulls to the seabed to evade the approaching boats, then, when these had pushed on overhead into the expanse, the dolphins went back to the surface.

Zhebi fixed his sickly eyes on the beach. 'Fusa want to wait?'

'It would be the wise thing to do,' she answered. 'But this may be our best chance. We go now.'

∽

Roopam had barely spoken all day.

No matter how Mako tried to cheer him, nothing worked.

Perhaps the reality of this whale's life was just beginning to sink in? Here was an animal whose whole family had beached because their leader's mind was poisoned with impurity. And now he himself had lost the only thing he had left: his freedom. His glumness wasn't surprising in the slightest.

Hungry and bored, Mako went into the corner to nap a while, and when the sound of boats whirring into life roused him back to life some time later, he found Roopam as morose as before. Mako wondered whether his friend might like to see his backward somersault. It was an excellent move – Fusa and Kikuko both agreed – and was sure to bring a little cheer to his weary heart. But just as he was about to launch into it, footsteps sounded.

The short human was back. This time, he held a box, and with the thing pressed to his ear, he spoke. 'Many thanks for returning my call.'

He went silent a moment.

'Pilot whale, yes. A long-fin, that's correct. You have some already? Very well, we'll release ours. And the bottlenose?'

Another moment of silence passed, before:

'You *don't* want him? Ah, that's too bad. No, no, I

understand. If he's too old, he's too old. I'll call again in a few days. Hopefully we'll have news of the albino by then.'

The short human turned to his companions. 'No. My buyer doesn't want them. When the fleet comes back in, let the whale go.'

'And the dolphin, Mr Ito?'

'Shuttle him to the beach and process him for meat with the others.'

∽

Fusa's rescue party glided into the cove with their bellies to the seabed. On the beach ahead of them, humans were busying themselves with a wide range of tasks.

The murky water was now so shallow that Fusa could feel her dorsal fin sticking out through the surface, but so far they'd evaded detection. Again, the water was rich with the bloody taste of minerals – so similar to the stuff that filled up Snow Crab Lagoon, but natural, at least.

Keeping tight together, Fusa and the bulls manoeuvred closer to the beach. The boat laying across the outflowing river confirmed her worst fear: her way to Mako's pen was blocked. She was just going to have to try and muscle it out of the way.

She steadied her heart rate and took air deeply into her lungs. Whatever happened now was out of her control. She made to thrash her way into the boat, but Zhebi suddenly let out a squeak.

'The hunters are back already!'

Fusa froze.

Yongsa's eyes widened, and even Flad, with his permanent scowl, appeared softened through fear.

Some of the humans began shouting to the returning boats. 'What are you doing back so soon?' and another called out:

'It's snowing again out there!'

Hanging in the Balance | 207

Right at that moment, the humans on the beach spotted Fusa and the bulls. A frenzy of activity broke out, as the land creatures scrambled to hoist up their spiked poles from off the pebbles.

Fusa made a rough calculation. The distance to the safety of open water was equal to the distance between the returning boats and the cliffs.

It was going to be close.

But as the hammering of metal sounded, the speed of the approaching boats then picked up: before she could even make it halfway out of the cove, the nets were already spread wide.

The cliffs were now closed off.

The humans had succeeded in sealing Fusa and the bulls into Blood Cove.

The dreadful, deafening, clattering continued.

But then another loud noise sounded, louder even than the hammers.

To Fusa's ears, it sounded like barking.

She looked ahead, through the gaps in the nets, and was astonished to see that Kikuko had returned.

And she had brought a most unexpected army with her.

21

A SICKENING VICTORY

So transfixed was Fusa by what was unfolding in front of her, she forgot all about her mission to the river.

From around the sides of the humans' nets, a multitude of sea lions, with Kikuko at their helm, came gliding in.

The chaos was instant.

Though the hammers fell silent, the humans hollered from off the water as loudly as their tiny mouths could manage. 'They've pulled the nets away! Get those boats out here at once!' With this, the humans on the beach began hauling the wooden fishing vessels along the pebbles towards the surf, with the one blocking the river hoisted away first.

Fusa barely even acknowledged this happy outcome, however. All her attention was fixed on the boats further out. The sea lions had left the water and were now aboard the vessels, rocking them from side to side and thrusting their heavy bodies into the panicking humans.

Through shallows made murky with the blood of slain dolphins, the rest of the sea lions suddenly emerged. A bulky bull with big, sad eyes brought his whiskered nose right up to Fusa's beak. He made no barks, but his intention to help was unmistakable.

Kikuko was clicking frenziedly. 'The beach, auntie! Stop them getting those boats out!'

Fusa turned to see the humans still dragging their vessels into the surf. In moments, they'd be on the water, helping to restore the broken wall of netting, shutting in every animal.

That couldn't happen.

Turning, Fusa gave the sea lion bull a pleading look, then, with a thrash, she glided up to the water's edge. The stones scraped along her underside, but she forced her way up the beach until she could go no further.

The bull gave a shout – 'Aarrrrrck!' – which rose up out of the cove and echoed off the cliffs. Then, joined by other members of his colony, he leapt out of the surf and onto the beach.

Tramping past Fusa on their wing-like flippers, the sea lions proceeded across the pebbles, hurtling themselves into the boats, sending the humans scattering away.

Zhebi gave an alarmed chirp. 'Fusa come back now!'

But there was no way she could. In order to show the sea lions what she needed them to do, she had stranded herself.

More humans were on their way. Along the river wall they came, yelling furiously. The shortest of them was especially animated, and was pointing at Fusa directly. 'That one!' he called. 'My buyer in Dubai wants one of those! Get it!'

Blind to what was going on behind her, Fusa listened while Zhebi and Yongsa chittered away for the briefest of moments. Her dolphin companions then went quiet, before a rush of water came splashing over her tail. As though they were strand fishing, the three bulls had hauled their bodies ashore in perfect unison, using the wave they created to swoop in and scoop Fusa back out with them into the shallows.

'Thank you!' she cheeped, but the moment of

celebration was short-lived, since a hail of stones suddenly landed upon them. The humans were attacking.

The four dolphins recoiled back into the cove, clambering up into a sky again specked with snow. On the beach, humans were swinging their metal poles at the sea lions who'd taken up residence inside their boats, while out on the water, the people on the fishing vessels were making a good job of casting the invading animals back into the water.

Fusa whistled out to Kikuko. 'I'm going to Mako now. Stop them getting their nets back out.'

Turning sharply to the right, she accelerated across to the beach's centre. She pushed past the wall, and up the unobstructed river, and was soon making her way towards the floating pens.

∽

From the walkway, the humans were lowering the fabric into the enclosure. Mako was buoyed: had they come to release him at last?

Roopam's eyes had grown glassy with distress again.

'Don't worry,' said Mako. 'I'm sure they're coming for you, too. You're just a bit big, that's all.'

Just then the sound of hammering rose up into the valley. The whale moved closer to Mako and held his large flipper against him. 'They're not releasing you, my friend.'

Mako twisted his beak to the side in confusion.

'You need to make peace with your Moshiri.'

Still, Mako remained perplexed.

'They're back,' said Roopam. 'With their catch. This pair is taking you to the beach now for the slaughter.'

A ball of ice sat beneath Mako's ribs where his heart should be. Blood Cove was waiting for him.

But the clanging of the hammers suddenly ceased,

and a commotion of human voices from down at the beach pierced the sky. Then a curious sound came skipping along the cliffs in a drawn-out 'Aaaarrck!', and the two humans hurried off the walkway and sped away in their boat.

For a short while, neither Mako or Roopam spoke. But then Mako noticed just how much the whale's spirits seemed to have cheered. 'That's the first time all day your eyes have had any joy in them,' he said.

'Listen,' said Roopam.

A voice was whistling below them, on the other side of the roped bottom.

'Mako!' it went. 'Down here!'

With Roopam beside him, Mako dived to discover Fusa's beak poking up into the pen.

'Auntie! What are you doing here now? Isn't there a slaughter taking place?'

'We've taken over the cove to get you out. This is your one chance, Mako. Is there *any* way you can get through this rope?'

'None,' quacked Mako. 'Believe me, I've tried. The only way out is if the humans pull me up with their machine.'

'That's not the *only* way,' clicked Roopam. 'I could fling you out.'

'Fling me? How?'

'Look at his tail, Mako,' said Fusa. 'He could toss a boat out of there with that thing.' She turned to meet the whale's eye. 'Hello,' she said. 'My name's Fusa.'

'I'm Roopam. I know all about you, auntie.'

'You do?'

'My friend here says you're the best big sister a dolphin could ever hope for.'

Mako began to fret. 'But Roopam. What about you? I won't leave you in here.'

'They don't want me, Mako. I'll be let out soon enough.' The whale dipped his head to face Fusa. 'Mako is sorry he doubted you before. He understands now the special gift you have.'

For just a moment, Fusa seemed overcome with distress. It was as though mention of Moshiri had reminded her of something awful — something, no doubt, in one of her sleeping visions. But she quickly regained her focus, and squawked up through the rope. 'Now, Mako! It has to be now!'

Mako and Roopam held their faces close together, then went to the surface.

'After we've crossed the western sea to see the trout-god,' said Mako, 'we'll be going to Squid Hood Bay. Come find us there.'

Roopam smiled sadly. 'Don't get carried away, little friend. You've got to get out of the cove first. Are you ready to go?'

Mako, fuelled by excitement and fear in equal measure, nodded his beak. 'What do I have to do?'

'Go right back to the walkway and get yourself the best run-up you can. When you make it onto my tail flukes, I'll launch you. Hopefully you'll clear the walkway. Ready?'

'Ready.'

While Roopam got into position at the edge of the pen, Mako glanced down to the rope floor where Fusa was nervously watching, and quacked down an instruction. 'If this doesn't work, auntie, you need to get out of the cove as fast as you can.'

Fusa let up a bubble and smiled broadly. 'Good luck,' she said, and swam out into the middle of the river.

Mako steadied his nerves. With his heart heavy with sorrow, he went to the back of the pen. There was barely any space between him and Roopam, and he worried he might not be able to reach a decent speed, but he thrashed as hard as he could.

'Thank you, my friend,' he said, as his body glided over the whale's flukes.

And with that, he was up in the air.

Mako simply couldn't resist. Sailing through the snow-dappled sky, he went into a forward somersault – then another. And, since this might be the highest he'd ever get to soar for the rest of his days, he added a twist into the routine too, before finally splashing down into the open river.

Fusa gave squeals of delight, but Mako knew better than to celebrate prematurely so, following a single, sombre nod to Roopam, he glided quietly downriver with Fusa into the cove's surf.

The scene ahead of him made no sense at all. A pair of sea lions lay dead on the pebbles of the beach, while others occupied boats and fought off furious humans. Further out, muscular dolphins that looked like Zhebi – one of them was Zhebi! – were making a nuisance of themselves by pulling away the fishing nets.

A loud shriek came through the water. 'Mako!'

A wave of joy rippled along his spine to see Kikuko, who was speaking to the sea lions.

'Back into the water!' she clicked at them. 'We need to get out of the cove – all of us!'

Mako, Fusa and Kikuko led the way and, followed by the herded dolphins and too many sea lions to count, they swam right past the enraged humans on their boats and out into the open waters of the ocean.

∽

For now, any joy at Mako's escape had to be strictly private: boats were pursuing the rescue party.

Fusa swam between Mako and Kikuko, holding fins with both. This was one of the happiest moments of her life so far, yet a pain lingered in the eyes of both her friends, whose juvenile spirits had been shattered today.

There were some events, she supposed, that brought on a change which couldn't ever be reversed. Just as time flowed forwards and never back, there was a certainty to the suffering that awaited each of them. It would be, perhaps, that it made them physically broken, as Zhao had been. Or that it would cause their minds to split apart like the seabed in a quake and they'd end up like Flad – curiously absent from each present moment. Then again, it may simply be that they remained much as they'd always been, minus only the lustre of their innocence. Perhaps that was all growing up really was: learning to manage an ever-swelling sense of loss.

Kikuko was trying to conceal the true scale of her upset, but as she repeatedly counted the sea lions around her, it was clear that their diminished number weighed heavily upon her.

'They're very brave,' Fusa cheeped, noticing the girl's eye wander across once again to where the colony was gracefully gliding around the headland.

Kikuko let out a mournful bleating. 'When I reached their rocks this morning, they didn't hesitate to come back here with me. Even when I warned them of the danger.'

On Fusa's other side, Mako's energy suddenly shifted. 'It's more than I deserve,' he said.

Kikuko's beak twitched. 'Not to them. They see you as one of their own.'

Below, the ocean floor was beginning to fall away in a chasm. They'd come soon to the start of the gullies, and would be back at the spot where Fusa had left Daeli nursing Kiyo.

Zhebi led the group into a dive, but Yongsa gave a sudden whistle and the three bulls came to a halt.

'What is it?' said Mako.

'Look.'

Fusa threw a click train ahead of her. When it rebounded, her screen displayed a single dot: a boat.

'Human will make trouble now,' said Zhebi.

Cautiously, the party dipped down into the trench

and proceeded along its walls until they came to Daeli. Fusa went up to the cow and held her face next to her, terrified at the sight of the wound along her side.

A steady trickle of blood was pouring out of her.

And there was no sign of Kiyo.

'Humans drop down in water,' said Daeli. 'Spear me, and take calf.'

Kikuko clicked frantically. 'Took him where?'

'Boat.'

'That one?' asked Mako, looking up at the silhouette on the surface above.

Daeli nodded while she held her body against the rock of the gully. She was doing well to stop the bleeding; the wound had caused some damage, but it was clear their spike had glanced along her side instead of puncturing her flesh.

Wasting no time, Kikuko swam around to the sea lions. She held her beak against the whiskered nose of the biggest bull and, much as Fusa had done before she beached herself, she spoke to him with her eyes.

The bull gave a bark, and the other animals gathered beside them. Then, altogether, the sea lions and the dolphins propelled their way upward.

The humans became flighty the moment they saw the animals break through the surface, with one reaching for his spike. But the party remained as they were, surrounding the boat.

In perfect synchronisation, the dolphin bulls leapt in the water and thrashed their tails down to create a wave, causing the boat to rock from side to side. Again, Zhebi, Yongsa and Flad went up and over the surface, pushing another wave towards the boat, whose sides now dipped closer to the waves as it bobbed this way and that.

The sea lions had waited for just the right moment. Pulling themselves up onto the boat's far side when it tipped to its lowest point, the heavy bulls climbed aboard the vessel, and in the pandemonium that followed, both the calf – and a single human – fell into the water.

Fusa and Kikuko went straight to Kiyo, who was crying with distress. They dived down with him into the gully, and though Daeli was injured, she wasted no time rolling her body over to nurse him with milk and comfort.

In the ocean above, however, something awful was happening.

Zhebi, Yongsa and Flad had each seized a hold of one of the submerged human's limbs, and were pulling him into deeper water.

The human fought as hard as he could, and for a moment wrested himself free of their jaws to snatch a breath above the surface, but the persistent bulls clamped on again and dragged him below the waves. At that moment, a spike of metal came whizzing into the water, spearing Flad directly in the head. The muscular bull turned instantly over; belly-up, he floated on the surface, blood streaming out of him.

The other bulls were undeterred though, and dragged the human further down, one leg apiece.

'Mako!' whistled Zhebi. 'Fusa! Take hold of arms!'

Mako turned to Fusa with horror, and in that moment Fusa knew she was witnessing one of the most important moments of this young dolphin's life.

Zhebi and Yongsa had pulled the land creature halfway to the seabed already. Frantically trying to get away, the human was striking their heads limply with his free hands.

Fusa watched as Mako moved into range of the human's flailing upper limbs. He looked at the drowning creature intensely, then at the bulls, and for a moment it seemed that he was about to act. But the masses of bubbles cascading out of the human's mouth suddenly ceased coming. The effort to escape the clutches of the dolphins had come to an end.

Still, though, the bulls held on, and dragged the lifeless thing all the way down to the others, as though they wanted Daeli and the calf to see what they'd done.

The sight of yet another human body in the water nauseated Fusa. Unlike those other ones, who'd been overcome by a surge of water so extraordinary it would be discussed for generations to come, there was nothing natural about the death of this individual. This was killing for killing's sake, and confirmed what she'd suspected about these strange dolphins who lurked in dark places: though it was through no fault of their own, their nature had been truly corrupted.

Kikuko gave a whistle. 'More boats are on the way! They've just rounded the headland!'

After drowning the human, Zhebi and Yongsa had gone to the surface to rest beside the body of Flad. The sea lions were enjoying themselves in the network of trenches below, while Mako, in a kind of daze, was seemingly attempting to make sense of what had just happened here.

Fusa looked about herself for a cue as to what to do next. But then she noticed Mako was staring at her. As was Daeli and Kiyo, and Kikuko.

They were waiting for instruction.

How had this happened? She was a young mother whose life had been thrown into chaos by a force of unimaginable ferocity. She'd been beached, blinded, befriended by mysterious animals; had spent nights alone in the expanse of the ocean and had taken a helpless calf under her flipper. Her love for her friend had driven her to take the kind of risks that, not weeks ago, would have turned her organs to ice to even consider. But she had done it. Against all the odds, she'd got him out of there.

And for doing so, she had won their total trust.

Mako came close to Fusa and held his face beside her. 'There's something you need to know, auntie,' he said.

'Roopam told me where west really lies. It's not through the strait on the other side of the island. We won't find the great trout-god over there. The west of the world is so far away, a dolphin could never swim there.'

Fusa let up a single bubble and steadied herself. 'It doesn't matter,' she cheeped, with a curious blankness.

Kikuko recoiled in shock. 'How can you say that? After all this travelling?'

Mako, too, was overcome with angst. Yet as he swayed his beak away, it was guilt that resided in his eyes. 'I insulted him though, auntie.'

'Taking the fish from the shrine *was* bad, Mako. But Moshiri's thrashing was never about you. I see it now. We were wrong.'

'What do you mean?'

'All this time, we thought it was wrath,' said Fusa, her beak drooping. 'But he's not angry at all. Moshiri is *hurting*, and what creature doesn't thrash when they're seized with pain? The impurities in the water are killing him, Mako. And as he dies, the oceans he bears on his back are turning slowly back to swamp.'

'But why didn't he make that clear in his visions to you?'

'I think he did. Always, it was a warning for us to stay away from the human habitations on the coasts, where the decay is worst. That was the message. And if we don't get that message to our pods, I'm afraid the suffering of every creature who dwells below the waves will grow more as each new day dawns.'

Barely perceptibly, Mako flinched. 'Are you saying—'

'Yes, Mako. It's time. We must head back now to Squid Hood Bay.'

22

PARTING

The goodbyes began with Zhebi and Yongsa.

Fusa, down in the nooks of the seabed with the others, had waited for the pair to come down again. The light of day was fading, and more boats were approaching, and she knew she couldn't delay any longer.

The time to begin the journey north had come.

Flad was bobbing on the waves, his body as firm and inanimate as a chunk of tree come into the ocean after a storm. A serenity marked his face — one that had been absent in his life — and all found in it a comfort, of sorts.

The memory of the deliberate killing of the human was still sickening, but Fusa reached her flippers out to Zhebi and Yongsa nevertheless. 'I'm very sorry,' she cheeped, 'for what they did to your friend.'

She recognised the intensity in Zhebi's eye as he looked on at his fallen companion. As he'd done with Zhao, he was waiting to witness the spirit ascend.

Mako had been lingering forlornly near the lifeless human, but turned away for a moment to face them. 'Thank you for helping me get out of that terrible place.'

Zhebi and Yongsa, however, were lost in the dark gullies of their own minds. Though she knew it was unlikely, Fusa hoped they might one day find themselves in worlds filled with light, and fun, and peace.

A whistle from Kikuko urged the party to look up: the approaching boats had drawn close enough that voices were becoming audible up in the snowy evening sky.

'The albino is with them!' the humans were yammering, frantically. 'Get down there after it!'

A splash sounded as one of the riders from the boat dropped into the ocean. Fusa, driven more by what the dolphins might do to him than what he might do to them, rounded up the others, and their entire party pushed off, into the expanse.

Putting as much distance as possible between themselves and the cove was Fusa's prime concern. So, on the north-flowing currents, they swam without resting once, until, with a bright moon shining in the dead of night, the sea lions could journey no more. Thankfully, a large island of items discarded from the human world spared them having to go to shore — they leapt out of the ocean and, on beds of plastic detritus, went straight to sleep.

As the sea lions rested, the dolphins hung below the surface. Kikuko and Mako napped on either side of Kiyo, leaving Daeli and Fusa to chat quietly together between naps of their own.

After the drowning of the human, Fusa was weary now of Daeli. The same vacant glare resided in her eyes as had in Zhebi's, and Fusa wondered if she too harboured such deep hatred of that species that she might one day be compelled to take one of their lives. The older cow had observed the bulls with complete blankness when they committed that terrible act, making it impossible to tell whether Daeli approved of their deed or, like her, had been appalled by it.

Of course, there was always a chance that the cow was simply too focussed on protecting Kiyo to pay much mind either way. They had certainly bonded in their short time together. It was even possible, perhaps, that Daeli may wish to raise the infant as her own.

Fusa put this to the older cow, but Daeli, with a tenderness until now not seen, gave a shake of her beak. 'Not possible to take Kiyo. Already, human make too much damage for Daeli.'

There were a number of things that could have meant, but Fusa thought better of prying. 'Will you come with us across the strait, at least?'

'Daeli will take Kiyo to Fusa's pod. Then Daeli's time will end.'

A ripple of pity ran through Fusa. Some animals, it seemed, really did come into the ocean to suffer. It was a risk travelling with a dolphin as tortured as Daeli clearly was, but the cow was devoted to the calf – and Kiyo *did* require a nurse – and she had earned the right to accompany them for however long or short a journey she saw fit.

When the sky began to blush in the east with the first rays of dawn, the sea lions leapt back into the ocean, signalling their readiness to voyage on. Following the current once again on a northern trajectory, the party swam until hunger slowed them; by the time the sun was directly overhead, they left the open ocean and made their way to where the craggy coast was fringed with beaches.

They proceeded along the headlands after eating their fill, and soon Fusa recognised the rocky promontory where they'd first met the sea lions.

It was time for their next parting.

Fusa's gratitude sat in her heart like a pain. Nuzzling her beak against the face of the largest bull, she kept her gaze locked on his round eyes. 'We couldn't have done it without you,' she chirped.

Mako enjoyed a quick race with the younger members of the colony, as he'd done on their first meeting, then made a point of thanking each and every animal who'd given up their time to help spare him from a truly wicked fate.

Of course, it wasn't only their time they'd given up and Kikuko, for her part, hung low in the water at the rear of the party, unwilling – or unable – to join in with the goodbyes. Fusa had seen anguish in Kikuko before, but never to this degree, and it was clear that she felt responsible for the lost lives of the four members of their colony.

The sea lions, however, wouldn't let her wallow. They coiled their sleek bodies around her and tickled her chin with their whiskers and, before they leapt up onto the rocks to conclude their part in the journey, held their faces close to hers. And while they gave no barks, it seemed to Fusa that they communicated not to be sad for what had happened, and to carry no guilt.

Whatever it was they imparted with their big eyes, it worked: Kikuko's spirits picked up, and the dolphins left them in good cheer.

But a shadow darkened the carefree mood.

Awaiting them further up the coast was a place that had haunted them ever since they'd left it behind.

~

Kiyo was the first to complain of a prickling sensation.

A calf's skin was more sensitive to changes in the water, so Fusa wondered if it may just have been his age. Before long, however, Daeli began complaining that her eyes were burning, too, and Fusa knew they'd come at last to the stretch of coast she'd been fearing.

Snow Crab Lagoon, sheltered from the expanse behind a long sandbar, was there now on their left side, and beyond it the menacing human buildings which even now were billowing smoke up into the dusky sky.

Fusa recoiled. Her last vision was of this very place, this long ribbon of coast, which, with Moshiri's waning life, had become lit up with an infectious – and spreading – impurity.

Swimming with caution through these needling shallows, that dream replayed over and over in her mind, of voices made heavy with pain, where even Wakka Totto, usually so measured, had been unable to disguise her agony.

But Fusa knew she couldn't afford to get lost in her angst. Not while there was journeying still to be done.

She went up into a spyhop. The humans hadn't concluded their business on the land, yet. They were just frames now, the cube-like structures which had exploded, but still the land creatures scurried urgently around them. It was apparent they'd come some way towards fixing this mess — but so too was it obvious that more anguish awaited them.

As the dolphins milled together near the shore, Mako gave a quack. 'Taste that? Reminds me of the water in Blood Cove.'

Kikuko spat a jet of water into the air. 'Was that what this horrid stuff was all along? Blood?'

A bolt shot along Fusa's spine as she looked toward the ruined buildings. 'Do you think they're massacring animals in there?'

'Must be,' said Mako. 'The water isn't cloudy here like it was in the cove, but it's got the same kind of bitter taste. The river beside the shrine must be carrying down blood.'

Just then Daeli came forward. 'No,' she said. 'Not blood. Impurity is human creation.'

The others looked at her, confused.

'When human keep me across western sea, they make many weapon.'

Mako shook his head from side to side. 'What's a *weapon*?'

'A tool,' said Kikuko, 'for inflicting pain on others. Like the spear that struck Flad.'

'Yes,' said Daeli. 'Me... Zhao... Flad – we are weapon, because human teach us to hurt others.'

Fusa expelled stale air from her head. 'And Zhebi and Yongsa, too?'

'Zhebi and Yongsa different. Human teach them for spying only.'

Kikuko drew closer to Daeli, fascinating by her odd words. 'So, your captors made weapons – and those weapons had something inside them that tasted bloody like this?'

'Yes. Bad thing. Not like nature. Big danger for all life.'

Mako, who'd been busy scanning the open water to the east, turned back to them. 'The currents were teeming with orca last time we were here. But there's nothing out there now except a few ships.'

'Then we can go round this polluted stretch,' said Fusa.

Kikuko let out a chuckle. 'A few ships, huh, pretty boy? You'll be wanting to indulge in a spot of bow riding while we're passing, I suppose?'

But Mako didn't seem very keen on that idea at all.

∽

Moshiri had been on his mind less and less over the past days. Even while he'd recounted the circumstances to Roopam of how he'd come to be pursued by so much hardship, Mako felt curiously ambivalent towards the trout-god.

Their journey onward from Snow Crab Lagoon had brought them to a stretch of coast familiar to Mako, and when his scans came back with echoes of a gate, he winced.

This was the very spot where all his troubles began.

On the wall of the promenade, at the foot of the shrine through which the great backbone fish could be reached, were the three stone plinths, and his heart quickened for his closeness to it.

It was difficult to conceive that he was even the same dolphin that had been here weeks ago. Then, all that mattered to him was finding the next thrill, and he'd known the moment he laid eyes on it that he'd found one in this towering gate standing out from the waves with its eagle's wings outstretched. He'd so wanted Hideki and Karoo to see his mischief then, but after they darted off back to the pod, he wished only for the humans to see it instead.

Nothing could have prepared him for what *their* praise had caused. It was as though his entire life were given purpose by their applause. He wanted nothing more than to be loved by them – and for that, he had endangered himself, and the lives of countless others. Whether it was riding in the wake of boats, deliberately beaching himself, or trying to earn a snack by entertaining them in some shallow cove far to the south, he had greedily courted human affection.

What did it matter that he had been warned to keep away from those peculiar, upright beings? There were some lessons, it seemed, that couldn't be learnt through the suffering of others. Sometimes, a dolphin had to suffer himself in order to really understand the truth of the world he lived in.

And now, finally, he did understand.

As he swam in the choppy waters around the bright legs of the gate, Mako cast a glance at Fusa and Kikuko. Neither had said anything about this moment over the course of the voyage, yet both had known it was coming. Now that it was here, they simply looked on, awaiting his move.

Unlike the anxious girls, Kiyo was so excited that he was spinning in the water as he darted between the others. The story of how Mako had put back the fish in the riverside shrine had entertained the calf no end – did humans *really* pick him up and carry him through the site?! – and he hadn't stopped enquiring whether the older boy was going to do it again when they made it back to the original one.

As the dolphins lingered in their spyhop, some boats came puttering around a bay, and its riders began to wave. Mako watched them nearing. Before, his first thought would have been to show off for them. But instead he retreated now below the waves to join Fusa, who refused to be seen by humans while something from their world was affixed to her.

He put his flipper on her. With time, this brave young dolphin would know just how much he regretted the terror she'd endured. Yet, in an odd way, he suspected the anguish of the journey they'd shared had done her at least some good.

Letting up a bubble, his smile broadened. She was probably thinking the same thing about him this very moment.

And she would be right.

If the horror of his experience had helped him, it was no more evident than in the final act of violence he'd been forced to witness. In those moments when Zhebi and Yongsa invited him to help drown the land creature, when time seemed to freeze, everything changed for him. Humans had inflicted such terrible trauma upon him, yet he wasn't even tempted to participate in that wicked deed.

He knew it was wrong. Not because the trout-god decreed it so, but because his heart had told him. Caught in that suspended patch of time, he understood that he mustn't respect the ocean simply because he was afraid of what Moshiri would do if he didn't. He knew he had to respect it for the sake of protecting it. Because it was his home.

The guilt he'd carried had seemed destined to be with him forever. Since taking from the backbone fish was an offence against nature, it was clear that he owed a debt. But perhaps, in refusing to join Zhebi and Yongsa while they committed another such offence, he had paid it back already.

'Go on, Mako!' chirruped Kiyo, eagerly. 'Go put the fish back!'

He looked up to see his friends making their way to the rocky bottom, and Daeli scooping Kiyo beneath her fin. And as he observed the cow, another truth became clear to him.

Daeli, like the other dolphins who skulked in hidden places, was the way she was for one reason: humans. Land creatures had changed these dolphins into something they were never meant to be; it was doubtful that anything could ever put them back again. Zhebi and the others were what human interference looked like at its worst.

And yet the lives of every dolphin he knew – not least himself – had been shaped in some way by that land-dwelling species.

'Go into the shrine!' chirped Kiyo again.

Mako looked at his friends one by one. 'No,' he said.

The calf was inconsolable. 'Oh! Why not?'

'Moshiri belongs to humans,' quacked Mako, and the wisdom in Fusa's eye as she nodded her beak told him she knew exactly what he meant.

~

At the northern cape of what Kikuko called the 'big island', the ocean had become dense with marine life.

To Fusa's amazement, word of their journey had gone around, and now, resting in the shadow of a perfectly round tower at the very tip of the cape, many animals came across to see for themselves this travelling mini-pod.

Having crossed the strait several times already, Fusa

was familiar with the rocky cove where they'd agreed to rest for the night. The volume of pods was anything but usual, however.

When a group of cows came over to nose at the small party, Fusa asked them just where everyone was headed.

'The spawning,' replied one, after some moments staring at the curious box fastened to her head.

Mako gave a shake of his beak. 'Wasn't that weeks ago?'

'The mackerel spawning, yes. But something's turned the fish strange in the south and whole shoals have travelled up to Squid Hood Bay. Almost every family we've met are saying it's unlike any spawning they've known.'

Fusa sent a shrill whistle through the water to bring her friends back from chasing fish. 'All these pods are crossing the strait now,' she announced when they'd gathered. 'Something has made the fish travel up from the south.'

'Something?' said Mako. 'You think it's the corruption in the water?'

'Perhaps,' said Fusa, waving her beak. 'I know we said we'd rest here tonight and make the crossing at dawn, but we'd be safer against orca attacks if we went with these pods. Besides, some of this lot are bound to want to sleep during the crossing, so we can get some rest then.'

Fusa faced Mako. Since he heard of the spawning, his beak had begun to droop and a melancholy resided in his eyes. 'What's troubling you, little brother?' she asked.

'He's just realised his own pod will be there,' said Kikuko. 'You're worried about seeing them again, aren't you, pretty boy?'

Fusa let out a sad squeal. 'Is that true, Mako? After all you've been through? Surely you want to meet your family again and tell them all about it?'

'It doesn't matter what I want. They won't wish to see me again.'

'You know something?' said Fusa, pressing her fin against him. 'You've grown up a lot since we first met. But you're still a very silly thing. I know you think you don't deserve to be happy because that little girl got taken by the orca. And maybe you do bear some of the responsibility for what happened to poor Chizuko. But if a dolphin is defined only by a single moment, why can't it be the moment you saved me? You've done wonderful things, Mako, and for that, I think you *do* deserve happiness.'

'She's right,' chirped Kikuko. 'So stop fretting, krill-for-brains.'

Mako smiled. 'Let's make this crossing now.'

'It's agreed then,' said Fusa. 'We'll wait until Daeli comes back, and then we'll set off.'

But Daeli never did return.

23

THE OCEAN OF THE FUTURE

It was noon when the travelling dolphins made it to the wide basin of Squid Hood Bay.

The sun that broke through the clouds shone warmly on a spectacle of nature. The waters were rich with more fish than Fusa could ever have imagined, and visitors from the north – bulbous-headed belugas and sharp-toothed seals – had arrived to feast alongside a multitude of dolphin and whale pods.

At the sight of the maternal pod, it was as though everything Fusa had been through since the wave washed her ashore had been merely imagined. She approached with the same wariness as when she'd last swam with them, unsure how she stood to be received. 'I'm guessing you all thought you'd never see me again?' she said, awkwardly.

'Not at all!' chirped Turem, who'd come thrashing through the water to see her cousin and her new friends. 'We know all about your adventures!'

Fusa jolted with the shock of it. 'But... how?'

'The whales! They've been watching you almost since you left. We've had heaps of reports from them.'

'You mean, this whole time you *knew* I was alright?'

'The whole time, mama!' said Misa, who'd come gliding into the party with the other youngsters.

At the sight of her daughter, Fusa began to weep. Though she'd done nothing deliberately wrong, she ached with such a deep remorse she could hardly bring herself to look the calf in the eye. 'I'm so sorry, Shrimp,' she groaned.

The smile on Misa's face grew even wider. 'Don't be sad, mama. It only happened because you risked your life for the safety of your pod. We're all so proud of you.'

'All of you?' asked Fusa, scanning around to see that Toshi was here among the feasting hordes too.

Catching her eye, the bull came over and gave their daughter a playful nudge with his beak. He then twisted away from Misa to face Fusa head on. 'You're back then?'

Fusa nodded.

'Bet you wish you'd split off with me after all.'

A pang of emotion flashed inside Fusa. Her heart had indeed ached for this bull when he left, and she'd felt his absence like a bereavement.

Yet it was only anger which stirred her now.

'Split off with you? And leave my pod to face danger without us? No, Toshi. You showed me who you really were that day – and I'll be forever thankful for it. Now excuse me. I've got loved ones to be with.'

With Mako, Kikuko and the calf watching on from the back, Fusa swam around to bring them in closer to the maternal pod. 'I'd like you to meet somebody,' she said.

'Oh, we know all about this fine boy,' said Turem, bringing her face close to Mako's. 'How can we ever thank you for looking after Fusa the way you have?'

'Look after *her*?' quacked Mako. 'Auntie looked after me!'

'And this,' said Fusa, 'is Kikuko.'

Misa, enamoured with the older girl, twisted in excited circles around her. 'Thank you, Kikuko! Wouldn't you like to stay up here with us?'

'Well?' said Fusa. 'You'd be welcomed as one of our own.'

Kikuko arced her back up and spat a jet of water high into the warm sky. 'That's very kind of you,' she said. 'I'll stick around a while. But my life is in the south.'

Just then, Mako pulled away from the group with a bashful glance. 'I think I'll leave you to it for a while.'

Fusa looked at him with tenderness and sympathy. She knew what he had to do.

Scooping Kiyo away from Fusa's girlfriends, who were fawning over the calf, Mako gave a gentle whistle. 'Come on, little one,' he said. 'You're coming with me.'

∼

As they swam through the feasting pods, Kiyo couldn't stop crying.

Mako, however, was very patient. The poor thing had suffered so much and, once again, felt abandoned. 'You're such a good boy,' he said, consolingly. 'And you're going to have a really good life from now on. I promise.'

Mako, turning his beak this way and that as he navigated through a vast throng of bodies, at last found who he was looking for.

He'd gone through this moment so many times. Practiced what he would say if he ever had the chance to come before them again. There were times when he was certain he simply wouldn't be able to face them at all, that he'd simply speed away rather than put himself through the discomfort of it. But now that it was about to happen for real, he felt no compulsion to flee.

This had to be done.

'Hello,' he said to the parents of little Chizuko.

Their sad eyes brightened the moment they turned to him. 'Mako! You're back at last! We were all so worried about you!'

His beak drooped. 'What I did was unforgivable. I

truly am as sorry as I can be. Chizuko was just a podling and I—'

'So are you, Mako,' clucked Chizuko's mother. 'I know you think you're all grown now into some big, strong bull, but to the rest of us you're still just a little thing, too. What happened was a tragic accident. We know you didn't mean for it to end up that way.'

'Really?' quacked Mako. 'Because I thought everybody would be so mad that they would want to send me away, so I went off on my own so you didn't have to—'

The voice that cut him off was instantly recognisable. 'We know, Mako.'

From behind him, his parents had appeared and Mako, who always liked to appear brave, suddenly began to whine.

His father continued. 'All of us knew. And we were about to come and fetch you back when the enormous quake struck and the water surged. After that, there was nothing we could do.'

'I'm sorry for punishing you so harshly, Mako,' said his mother. 'You're hard work, but all of us know you don't have a wicked bone in your body.'

'I'm going to be good now, you'll see. I won't cause you any more trouble.' But even as Mako said it, he suspected the promise would be broken by day's end.

He turned away, almost too embarrassed to broach the next topic. 'And as for the humans, I know why you were so upset, mama. For a time I thought I was just like my grandfather. But I'm not at all. I won't bother with those strange creatures again for as long as I live.'

Mako felt a nudge in his side from Kiyo, who was, as always, hungry again. With a fin, he brought the calf into the group, and turned to Chizuko's grieving parents. 'If there was a way to bring Chizuko back,' he said to them, 'I'd do it in an instant. I know that she can never be replaced, but this little one has been through the most awful hardship. Humans slaughtered his whole pod, right beside me.'

Chizuko's mother and father rushed to comfort the crying calf.

'He desperately needs parents to love him and help him get over his grief. And I was wondering—'

But he didn't have to say anything else, for in their chirping and their cooing, it was clear that the cow and the bull had already made their minds up.

A lightness like he'd never before encountered came over Mako. He'd meant it, when he promised to be good from now on. There was no question he'd been lucky, but if he went on pushing boundaries the way he'd always liked to do, that luck was going to run out. Now, all he wished for was to enjoy his life with the friends he'd made.

He took himself off to snack on some mackerel, then went to the shallows alone to rest. Just as he was about to fall into a nap, however, a clicking came through the clear waters of the bay. It was an odd voice – not quite dolphin – and was one he hadn't dared to hope he might hear again.

He thrashed his tail into action and turned to meet the approaching animal. 'Roopam!' he called out. 'You made it!'

The whale's face opened wide with a toothy smile. 'I've been on your tails for days. Half the ocean is on their way up here!'

Since the pair had only known each other in the confines of the pen, they revelled in the space of the shore, chasing each other and leaping and twisting through the surf. 'Should we try it again?' asked Mako, whose appetite for play simply couldn't be satisfied.

Roopam chuckled. 'Get a better run-up this time.'

Mako gave a nod and went to the rear of the whale. Then, as he passed over Roopam's wide tail flukes, he was launched high into the sky, where, to the delight of the spyhopping dolphins around them, he performed the most spectacular double somersault ever witnessed.

∽

The sun was hanging low by the time the reunions were concluded, and Wakka Totto was now leading a ceremony in the squid-rich waters surrounding an island.

The elder, her eyes misted with the effects of the pufferfish, was giving thanks for the bounty and the safe return of one of the pod's youngsters after a time of trial and ardour. Special thanks were reserved for humans: praising their ingenuity and their superior intellect, Wakka Totto informed the pod that Fusa was able to once again echolocate with the miraculous machine tied to her beak.

Turning her attention to the great backbone fish of the world, Wakka Totto concluded proceedings by reassuring the audience that Moshiri had at last begun to settle. His fretful period, she asserted, was coming to an end, evidenced by the relative calm of the ocean bed in the preceding days.

This caused a ripple of relief around the pod.

But Fusa felt curiously detached.

Wakka Totto must have spied her indifference, for when the dolphins dispersed to head off back to the shoals, the elder glided across to where Fusa was hanging with Mako and Kikuko.

Locking her bulging eyes with Fusa's, she spoke slowly. 'I understand how tempting it must be to blame Moshiri for your terrible ordeal.'

Fusa, still somewhat ill at ease in the company of the old leader, remained quiet.

'The great backbone fish of the world,' continued Wakka Totto, 'who makes the very tides ebb and flow, took you in his mighty inhalation and spat you back out on a surge which devastated the shore. But you were not the target of his ire, young Fusa. You were merely caught in something far bigger than you can yet understand.'

'As awful as it was,' cheeped Fusa, shyly, 'that terrifying wave was nobody's fault. It was just nature, doing what it has to do. But the impurity that's spreading from the shore – *that* is different.'

Wakka Totto lowered her beak, anxiously. 'You have had another dream vision, have you not?'

Fusa turned away.

'What was revealed to you, young Fusa?'

Resting her flippers upon her friends, who kept their eyes away in reverence to the elder, Fusa hesitated at first in her response. But, gradually, she began to share it. 'I've seen the waters of the coast boiling with poison. You're there. Only, it doesn't quite look like you. But it must be, since others are calling you by your name.'

The elder gave a chuckle. '*Rain* is my name, young beauty, as I came into this world during a downpour. *Wakka Totto* is merely a title.'

Fusa twisted her beak to the side in confusion.

'It means *Water Mother*,' explained the elder. 'The dolphin the others are addressing in your vision is *you*, young Fusa. It is the future, when you have become the Wakka Totto.'

Fusa's heart began to beat heavily. Something suddenly made sense, but it was so unsettling she could hardly bear to dwell upon it. When they'd reached the humans' smoking buildings yesterday, she'd thought the place in her vision was simply Snow Crab Lagoon. But while that bay's waters were still impure with a substance like blood, they had improved.

Snow Crab Lagoon was *not* the water she'd envisioned.

The scorched expanse in her vision was the entire ocean of the future.

'You should rest now,' said Wakka Totto. 'All three of you have travelled far.'

Fusa didn't wish to rest, though, and instead led her friends out into deeper water.

Mako broke the silence after some time, transmitting an inquiring whistle. 'You told your elder that the wave was just an act of nature. But how can you *know* that?'

Fusa glided to a halt and hung at the surface, watching the sun as it dipped over the horizon. 'Because there is no Moshiri.'

Kikuko flicked up water with her tail flukes. 'Then who's putting visions into your dreams, auntie?'

'I don't know. I think… it sounds crazy. But I think it's coming from the ocean itself.'

'But why do the humans have their own shrines, if there is no Moshiri?' asked Mako.

'They invented the trout-god to help them understand our world. They're land creatures – they can't possibly know the oceans like we do. But by letting ourselves get close to their kind, we let their ideas into our own way of thinking.'

'Then, all those thanks and prayers to him were just a waste of time,' said Kikuko.

Fusa swayed her beak. 'Not if we remember that *Moshiri* isn't something separate from the ocean. Moshiri *is* the ocean: a living thing, whose life, like ours, will decay if it's not properly cared for.'

A few moments of contemplation passed in silence, then Fusa twisted away and led her friends off again.

Swimming off farther into the expanse, Mako turned to Kikuko. 'So you're going south again, huh?'

'Yep,' clicked Kikuko. 'Back to the islands where I was born. I'll see if the sea lions want to come with me. How about you, pretty boy? Want to join us?'

Mako edged his beak bashfully away. 'I kind of do, yes. But I think I'll stay here a while. I've missed pod life – especially getting told off. I'm just not ready to go off on my own yet.'

'Well, you stay here and annoy everybody and get

punished all you like,' said Kikuko with a grin. 'I know where to find you. And how about you, Fusa?'

'*Coral*.'

Mako and Kikuko turned to each other. 'What?'

'I don't wish to be known as Fusa anymore.'

'Why?' asked her friends in unison.

'*Fusa* is of their tongue, not ours,' she said, and let up a bubble. 'Humans are a very mysterious race. They might just be the kindest creature of all. You only have to look at them when they wave from their boats to know their hearts are filled with love and goodness. But there's something in their nature that makes them take for granted the world they inhabit. The ruined ocean of my vision is not Moshiri's doing – it is theirs. And that's why, from now on, we must have nothing more to do with humans. Any of us.'

She moved her body in between her friends. 'Now,' she cheeped, 'help me get this box off my head.'

'But, auntie!' quacked Mako. 'You need that to guide you!'

'Please. Just do it.'

Mako and Kikuko pulled at the strap around Fusa's beak, detaching the device from around her.

Holding it between her jaws for a moment, Fusa then let the device drop. 'Dolphins will show me the way now,' she said, 'not humans,' and the curious metal box sank all the way down to the bones of the whalefalls laying silent and still on the seabed below.

THE END

HISTORICAL NOTE

The earthquake which struck off Japan's Pacific coast in the spring of 2011 remains the largest to hit the country since records began. It was powerful enough to move the island of Honshu by eight feet, shifting the planet off its axis by some 20cm, and it shortened the length of a day by about a microsecond.

The upthrusting seafloor caused a tsunami which reached almost ten storeys in height, a surge which travelled towards Japan at a speed exceeding 400mph. While the waves both slowed and shortened before hitting the coast, they inundated a total area of over 200 square miles and, in places, reached six miles inland.

The combined impact of the earthquake and tsunami resulted in over 15,000 deaths. Almost half a million people were made homeless.

As well as being the most expensive natural disaster in history, it was also very nearly one of the deadliest. The impact of the tsunami waves upon the coastal Fukushima Daiichi Nuclear Power Plant caused three nuclear reactors to melt down. Japanese officials consequently declared it a Level 7 accident – the highest level of danger on the International Nuclear Event Scale.

To remedy the unfolding crisis, the Tokyo Electric Power Company (TEPCO) pumped seawater into the plant. In the weeks it took to cool the reactors, however, large amounts of atomic material contaminated the environment. In 2013, TEPCO admitted that 300 tonnes of highly radioactive water had leaked into the Pacific every day. At the height of the crisis, radioactive material in the ocean near Fukushima's reactors was found to be 50 million times higher than before the accident.

At the time of writing, over one million tonnes of contaminated wastewater remain at the stricken power plant, stored in over a thousand giant tanks. This water, which has undergone a rigorous treatment process, is scheduled to be released into the ocean over several decades.

Japanese authorities insist that the impact of releasing the water will be minimal, and that it is in line with international standards; environmental groups, however, are sceptical, with fears of significant harm to marine life.

Time will reveal who was right.

Militarised marine animals have been a feature of our oceans for well over half a century.

In the US, dolphins have been trained since the late 1950s to assist in naval operations. Used primarily to locate and report the whereabouts of sea mines to their human handlers, the US Navy has made no secret of its marine mammal programme.

Other nations, however, are not quite so upfront. When, in 2019, a beluga whale surfaced in Norwegian waters wearing a camera harness, speculation was rife as to its origins. One clue was the writing on the harness itself, which proclaimed: 'Equipment of St. Petersburg.'

(At the time of publication, during the ongoing war in Ukraine, further reports of military-trained dolphins have surfaced; satellite images have revealed dolphin pens in a Russian naval base in the Black Sea.)

ABOUT THE AUTHOR

Welsh author Justin Morgan has been lucky enough to have glimpsed some of nature's most elusive and spectacular species.

From jaguar and giant otters in the Brazilian Pantanal to a wild dog hunt in South India and humpback whales in Australia, he has suffered insect bites, punishing temperatures and seasickness in the hope of snapping some photographs and spinning a few yarns.

He currently lives in the UK with his very clever and very patient wife, Charlotte, where he is readying the final title in the *Animal Eyes* series for publication.

Get a FREE EBOOK @ justin-morgan.mailchimpsites.com

ACKNOWLEDGMENTS

I would like to offer my sincere thanks to editor Lisa Edwards for her incisive feedback on story development; to my friends and family, for all their encouragement and kindness; and to Charlotte Morgan, whose belief in my work and ongoing efforts to support it motivate me to keep writing.

I'd also like to acknowledge the great nation of Japan, whose creative people, spectacular natural scenery and rich culture keep me coming back time and time again.
どうもありがとうございます

Made in the USA
Thornton, CO
12/15/22 09:50:29

64010707-290e-4a82-93bc-8772bab1b30dR01